HALF-BLOOD'S BETRAYAL

S.C. STOKES

PRESCIENT PUBLISHING

CONTENTS

CHAPTER 1

Of all the places I expected to die, I never thought it would be here at Weybridge Manor. The manor had always been a safe haven. I may not have always been welcome in it, but the Caldwell family home was a bastion of safety reinforced by the sheer stature of my father.

Few people on earth were willing to pit themselves against the massive industrial complex that he had built.

Call it a talent, but I'd managed to find one.

Or rather, he'd found me.

Now, as my father's health waned, the vultures circled, ready to pick at the carcass.

Foremost among them was Andrew Lynch: chairman of the Brotherhood, and one of the most powerful men in the known world.

Founded by my forebear, Francis Drake, the Brotherhood had been established as a guiding influence to prosper mankind. Lately, its focus seemed to be shifting. The organization I'd watched my father participate in since I was a child was no longer a benevolent hand so much as it was a gauntlet, crushing those who stood against it.

The Brotherhood held influence in any room that meant anything, anywhere in the world. Their payroll included politicians, princes, and people of influence and means around the globe. For centuries, the Brotherhood had built their organization, bankrolled largely by my family and our gift.

We'd turned stone into gold and built an empire for them. How ironic that the engine my ancestor had unleashed seemed destined to grind his own descendants to dust.

That was what happened when you said no to Andrew Lynch.

Not that I'd had a choice. Lynch had too much power already; giving him the Grail would have created a monster. I'd seen the tyrant hiding behind those smiling eyes.

He was exactly the sort of man the Holy Grail needed to be hidden from. Power and immortality? Humanity simply couldn't afford for him to have that. Given the choice between handing the Grail over and gaining my freedom, or sparing the world his enduring tyranny, I'd chosen the latter. And now I was starting to feel like I was being crushed by the weight of the inevitable consequences of my actions.

Lynch was inevitable.

Now that blood had been spilled, there was no chance that he would be willing to leave my family alone. If our familial gifts had built the Brotherhood, we could fund any effort to thwart it.

Lynch didn't strike me as one who left loose ends.

We knew too much.

"What are you thinking?" Lara squeezed my hand and drew me back to the present. Our walk through the manor grounds should have been holding my focus, but Lynch was a Damocles sword hanging over us both.

There was no hiding my feelings from her.

"You have that look in your eye," she said. "It's the same look you had the day you took the mask."

She was right. The day I'd stolen the mask from her I'd been on edge. I'd had every reason to be. I had been about to light a match that could have cost me her love, all in the hope of curing the curse so that I had a life and future to spend with her.

It was the biggest gamble I'd ever made.

Now I stood on the precipice of another.

"I'm starting to wonder if I made the right choice," I replied. "Lynch offered me a seat at the table. Even told me I could have his seat when he was done with it. In another life, the Brotherhood, and its influence, might have fallen to me. Perhaps I might have done some good with it like my ancestors did."

"You give him wholly too much credit," Lara replied. "Lynch is a career climber. Now that he's at the top, he has no intention of relinquishing his power. Why do you think he wanted the Grail? A man like Lynch just wants all the power he can muster, and he will hold onto it until it's pried from his cold dead hands. So stop doubting yourself. You made the right call. We both know it."

We strode along the bank of a small lake on the estate. The cool breeze whistled over it, troubling the leaves on the oak trees providing our shade.

Lara had a point, but I was struggling to deal with the guilt. I'd made a choice. I'd been true to my word and given the Grail to my friend, its guardian.

That made me honest, sure. But the collateral damage of that decision had placed everyone I cared about in Lynch's sights.

"You're not wrong about Lynch. But we can be both right, and dead. They aren't mutually exclusive."

Lara pulled me up short.

"Enough." Her voice grew louder. "You've been growing more morose by the day. I love you, but you need to get your head back in the game."

"What you mean? I am in the game." I shook my head. "This is all I've thought about since we got his call."

"I know, but instead of thinking like you normally would, instead of challenging the impossible and finding a way, you seem to already be in mourning. I'm not ready to give up. I want my life, Seth."

The words hurt, mainly because she was right. I'd been ready to blow up our life together just for a chance to cure the curse and live another day. Now the Brotherhood was coming, and the inevitability of that was weighing on me.

I felt like Atlas, only the world was crushing me.

The curse seemed almost irrelevant now. I doubted I would live long enough for the curse to kill me.

I was making plans, but she was right. The pressure was getting to me.

"I'm doing my best," I said. "I'm fortifying the estate, expanding our influence, calling in every favor. Literally centuries of them. If Lynch wants a fight, we're going to give it to him."

Lara poked her finger into my chest.

"You can't wait for him. If you insist on fighting him on his terms, he will win. He is the Director of Clandestine Affairs. He has access to the greatest intelligence networks in the world. He knows where we are. He probably has a satellite tasked over us as we speak. The moment he can get away with it, he's going to bury us. I don't think you should wait for him to pick his battle."

"Andrew Lynch has been warding off threats for thirty years," a voice called. "A direct assault is only going to get you killed."

I would recognize my father's voice anywhere. I turned as he hobbled over to us.

My father and Lara seldom agreed on anything, and that seemed unlikely to change today. The two of them exchanged an awkward glance and Lara pushed her hair back out of her face.

"Waiting for him to come for us isn't going to be any better." She sighed. "But what would I know? I'm going to head inside and finish checking our RSVPs. Come hell or high water, this wedding is going ahead. I'll leave planning the honeymoon, and ensuring we survive to see it, to you, then. Got it?"

She was speaking to me, but we both knew she was including my father in the mandate.

She was right. I needed to step up my game, and I couldn't leave it to Lynch to decided when and where the matter would be decided.

"Got it. See you soon." I spoke softly, managing a bit of a smile. She hadn't given up, and I took both comfort and encouragement from that.

"Good," she said, then pressed her lips to my cheek. The warmth in that kiss flooded my entire being. "I'll leave you two boys to talk."

My father was silent as Lara headed for the house. He didn't say a word until she was out of earshot. "If you let her goad you into action, she'll get us all killed."

"Dad, please. I don't have the bandwidth to deal with you two bickering as well."

"I'm not bickering. I'm just trying to open your eyes to the fact I've been dealing with Lynch for my entire life. She's only been aware of the magnitude of the threat he poses for a few weeks. I don't want love blinding your better judgment. We need to present a united front."

"United front?" I tried not to laugh. My father and I had barely agreed on anything since the day I turned eighteen. I gestured at the fortified walls. "I'm playing my part, aren't I? I've done nothing but plan the defence of this place for weeks. What makes you think Andrew won't just throw men at the walls until everyone inside them is dead?"

"Because we'll make the price of doing so more than he can bear," my father answered as he hobbled on. "There is only one thing Lynch fears. That's losing his power. The rest of the Brotherhood's inner circle will be warning him against overt action. They are only effective at influencing others, because their true loyalties remain a secret."

"What do you mean?" I asked, starting after him.

"They might sit in governments and organizations around the world, but if those they served discovered the extent to which they had been manipulated in the pursuit of the Brotherhood's agenda, their lives and power would be eroded."

"Then why not expose them?" I said as we crossed the perfectly manicured lawn. "Blunt their influence. You would have enough dirty laundry to air that they could never cover it up."

"Because right now, Lynch is trying to convince them that killing us is a net gain for the organization. The others will be holding him in check. He might be the chairman, but if we can continue to fortify our position, we make it untenable for him to attack us. If doing so would draw too much attention, they will veto his efforts in the interest of their own self-preservation."

My father's plan made sense, but it also hinged on the assumption that Lynch was in his right mind. It also gambled on a handful of men I'd never met having the clout to prevent Lynch from coming after us.

I ran my hands through the tangled mess that was my hair. My father's plan was reasonable, but I didn't have enough faith to stake my life on it.

"What if their influence isn't enough and he comes for us regardless?" I asked.

"Then we meet fire with fire and are no worse off for having tried a tamer course of action," my father replied as he pointed to the borders of the estate.

Reinforced walls ringed the manor grounds. Behind them, anti vehicle tank traps had been erected, with razor wire spaced between them. The additional layer of defence wouldn't be discovered until attackers penetrated the massive perimeter fence. At least at ground level, the manor was being turned into a citadel.

Throughout the estate, gun emplacements and sniper nests had been concealed.

There were certainly perks to the Caldwell industrial complex.

Lynch would need an army.

The real question was, would those around him let him deploy one.

I wondered if my father would ever muster the courage to strike back at the organization he'd spent his entire life serving, protecting, and prospering. Or whether when the time came, he would capitulate to Lynch's agenda as he had in the past?

He seemed committed to the current course, but he was as wily as he was wealthy. I couldn't help but think he understood Lynch because they were both so alike.

I looked at my father. "You didn't come all the way out here to tell me to stay the course. What can I do for you, Dad?"

We hadn't been that close in recent years but calling him Frank to his face didn't sound right either.

"I wanted to talk about the curse," he said, his voice little more than a whisper.

My jaw dropped. "The curse? Now? With Lynch breathing down our neck?"

"Look, son, I know we haven't always seen eye-to-eye, but I've always tried to keep you safe. Soon, I am not going to be able to do that anymore. I won't be here forever, son."

Oh, hell no. I wasn't ready for this. I was emotionally drained as it was. Living for weeks with the possibility of my own imminent demise had grated on my nerves enough without my father wanting to confront his own mortality. I'd spent my life wanting to cure the curse; he'd only recently got on board.

"I can't do this right now, Dad. Besides, if Lynch comes for us, the curse isn't going to matter. We'll both be dead and it will die with us."

"I'm working on Lynch," my father replied. "He's the devil I know. I want to talk about the one I don't know so well. You do though. You were there."

"Where?" I asked, not quite following.

"Panama. That's where it all began." He leaned against a nearby oak tree for support.

"What about it?" I turned away, preferring the ripples in the pond to the weathered and worn look on my father's face. He looked tired and stressed out. The weight of the curse seemed to be grinding him down of late.

"Well, with everything that we've learned about the curse, I think what transpired in Panama is the key to breaking it. We know Aleida used that knife. You said it tears the spirit out of the body. That's progress. Now we just need to work out how she managed to anchor her spirit in our world and we can be rid of her, once and for all. Was there anything in the temple she might be using to keep herself in our realm?"

I thought of the time I'd spent in Panama. It wasn't exactly a Sunday stroll.

"I don't know, Dad. To be honest, there was a lot going on. I had an army of Inquisitorial nutjobs chasing me in the hope I'd make an agreeable sacrifice to usher in the Apocalypse. I didn't really have the luxury to search the place."

"But you found the blade," my father replied, "and what was left of her."

"Yes, I found her on an altar with the knife buried in her chest. I think she used it to separate her spirit from her body, and then the magic of that site of power to affect some sort of binding ritual. But what she used as an anchor is beyond me, because there was hardly anything left of the temple when I was done."

"Well, if it wasn't the temple, it has to be something else," he mused. "Any thoughts?"

"Not particularly," I answered. "I haven't exactly had the time to focus on it of late."

My dad tried to hide his disappointment by scratching his jaw but failed miserably.

He nodded slowly. "I know you're focused on Lynch. I'm working that angle as best I can. But there's a part of me that sees a future where I once didn't. I want to be free of this. I want to be free of Aleida and her insidious voice in my head."

"Well, what do you want from me?" I asked, balling my hands into fists. I'd been trying to actively break the curse since my eighteenth birthday. This was deathbed repentance on his part, and poorly timed at that.

"I'd like to borrow her knife. I didn't want to take it without asking."

"Dad, if you want it, it's yours. I can't deal with this right now. I need to focus on Lynch and then I swear if we survive him, we can put every waking moment into curing the curse."

"I appreciate that. In the meantime, I've given you my power of attorney. The resources of this family are at your disposal. Do with them as you see fit. Just remember that we'll all bear the consequences of your actions."

My heart skipped a beat. Had my father really just given me the keys to the kingdom?

"Why now, dad? What are you up to?"

"It's time you took your place. I'm losing the ability to keep things in check. Even if we survive Lynch, sooner or later, others will come. They need to know they'll be met with youthful vigor, not a tired old man."

"I don't know what to say." I started toward my father.

"On that, Lara and I are in agreement. Get your head straight. Lynch has no idea what he's started with you. But you need to stop dragging your feet, and ensure the future of your family. You have more to fight for than Lynch will ever have."

My family. It was words I didn't dare utter aloud for fear the universe might take it as a challenge and crush my dreams. It was also perhaps the most encouraging thing my father had ever said to me.

A lump formed in my throat. Tears threatened to find their way down my cheeks.

My dad turned to leave but paused. "Have you considered calling on your friend?"

"Friend?" I raised my head.

"The one in New York, Kasey Chase. She has as much an axe to grind with the Brotherhood as you do. Akihiro was a member of the Inner Circle when he tried to have her killed. Perhaps now you can find common cause against them."

He was right. The night I'd met Kasey, she'd certainly been interested in their existence. I didn't know that I wanted to drag her into my mess.

"I'll think about it," I replied. "In the meantime, don't do anything rash, Dad."

He smiled. A rare occurrence, but there was a twinkle in the corner of his eye that told me Frank Caldwell had not given up on life just yet.

He headed for the house. I considered going after him, but I still needed time to think.

I turned and headed in the other direction. Walking through the oak trees, I found my mind clearing.

It was almost as if a weight had been lifted from my shoulders.

I took my phone out of my pocket and tried to call Kasey. Dad was right, she would be a powerful ally if I could prevail on her to make the trip.

Unfortunately, the phone just beeped in my ear and played a message about it being out of the service area.

With no other choice, I recorded a message and jammed my phone back in my pocket. In spite of not getting through, my mood lightened. I was taking action. I wasn't sitting back waiting for the inevitable.

My father had just given me the Caldwell war chest to work with. The further I walked through the trees, the more ideas came to me. Ideas that were going to cause Andrew Lynch no end of problems.

My mood continued to improve by the moment. It was like a ray of sunshine had pierced the storm clouds that had been hanging over me for weeks. I hadn't felt this good since...well, since my friend had left me.

A tingle ran down my spine and I stopped dead.

That sensation could only mean one thing. I'd only ever felt it in his presence. "Are you just going to stalk me through the shadows, or are you going to show your face?"

CHAPTER 2

A stiff breeze whistled through the oak trees. A twig snapped somewhere off to my right and as I turned, my friend stepped out from behind the tree.

Murdoch, as I had known him, was a little under six feet tall, and wore an open flannel shirt over an old T-shirt, a pair of worn-out jeans, and a set of scuffed combat boots. His tanned complexion had no wrinkles, and his thick brown hair was kept in check by a faded baseball cap.

Murdoch was smiling. It was the same knowing smile that had often made me wonder how he could be so recklessly optimistic in the face of danger and certain death.

The only difference was now I knew why. He wasn't Murdoch at all. No, he was a much older being. One who had watched the world for centuries, possessed power I could scarcely comprehend, and for reasons I still didn't understand, had been content to shadow me on my reckless quest for the better part of a decade.

"How did you know it was me?" Murdoch asked, his voice soft as was his way.

"There is a feeling about you," I replied. "I always appreciated it when we were together. I just never realized how much your presence lifted my spirits until you were gone. I thought it was just who you are. Now I suspect it's what you are."

"It's hope," he replied. "We notice it most when we feel none."

He was an angel; I'd seen it with my own eyes. How did he have any idea what I was feeling? I didn't know what to say.

Murdoch scratched at the nape of his neck. "I was once a man, Seth. In my darkest days, I lived without hope, the light that I had followed for years taken from me. It is agony. I see your pain, Seth."

"Is that why you're here?" I asked, a little confused. I was happy to see my friend, but I still couldn't shake the feeling that things had irrevocably changed the day I'd seen him as he truly was. "Or are you here to explain why you left with the Grail and never said a word?"

Murdoch looked down at the ground, as he peeled his cap off his head. "I'm here to see a friend in need, is that okay?"

I nodded, feeling a little sheepish.

"Then let us walk for a moment. I imagine you have questions. I will answer what I can."

I fell in beside Murdoch and we walked together.

"Should I call you Murdoch? Or do you prefer..."

My voice trailed off. I wasn't really sure of the proper protocol for speaking with an angel.

"I have had many names, but Murdoch is one of my favorites."

We followed the path through the trees.

"Why are you so guarded, Seth? It's me. Ask what you will."

So many questions flooded into my mind, I wasn't sure where to even begin. So I started with the one that had been wearing on me since the day I'd learned the truth.

"Why me?" I asked, my voice threatening to crack. "You were my driver for crying out loud. Why were you slumming it with me?"

Murdoch laughed. "Slumming? You have a jet. I'd hardly call it slumming."

"You know what I mean. Surely you had more important things to attend to?"

"I go where I am needed," he answered. "I knew who your father was when he summoned me. The Brotherhood might hide themselves from the world, but they cannot hide from us."

"Us?" I asked.

"My master and those who serve him."

"You mean God?" I asked. Murdoch had been far too cryptic for too long. I wanted answers.

"Yes," he replied. "I've always been honest about that."

"Yeah, but..." I paused as I considered my response. "There's a difference between someone who likes to pray, and being a messenger for the almighty."

"Perhaps, but faith is personal. I wasn't going to reshape yours by imposing the burden of my knowledge upon you. Unfortunately, it became unavoidable in retrieving the Grail."

I supposed that made sense, though the implications of his admission threatened to overwhelm me. The existence of God was something I'd always struggled with. I didn't consider myself an atheist, but I did find it hard to believe in a divine plan when I'd been born cursed.

Perhaps I should have drawn that conclusion when I'd spoken to him about meeting Zeus, Hera, and Hades. He'd said as much, but in the context of the place and time, I'd heard it only as the sincere beliefs of a man of faith—not a statement of fact from a divine messenger.

The reality of his master was too much to take in, so I set it aside for the time being.

"And the Grail?" I asked. I didn't believe for a moment that it was the answer to my current predicaments, but I wondered what had become of it.

"I've placed it somewhere safe. Far beyond the hands of those who would use its power for evil."

A sensible course of action. The moment its presence had been known, men like Edward Knight and Andrew Lynch had made acquiring it their sole objective.

We approached the edge of the oak forest near the western boundary of the estate. The path led around the entire perimeter of the estate, so we weren't in any danger of running out of trail.

"Is the Grail the reason you've been able to live so long?"

"No, I've never drunk from it. While I was once mortal, my current state was a gift from my master. It is likely why I was entrusted with its care. I have no need of it."

His words echoed through my mind. He'd once been a man but was now an immortal, ageless angel, and exactly the kind of being I needed in my corner in the coming days.

But I still didn't understand how he'd come to be here in the first place. Or why he'd left with the Grail and not returned until now. I got the impression from the manner of his stealthy entrance, and the fact he was slumming it in his mortal form, that he wasn't planning to stay.

"You still haven't answered my question. Why me?"

Murdoch's voice was level, tentative, as he replied. "After the stories that ran in the paper about being shot down, I got more media attention than I had hoped. I was on the verge of changing my identity once more when I received an invitation from your father. I knew who he was, and figured it was best to hear him out before I made my decision."

"So he invited you to the manor?" I prompted. I had heard that much of the story before.

"He did. And knowing his connection to the Brotherhood and the range of his influence, I assumed he had figured out my secret and wanted that longevity for himself. Your family's curse was not news to me, Seth."

My jaw dropped. He'd known about the curse before he'd met me? What else did he know? Did he know how to fix it? Had he been holding out on me this whole time?

"You thought he wanted to harness your immortality for himself?" I replied. "Why risk falling into his trap?"

"Curiosity more than anything," Murdoch answered. "If your father tried to take me against my will, it would have ended poorly—for him. But rather than try something so foolish, he did something wholly unexpected."

That sounded exactly like my father. He was a shrewd negotiator on his worst day. What was it that he had managed to surprise an angel with?

"Instead, he offered me a solution to my problem. He promised to use his connections in the media and the military to have the story suppressed and in exchange, all he wanted was to offer me a job looking after you. It was selfless. And frankly, the offer surprised me, given all I knew about him and the organization he belonged to."

"And you said yes." My voice was quiet as I contemplated the question that had been bothering me for weeks. It wasn't like Murdoch needed the money, and if he could change his identity so readily that would have solved his problem without inheriting a babysitting job.

"I did," Murdoch replied.

"Why? I asked. I looked away from him, scanning the perimeter fence as we made our way toward the driveway.

"Because unlike your father, you weren't married to the Brotherhood and its agenda. You had the potential to do great things, Seth. But most importantly, I saw your heart. I saw the good in you. So, I lent my strength to your cause for as long as I could."

There was a bitter finality in his choice of tense that told me I couldn't expect much more of the companionship I'd enjoyed these last few years, let alone an angel fighting in my corner.

"Isn't that against some sort of rules? I didn't think angels could intervene in mortal affairs."

"Some rules are firmer than others," Murdoch answered, kicking a stone along the path. "My job is to watch over and protect mankind. You fit in that mandate."

A lump formed in my throat. "But I'm just one person. I've dragged you all over the world chasing cures to a curse and arcane trinkets. Why do that? Surely you could have had greater impact elsewhere?"

"Your influence is greater than you give yourself credit for, Seth. On very small hinges turns the destiny of man. A few small actions cause great impact. It is our way."

"What actions?" I asked, wanting to understand his perspective better.

"You stopped the invasion of our world by those creatures in Panama. You prevented the power of Ares falling to the Fae courts and upsetting the delicate balance there. And with little hesitation, threw in your lot to prevent the vampires from taking over New York City. Last but certainly not least, you prevented the Grail from falling into the hands of dangerous men. For as long as I have known you, you have risked your life for worthy causes. That's why I chose you."

"I'm not a hero. I've just been trying to cure my curse, you know that." I wasn't the saint he made me out to be.

"You're not the sinner you assume you are, either," he replied as if he could read my mind. "You will go far, Seth Caldwell. I've always known that."

We wandered along the path, an uneasy silence growing between us. He wasn't volunteering his assistance, but he was here, so I pushed him a little.

"Not if Lynch has anything to do with it. The Brotherhood are coming, Murdoch, and if they don't get me, the curse likely will. I don't suppose you could be of any help with that?"

"I cannot so overtly interfere." He pulled on the brim of his baseball cap, as if the shadows it cast over his face hid him from view.

"Perhaps your memory isn't what it once was," I replied, "because I can think of lots of times you interfered pretty overtly. You didn't get that good with a shot gun by watching from the sidelines."

Murdoch chuckled. "There is a difference between helping you discreetly and pitting my true nature against the Brotherhood. Besides, Lynch already knows of my existence. I cannot intervene. I already walk a line by being here. I cannot cross it."

"Why not?" I wondered out loud.

What stakes were so high he couldn't be a little more hands on?

"Because to do so would irrevocably break the rules that bind us. There is an order to things, Seth. It can't be done."

"Then why are you here?" I asked. The words came out of my mouth a little harsher than I had intended and as they lingered between us, I worried I had offended him.

"Because you're my friend," he said, "and I could not sit and watch you wallow in despair when you have come so far. You have never been one to take the easy road. Why stop now?"

"Because it feels like I'm taking on the entire world. Lynch has governments at his disposal. We might have money, but he has power. I've seen it at work. You were on the plane out of New York. He could have shot us down. What are we meant to do against that kind of strength?"

"He has friends, it's true," Murdoch said. "but so do you. A lot of them. Have you considered getting them involved?"

I had. A hundred times. There was a reason I hadn't made those calls. "I don't want to get them all killed."

"You presume to make the choices for them. How about you tell them the stakes and let them choose for themselves? No one wants to see a world where Andrew Lynch controls everything. Tyranny in the shadows will oppress their rights as readily as any dictator. You must drag him into the open and defeat him there if you want the freedom you've always spoken of."

"I've already called Kasey. She didn't pick up."

"She will," Murdoch replied. "She's just got her hands a little full right now."

"How can you know that?"

Murdoch smiled. "Because she's even better at getting herself in trouble than you are. I know where she's been. It's half the reason I cannot linger here."

"What does that even mean?" I asked. "Enough riddles, just give it to me straight, please."

He shook his head. "I've said too much and you have enough on your plate already. Other than Kasey, who have you called?"

"Well, no one yet."

"Then get to work. And when you start running out of friends, consider those who might benefit from your struggle. Your friend in the bar might help for the right price."

"Bar?" I rubbed at my stubble as I tried to recall the last time Murdoch and I had been to a bar together.

"You mean Smith and Wesson?" The demolition gnomes were mercenaries, and good ones at that. But I wasn't confident they'd take this fight.

"Think bigger. I was thinking Levi."

The mind-reading barkeep had not liked Murdoch one bit. Had Levi known what Murdoch was the whole time? Try as he might, Levi hadn't been able to read his mind. He'd also thrown Murdoch out in no uncertain terms.

"Levi never leaves the Panhandle," I replied, though I could certainly see the advantage in having someone with that sort of power nearby.

"He is a creature of single-minded focus. I'm sure he could be persuaded, and you would certainly have an advantage in that arena."

Levi did seem to like my coin. Perhaps he was more of a mercenary than I had realized.

"When you're done with the fence-sitters," Murdoch said, "consider those who might hate you, but despise Lynch even more. The enemy of your enemy is your friend. At least as far as it counts here."

"You'd have me call Edward Knight?" I could scarcely believe my ears. Only weeks ago, Knight had tried to steal the Grail from us. We'd reached an armistice, but each time I traded favors with Knight, there was a price to be paid. He was the devil I knew, but a devil all the same.

"I'd have you call them all," Murdoch replied. "You'll need them. Not all of them will come, but many will. If you put your mind to it, you will find strength you scarcely dreamed of. That's why I'm here."

"To give me a lecture?" I managed a smile.

Murdoch raised his eyebrow, not impressed. "No, to remind you of who you truly are."

I was on a roll, so I decided to push my luck.

"What about my curse? I don't suppose you can help with that?"

"Why would I help with that?" Murdoch replied with a shrug. "You seem so determined to die at Lynch's hands first."

The words hit me like a sucker punch.

"Okay, I get it. I have been whiny and morose and managed to irritate everybody from my fiancé to a freaking angel. I get it. I'm working on it. But if you could give me a straight answer, literally anything to help me, it could change my life."

A slow rumble of SUVs rolled down the road outside the manor walls. I could tell what they were from the unique noise the tires made as they passed over the asphalt. They slowed as they reached the gates.

That would be Mom returning from the Arcane Parliament. Much as Dad hated her leaving the safety of the estate, some responsibilities couldn't be avoided. When the governing body of the magical community calls you to session, you answer.

"You already have all the answers you need, Seth. You just need to face your demon. Choose the battleground carefully. You've been there before."

I blinked.

"That's all you're going to give me?"

I'd been hoping for more than the contents of a fortune cookie.

"It's all you'll need," Murdoch replied. "Trust me."

It was as succinct as it was unhelpful. "I'm surprised you didn't just send it in a text and save yourself the trouble of racking up more frequent flyer miles."

"That's not why I'm here, Seth." The tone of his voice was heavy, a grim note of finality to it that I was all too familiar with. I recognized it from every time my friend had dropped wisdom on me that I wasn't ready to hear.

I was about to learn a painful lesson.

Up ahead, the gates opened as the convoy rolled onto the gravel driveway.

"Why are you here, Murdoch?" I asked as he stepped toward me.

"To see an old friend," he said, wrapping his arms around me, "and to ensure you were close enough when she needed you the most."

A chill ran down my spine as Murdoch vanished into thin air. It felt like his arms were still around me, the warm embrace enveloping me for a heartbeat, and then he was gone.

I looked to the convoy, now less than fifty feet away as they rolled through the open gates.

In that moment of clarity, I started to run. I ran for the gates as a hissing roar filled the morning air.

My feet kicked up dirt and rocks as I sprinted for the convoy.

I was too late.

A projectile slammed into the middle SUV and detonated.

CHAPTER 3

The SUVs were no ordinary commercial vehicles. Their outer hulls were heavily reinforced and the windows were layered bullet-proof glass. My father had spared no expense, but the rocket propelled grenade made it seem like the car was made of tin foil and sugar glass.

The SUV flipped sideways, dragging along the driveway before it rolled onto its roof.

The world seemed to slow as the lead and trailing vehicles screeched to a halt. Gunfire from the other side of the road ricocheted off their armored shells.

Return fire erupted from the sentry towers along the outer wall. My father had built the watchtowers to provide advance warning of approaching threats. But the ambush had been sprung from the woodlands across the road.

Smoke plumed from the ruined vehicle as Murdoch's words echoed through my brain. I sprinted toward the car.

He had been crystal clear in his warning.

Her. He could only have meant my mother.

I had to do something.

"Mom!" I screamed over the chaos.

Bullets whizzed past me, as I slid behind the overturned car, using its frame to shield me from the fire. With the state of the car, it took me a moment to gather the courage to look inside.

My heart pounded as I stooped down to look through the ruined windows. The entire chassis of the SUV had been twisted, the weight of the vehicle slowly compacting it as the compromised frame gave out.

I had to crouch on my hands and knees just to look inside. The driver was dead; the shattered glass had cut him to pieces. Bullet-proof glass simply wasn't made to stand up to that sort of punishment. Nothing short of a tank would.

The passenger hadn't fared any better. I moved down the car, looking for my mother.

She was in the back seat, dangling upside down from her seatbelt, blood running down her hair before dripping onto the roof beneath.

"Mom?" I shouted as I pulled on the door. "Can you hear me?"

She twitched but didn't say anything.

"Hang on, Mom, I'm gonna get you out of there." I yanked on the door, but it was twisted and stuck between the weight of the car and the ground beneath.

More bullets slammed into the vehicle. It seemed the assassins were not taking any chances.

"Give me some cover, now!" I bellowed over the weapons fire.

The bodyguards in the other vehicles fanned out, using their vehicles as cover as they returned fire.

I set my boots against the panels and pushed against the car for leverage to open the door, but it wouldn't budge. I sat hunched over in the grass as another realization dawned on me.

The rocket propelled grenade I'd seen wouldn't be the last. And right now, the vehicle was a sitting duck with my mother trapped inside it.

I had to get the door open. I considered trying to use my magic to make a hole through it, but I didn't dare risk setting the car alight, so in the chaos I took the only other path I could think of.

Pressing both hands against the door, I whispered. *"Suelo."*

Pouring magic into the door, I transmuted it from reinforced steel to dirt. The power required made my head spin, but it was all I had. The door crumbled into soil that fell to the ground, leaving a gap for me to attempt to shimmy through.

With the door removed, the resistance against the weight of the car was that much less and it was compacting even faster.

I was running out of time, but I refused to give up. My mother needed me. I couldn't let her down. I scrambled through the shrinking gap into the back seat and undid her seatbelt.

She dropped into my arms.

Her hair was in my face, her weight pressing down on me awkwardly as I tried to reverse my course. Sweat rolled down my face. As I dragged myself backwards, I felt the pinprick of broken glass cut my arms and elbow, but I'd had worse. I pushed myself backwards, my hands under my mother's arms as I pulled her from the vehicle. No sooner had I got her onto the grass, than the vehicle's shell gave out completely, compressing against the driveway and crushing the bodies of the two men left inside.

They deserved a proper burial, but we would have to come back for them.

I looked down at Mom. Her white dress was in tatters and stained with blood. Most of it her own.

More shots rang out. This time, they came from within the compound.

A convoy of a half-dozen military grade vehicles rolled down the driveway. The two lead jeeps had mounted .50 caliber heavy machine-guns. Caldwell security personnel stood behind them, blasting away at the forest across the road.

They might not have been able to see the ambushers, but the machine-gun's rate of fire made that irrelevant. The heavy weapons shredded the foliage the cowards were hiding in.

I dragged my mother fifteen feet but didn't dare go further, for fear of leaving the shelter provided by the broken vehicle.

A faint whoosh signaled the approach of another RPG. I looked up and realized that rather than target the rolling convoy heading their way, the cowards had fired it at the ruined vehicle I'd just crawled out of.

The cowards clearly had orders to see my mother killed.

I threw myself over my mother's frame and summoned a shield.

The explosion rang out as it struck the car. Power leeched from me as twisted steel glanced off my shield. Debris rained down all around us, but I grit my teeth against the strain of the focus required to maintain the shield.

Sweat ran from my hairline down my chin, but still I held my focus. The ambush was quickly turning against the aggressors as more and more Caldwell reinforcements arrived.

The quick response team rolled like an armored spearhead. One vehicle, an armored troop carrier, peeled off toward us as the others surged toward the gates. No sooner had they cleared them than fire teams disembarked, pushing into the forest, pursuing those who had dared strike the cowardly blow against my mother.

Releasing my shield, I examined my mother's injuries.

Blood seeped from a series of lacerations. The shattered glass had acted like shrapnel inside the car. A four-inch tear across her stomach where a piece of glass or shrapnel had cut through her bled profusely. Another injury on her head looked shallow, but even shallow wounds bleed fiercely there. She was turning pale from loss of blood.

Fastening my hands over the wound in her stomach, I chanted loudly, tears rolling down my face as golden light poured from my palms. I had no idea how much internal damage had been done, but if I could stop her from bleeding out, there was a chance to save her. And right now, I clung to that chance with everything I had.

Moving slowly over her wounded body, I healed every cut or scrape of substance that I could find, my mother's faint breath against my cheek the only sign she was still alive. I labored as the armored troop carrier rolled up beside us. Its ramp dropped to reveal an interior that had been converted into a makeshift ambulance.

"Jillian!" My father called, his voice hoarse as he charged down the ramp out of the carrier.

Arthur, the family healer, was right behind him

"Is she..." My father's voice faded to nothing as he choked on the thought of what might have been.

"She's alive, barely," I whispered.

"What happened?" Arthur asked as he set down his black leather bag and went to work examining my mother.

"Ambush. Someone hit the car with an RPG. I've sealed it, but I have no idea how deep it went."

"You've done well." Arthur waved to two orderlies who were wheeling a stretcher out of the armored carrier.

"She's breathing but needs blood," Arthur said as he reached into his bag.

By the time the stretcher arrived, he'd inserted a cannula and had hooked up a bag of blood.

"We've got to get her back to the house, Frank," Arthur called.

My father stooped down and pressed his lips to my mother's head before pointing to the carrier. "Go. Take care of her. I'll deal with this."

We lifted my mother onto the stretcher, and the orderlies wheeled it toward the transport. Arthur tossed his bag on it and rode it the rest of the way, his hands glowing white and gold as he continued what I'd started. Arthur was a savant and my mother's best chance at survival.

My father and I watched as the carrier raced back to the house, leaving massive furrows where it tore up the lawn.

My father shook, not with fear but with unadulterated rage. I could feel the arcane energy building within him as he channeled his power. The pallor of his face was tinged an angry red and he seethed as he stalked toward the front gates of the estate.

He didn't say a word, so I started after him. "Dad? Where are you going? It's not safe out there. Let the team do its job.

Gunfire chattered as the quick response force pushed deeper into the woodlands across the road.

My father didn't answer me. He just kept walking, his eyes fixed on the tree line.

"You're going to get yourself killed," I shouted as I went after him.

"This was Lynch," my father called over his shoulder. "This stinks of his cowardice."

I quickened my step, leaving the safety of the shattered husk of my mother's SUV.

"Of course it was Lynch. For weeks I've been telling you he won't be content with letting us live through this. I turned him down and I snatched the Grail from him. We're a threat. I'm a threat, you're a threat, our family's continued existence is a threat to his precious little Brotherhood. If he lets our defiance stand, he'll lose the fear he's instilled in others. He's a dictator, not a diplomat."

"This is more than that," my father shouted back. "It was a message. For me"

"What do you mean?" I asked, scanning the tree line for signs of hostile forces.

"He wants us to know that he has enough clout to drag us out of our safehaven and before the Arcane Parliament. Look at the cars. He only hit one. He knew exactly which vehicle she was in, which meant he tagged it while the convoy was waiting. He could have killed her anywhere, but he waited until she was almost home so that she could die in our arms. Lynch is a sadistic bastard. This is the measure of his resolve."

"He wants to get in your head," I said as I rushed to keep up with him. "Draw you out of the estate, where one of his snipers could kill you. This is madness."

"If he wants into my head, he's going to be bitterly dis-appointed," my father answered. "That spot is already taken with a four-hundred-year-old witch and she informs me she isn't going anywhere."

Clearly, Aleida was still present and taking the opportunity to sink the boot in.

There was no reasoning with him when he was like this. My father had a temper, and Aleida knew how to stoke it. Hell, she was probably goading him as we spoke, doing her best to get him killed.

The thought caused my heart to leap into my throat.

I'd experienced her voice in the temple in Panama. I was in no mood to have her take up residence in my head.

"Dad, this is reckless." I moved faster, trying to get between him and any potential threats.

We reached the safety of the armored vehicles of the quick response force. They were now blocking the street outside the manor. My father called to one of the staff who was sitting at the heavy machine gun mounted on top of the nearest Humvee.

"Relay orders to the team—kill them all," my father called.

"Dad, wait," I said. Perhaps if we could capture one of them, we could learn what else Lynch was planning.

"With extreme prejudice," my father added.

"Roger that," the security officer replied.

He relayed the order through the radio. There was a crackle of static and a garbled confirmation I struggled to make out.

"Sir," the security officer replied, "the assassins made no effort to flee. The team are rounding up the last of them now."

"Where?" my father asked.

"About a hundred feet into the woods," the radio operator replied. "If you wait here, we'll bring them to you."

"Negative," my father replied. "Sweep them for explosives. I'll be with the team in a moment."

He charged into the woods as quickly as his weary legs could carry him. I started after him, both out of concern for him and a fear of what he would do. I'd only seen him this angry once before in my life and he'd tortured an inquisitor to death in front of my eyes. Right now, he had the same murderous glare.

"Don't you want to question them?" I asked, trying to appeal to his usual sense of strategy and cunning. "Lynch might have other pieces in motion."

"No," my father replied. "We know who they are, who sent them, and why they were here. Lynch wouldn't be so foolish as to confide his greater scheme in them. There is nothing left to learn. They must pay the price for their actions here. We're going to send a message of our own."

I wasn't going to dissuade him and after the cowardly attack on my mother, a big part of me didn't want to. These monsters had hurt my mother. They'd tried to kill her in our driveway.

I felt my own temper rising. My mother was a saint; she didn't deserve any of this.

My father and I crossed the road together and pushed into the woodlands. The brush wasn't thick, just a lightly wooded set of hills that formed a nature reserve across from the manor.

Weybridge Manor didn't have many neighbors. We preferred it that way.

As we ran, a dozen shots rang out.

They were close enough that I startled a little as they cut through the cool air.

Then silence descended on the forest. All I could hear was twigs and dead fall crunching beneath our boots.

My father didn't slow. Clearly, he had every confidence that the quick response force had done the job.

I wasn't quite so confident, and I held my power close at hand ready for a shield if needed. It wasn't that I doubted our team's competency, so much as I wasn't about to underestimate Lynch again. I'd seen the savage intensity of the initial ambush and wasn't convinced it was over. I would relax when we were all safely back inside the manor itself.

"He could be baiting you," I said. "What if there are more of them?"

"I doubt it," my father replied. "Our teams are already sweeping the forest and it is unlikely that they were able to sneak a large force past our outer sentries. I doubt there is more than half a dozen of them."

We found a dozen men dressed in body armor bearing the Caldwell family crest. At their feet, laying in the dirt, were five men in camouflage fatigues. All of them were dead.

Two had been cut to ribbons by the heavy machine-gun fire of the Humvees. The other three had been wounded and then executed, on my father's orders. The team had been most thorough.

The ambushers' weapons lay in a pile, including a pair of RPGs.

"I think this is all of them, sir," a security officer called as he approached my father. I couldn't make out his features beneath the tactical helmet and scarf that obscured most of his face. Most of the men worked to obscure their identities, a safety precaution now that they were pitting themselves against the Brotherhood. They might be willing to risk their lives for a massive paycheck, but they didn't want their employment to be taken out on their families.

"They had this on them, though." The officer held out a satellite phone.

My father took the phone and pointed to the bodies. "Dispose of these. Then secure the street. When you're done, I want these woods cleared back to rifle range. I don't want any cover left where scum like this can hide within spitting distance of the manor perimeter."

"Sir, we don't own the land. The county does."

"I don't care. Get it done. I'll take care of the government. We'll restore them when we are done."

"Done?" the man asked.

My father waved him off, not interested in a debate. The security officer barked orders to his men, and they started clearing up the evidence of the skirmish.

My father worked the keypad of the satellite phone, and put it on speaker mode.

"Is it done?" Andrew Lynch's arrogant voice carried through the woods. The cold calculated manner in which he asked after my mother's attempted assassination made me clench my fists. I found myself wishing I'd done something about him when I'd been face to face with him in his estate. Of course, I hadn't known how things would deteriorate, or perhaps I'd just been too optimistic.

"You have made your last mistake, Lynch." My father's voice was cold and rang with grim finality.

"Oh Frank, is that you? How are things? How's the family? I haven't seen Jillian in months. Please give her my regards."

"You smug bastard," my father said, spit flying from his mouth. "Our family built the Brotherhood. I was content to leave it in your hands and die in peace, but you had to get greedy. And for what? A little more power. This cowardice will cost you everything."

"Frank, Frank," Lynch tutted. "There was a time those threats would have brought men to their knees, but the years have not been kind to you. You've lost both your nerve, and your mind."

"You have no idea the pain I will rain down on you," my father growled. "You should have come for me and left my wife out of it. The inner circle will hear of this."

"They already have," Lynch said with a laugh, "and we are in agreement. We have outgrown you and your family. You've become a liability. When you bury your wife, leave some plots beside her for you and your meddling son. I'll see you soon."

Lynch cut the call, leaving my father gripping the phone until his knuckles turn white.

My father chanted, *"Polvo."*

The satellite phone was reduced to dust which he hurled at a nearby tree.

"He thinks she is dead," I whispered.

"And I let him believe it," my father replied. "Let him revel in his false sense of victory while we burn his world to ashes."

"What are you going to do?" I asked.

"Not I. We," my father replied. "Son, we're going to destroy the Brotherhood."

CHAPTER 4

The mood in the west wing of Weybridge Manor was understandably somber.

The west wing housed the manor's medical facility. With our family's condition, my father had long ago invested in the finest medical equipment and staff that money could buy.

Others, like the surgeons and healers that were currently operating, had been on call. They had been flown in from the finest hospitals in southern England.

It was times like this that the family name came in handy. There was no one who was going to say no to my father, or the considerable funds he was capable of paying them.

There were some things money couldn't fix though. I just prayed this wasn't one of them.

Murdoch's presence and preparation had given us a fighting chance, but now the waiting was taking a toll on me.

My father had been inside the theater with my mother since we had arrived back to the house.

I'd had nothing but fleeting updates from Arthur who was coordinating the efforts of both mundane and magical practitioners who had been working on her for the better part of two hours.

We sat on a bench seat in the wood paneled hallway, Lara clutched my hand in hers.

"She will pull through," Lara whispered, "you'll see."

I hoped she was right. I'd spent my life living with the almost certain reality that the curse would eventually cost my father his life, but I had always figured my mother would be there as she had always been.

For the last two hours, the same few thoughts had been playing over and over again in my mind. I examined every minute that I'd spent talking with Murdoch, picked apart everything he had said.

I felt like a fool, thinking an angel had truly come to just lift my spirits. In one sense he had. If my mother had been killed, who knew how I might have responded. I had no desire to face that abyss.

Without warning me of the danger, he'd intervened to ensure I would be close enough to help when the time came. I thought of how I'd berated him and felt ashamed. In all the time I'd known him, he'd been a true friend and a stalwart companion.

Even in recent times, when I'd discovered he was more than he appeared and doubt had crept in, time had always proved me to be wrong for not trusting him. Even now that I knew who he was, there seemed a part of me that was inclined to doubt him. A fear that some other agenda had compromised my friend. Loyalty to a higher power.

I felt petty and grateful all at once. I was particularly appreciative that he persisted with a friend as frail and frustrating as I must be at times.

I wanted to do better, and as I sat in the well-furnished hall, I resolved to do exactly that. In the quiet of the west wing, a ticking clock was the only evidence time was passing at all.

I'd been lingering beneath a mountain of morose emotions while Lynch was slowly planning the extinction of everyone I cared about.

No more.

Murdoch had said the Brotherhood had gone astray. He wasn't wrong. They were miles from the ideals my ancestor had founded them on. They were meant to be a force for good, prospering the world to a better future. Now they were hoarders of power, content to let the ends justify the means until the only ideal they truly cared for was the accumulation of greater power and influence.

And when it came to Lynch, access to absolute power had corrupted absolutely.

I just didn't understand how among a circle of men so powerful, he had managed to wrestle control of the entire organization. It seemed Lynch had them marching in step to the beat of his drum, but each of them were powerful men in their own right.

As the clock ticked, I put my mind to work trying to understand what had occurred. Perhaps if I could figure out how Lynch had seized absolute control of a group that was intended to be a Council, perhaps I could undermine his position. One angry man was less intimidating than a collective.

I considered what I knew of them, and what had transpired in recent times. Every member of the inner circle was a person of influence and power, but even in such circles, power and influence varied widely. The director of Clandestine Operations brought with it considerable access.

Those who could realistically counteract his influence were few that I knew of. One had doubtless been the Shinigami, Akihiro, a centuries-old wizard who had spent his lifetime exploring the forbidden, insulated from the consequences of his actions by his ability to seamlessly assume new identities.

Akihiro had lived many lifetimes, wielded immense power, and was perhaps the only human who had almost found immortality. An agenda Lynch would have had interest in, much like the Grail.

Fortunately for the rest of the world, Akihiro had died in New York, the result of his maddened plot to simultaneously destroy the financial center of the United States while consuming enough life essence to elevate himself to immortality or something effectively approximating it.

He might have succeeded but for the intervention of Kasey Chase.

The other counter-influence was my father, the Brotherhood's bank and a descendent of the original founder. Unfortunately, the older my father became, the more advanced his condition became and the less reliable he'd been.

When I had met Lynch, he'd painted himself as my father's greatest advocate in the Inner Circle, when in reality he had likely been steadily undermining my father and lessening his influence.

My father's decline, along with the death of Akihiro, had created a power vacuum Lynch had expanded to fill.

I could see it now, Lynch's steady assent. Now he meant to cement that rise by showing what he did to those who turned against the Brotherhood. We were nothing but an object lesson for him to use to guarantee his future. If Lynch could dispose of the Caldwell dynasty, who would dare stand against him?

Only he hadn't succeeded yet. Even his first gambit, killing my mother, had come up short. It boded well for us. At least it would if Arthur and the others could keep her alive. My mother was a member of an old wizarding bloodline with allies and influence in both the Parliament and Congress.

Perhaps Lynch had been trying to sever any chance we would receive reinforcements from my mother's family. The savage efficiency to his actions sent a shiver down my spine.

The doors to the medical suite opened and my father emerged. His collar was undone, his usual tie absent. Blood stained his hands and shirt. No doubt it was my mother's. He looked to me and my heart stopped.

Slowly, he exhaled, his lips turned up into the slightest hint of a smile.

"She'll make it. It was close, but she'll make it."

Relief flooded through me.

"Told you," Lara nudged me as my heart soared. My father and I didn't often see eye to eye, but my mother had been a stalwart supporter of my choices my whole life. Losing her would have been losing the first person who ever believed in me.

"Can I see her?" I asked, my voice hoarse with emotion.

"She's in a medically induced coma for now," my father said. "She won't be awake for a few hours. But I'm sure she'd want to see you too. When you're done, I'll be in the den."

My father stepped aside to let me pass but held out a hand to stop Lara.

"Lara, would you walk with me?"

She looked at me and then at my father and nodded.

He motioned down the hall and they set off together. That I had not expected, but in spite of their frequent antagonism with each other, I knew Lara could hold her own.

I took a deep breath and stepped into the medical center. After washing my hands at the sink and sanitizing them, I pushed open the internal doors with my elbow and beheld my mother lying on a bed. White sheets were pulled up to her pale face. Her blonde hair rested on her shoulders, some of it still stained with her own blood.

Arthur sat in the corner of the room slumped in a chair. There were deep creases at the corner of his eyes, and his hair was mussed.

A team of four medical staff were clustered around the foot of the bed. Two women monitored a series of screens with my mother's vital signs illuminating them.

I made my way over to the bed, and the staff parted to allow me room.

The sight of my mother and her shattered body broke my heart. I felt competing torrents of emotions: giddy hope that she was still alive, and fiery rage that Lynch would so callously try to take her from us.

I thought of his voice as he gloated through the satellite phone. In that moment, there was no evil in the world equal to what Lynch deserved for this heinous act.

I placed my hand on hers, gently. She looked so frail, not the formidable matriarch I was used to.

"I don't know if you can hear me, Mom, but I'll fix this. They're angry with me and they took it out on you. But I'll deal with it. I swear. You just hang in here and get better."

I bent forward and planted a kiss on her forehead. A tear rolled down my cheek as I backed away.

Blaming myself wasn't going to fix my dilemma, but I couldn't help it. I'd made the choice. Giving Lynch the Grail was never an option, and I'd never considered it, not really. Sure, it would have solved one problem but created more. Lynch would have been ageless.

More importantly, I was a man of my word. I'd promised Murdoch I would help him recover his charge and I did. Now I'd sworn to fix this, and I would. I squeezed my mother's hand and fussed over the sheets, tucking them in.

Turning, I nodded silently to the staff and made my way out of the room.

There was purpose in my stride now.

Murdoch had said I should call everyone.

Andrew Lynch had enemies. No one accumulated that much power and influence without accumulating a few. As I headed towards the den, I vowed to turn over every rock, call everyone I knew, and gather every person who'd ever wished ill upon him.

It was not going to be cheap, but my family had spent generations building a fortune. Now I was going to deploy it all in pursuit of a singular objective: To ensure Andrew Lynch and the Brotherhood never hurt another living soul.

My mind was racing as I pushed open the doors to my father's study.

He sat in his usual place behind his desk. Lara sat opposite him in one of the leather chairs. But between them on the desk rested a slim laptop computer attached to a docking station. The docking station had a dozen memory sticks plugged into it. My father usually left manual work to others, so I wondered what he was up to.

"Lynch needs to pay for this." The words were out of my mouth before I'd even reached my seat.

"On that we are in perfect agreement," my father replied. "It's the how that must be considered."

I slid into the seat beside Lara. "Why don't we start by finding everyone who has ever had an axe to grind with Lynch and give them a focus for their ire? We could apply so much pressure, that piece of human refuse would be ground beneath the weight of it."

"You are thinking too small, Seth," my father said "We must do more than start a war. We must win it."

I blinked.

I'd suggested a war, but my father's response seemed to indicate he considered that a half-measure.

"Yes, Seth. We must undermine the entire structure from which he draws his power. Lynch is a cockroach. But a cockroach with more power and influence than any other man alive. We must cut it off, and then we can choke the life out of him."

I was liking where my father's head was at, but I had no idea how that was to be accomplished. The Brotherhood's power structure was, by its very nature, decentralized.

"So you're not content to just play defense anymore?" I asked. This morning he'd felt very differently.

"I never was," my father replied. "I knew Lynch would come. I just misjudged him. I thought his first attempt would be at your wedding, so I was making preparations to that end. Lynch is a theatrical son of a bitch. Destroying your life on what is meant to be your happiest day would be right up his alley. I just never supposed his hatred of you would be superseded by his desire to put me in the ground. I should have anticipated his cowardly assault on your mother."

"None of us saw it coming," I replied. "Don't get mad, get even."

My father shook his fist. "It's a visceral betrayal of my life's work. I built everything he wields like a toy. That he was so willing to countenance such a calculated assault on my wife, your mother, it shows the depths to which they have sunk. We are going to bring down the Brotherhood, Seth. All of it."

He'd said as much in the forest. I'd just figured that was the rage speaking. My father had been a part of the organization for his entire life.

"How do you intend to do that?" I asked.

He tapped the computer on his desk. "There is an advantage to having been the banker. I know every action of consequence the Brotherhood has taken in the last forty years. I know who is on the payroll, which officials have been bribed, what assassinations have been carried out, and what democracies have been destabilised. Lynch has installed tyrants and deposed despots to further his agenda. I know all of Lynch's dirty little secrets."

An uneasy silence descended on the study as my father rested his fist on the desk.

"He should have killed me first, because now I'm going to show the world what he is."

I could tell from the timbre of my father's voice that he meant every word.

"I'm going to take their dirty laundry and air it before the world. Lynch wants to kill us, but before the sun sets, the world is going to want his head. We will share this with every news station across the world. We will send it to every embassy and push it out across the Internet."

"The Brotherhood has operatives everywhere," I replied. "Surely they'll try to stop this."

"Oh, they'll try," my father said, "but their efforts will only add fuel to the fire. With every story, pressure will mount. The Brotherhood's operatives will be forced to go to ground and the truth of their existence will spread like a cancer through the world. That is how you destroy the Brotherhood. Proof of life, and I have plenty of it."

"How do you plan to distribute it? If you send it over the Internet, Lynch and his cronies are going to get their hands on it. Their data monitoring is second to none."

"That's why we're delivering the first wave in person," he said. "In one hour. We will be at the London Palladium with as much of the city's press as we can trick into showing up. They will think they have gathered for a surprise royal spectacle. We will deliver a story they won't be able to help but run. When we're done, we'll send copies of this information to key institutions around the world. Once the stories start to run, we'll dump it wholesale on the Internet. The broader the reach, the better."

"You mean to go in person?" Lara asked. "Surely they will be watching the manor?"

"I have no doubt," my father replied, "but our transportation is currently being arranged. Even Lynch can't hope to have enough resources on standby to deal with what I'm going to throw at him."

The plan was a more brazen and reckless course of action than I'd expected, but it had potential.

"I'm in," I replied, wondering how I might broaden the impact of his plan. "Have you ever heard of the Seekers?"

"Of course I have," my father replied. "Those little do gooder journalists have been seeking to overturn the Brotherhood since they first got a whiff of it."

"Exactly," I said, "and for once our interests align. I know their leader, Thomas. I met him months ago in The Run, and again at Glastonbury. If you truly want to spread this thing, you should get him involved. Their connections through colleges and learning institutions around the world will spread this news like the plague."

My father pointed to the phone. "If you can reach him, do it. But have him come alone. We don't need a scene."

Thomas had called me half a dozen times in the last month. I'd never returned his call, mainly because I'd had nothing to say. At Glastonbury I'd given him a few tidbits about the Brotherhood, hoping to pressure Lynch, but I imagined that he'd run into a wall trying to find any real evidence.

Now my father was offering them everything. I just hoped Thomas was still in town. I picked up my phone and dialed the number.

Thomas answered on the second ring. "Oh, the Caldwell heir, took you long enough. To what do I owe this unexpected pleasure?"

I didn't feel in the mood for trading barbs, so I just baited the hook to see if he'd bite.

"Thomas, you wouldn't happen to be in the greater London area, would you?"

"We never left," he said. "Not after Glastonbury. We're still waiting for the fallout."

"Good," I replied. "Be at the London Palladium in one hour. Your name will be on the list. Come alone and I'll give you everything you ever wanted. Tell a soul, and you'll likely get us all killed."

"Everything I've ever wanted." Thomas chuckled. "Don't make promises you can't keep."

He was less excited than I'd anticipated. So, I doubled-down. "How about the names and positions of those who make up the organization you've been chasing, as well as evidence of their crimes? All you've gotta do is show up."

"How do I know it's not a trap?" Thomas asked.

"You don't. Thomas, but of the two times we have met, it has always been you threatening to kill me. Trust that my disposition hasn't changed but my desire to see them burn has."

The phone went quiet, and I knew I had him.

"One hour," I said, and hung up. Setting my phone on the table, I looked to the others. "He'll be there."

"Hopefully he won't bring Lynch with him," my father replied.

"Tell me more about how you intend to get there without being murdered by Lynch." I leaned forward in my chair.

My father smiled. "I have the staff working double time organizing decoy opportunities throughout the city. My assistants are scheduling appointments with the Arcane Parliament, Westminster, and a dozen other institutions of power and influence. Lynch's intelligence networks are going to be reporting all manner of possibilities. By the time they can analyze everything, we will already be spilling their secrets. But we must move quickly. Every moment we delay adds risk."

In the past, Lara had entertained the idea of taking Lynch up on his offer, figuring that if we were inside the Brotherhood, we might use it to further better ends.

I turned to Lara. "And you're on board with this?"

She nodded. "Who do you think helped plan the decoy meetings?"

Well, at least my fiancée and my father were starting to see eye to eye on something.

Lara took my hand. "We're lucky we didn't lose your mother today. Lynch needs to go. I'm all in."

"Okay," I said. "I'll call Dizzy on the way. Tell her where to meet us. She'll need to stay with us until this is over."

"You'll need to steer clear of her family," my father replied. "Her father is up to his armpits in promises to Lynch. So tell her to come without a word to him."

My father shut the laptop and tucked it in his briefcase. He took out two of the memory sticks and handed one to me and one to Lara.

"In one hour, the Caldwell server will start emailing links to that repository to every news outlet of any substance in the world. They'll be reticent to run the stories until they see others carrying them. Once they do, it'll be wildfire. If anything happens to me, spread them as widely as you can."

"Understood," I said as I took the drive.

"If anything happens to me, you need to keep Lynch so busy chasing his tail that he can't come after you."

I tucked the memory stick into my jacket pocket. Lara slipped hers into her sock and pulled her pant leg down over it.

We left the office and headed for the front door.

Outside, I stopped. Forty identical SUVs were parked in the driveway. I'd been so preoccupied, I hadn't even heard them being gathered. They were armored and had an army of security personnel stationed beside them.

Some of the security personnel were even dressed like a body double for my father, Lara, and me.

"Lynch might be watching," my father said, "but with forty cars heading in twenty different directions, even Lynch won't be able to scramble the resources he needs in time."

Lara nodded. "He'll be expecting us to hunker down in the manor, like we have the last few weeks."

"And we just executed one of his teams in the area," my father said. "Your wedding isn't for ten days. The balance of his forces are likely still en route. This is our best chance."

On that, I was in agreement. "Let's do it."

My father, Lara, and I were led to different vehicles. No matter what happened, one of us had to make it to the Paladium for this plan to work. If we did, Lynch's life was going to become a living nightmare.

Looking out the window, I smiled.

We had a plan. It was as bold as it was dangerous, but it could work.

Lara caught my eye and waved. I waved back and the vehicles started to roll. Forty armored SUVs, a hundred plus security personnel.

I clutched the memory stick in my pocket. This little two-inch piece of steel possessed the power to shake the Brotherhood to its very core.

The question was, would Lynch have the resources and manpower to stop us in time?

CHAPTER 5

While our destination might have been the London Palladium, the route we took to get there was the scenic one. The further we got from Weybridge Manor, the more the convoy split and fragmented, with armored cars heading in every direction.

I had tried a similar tactic when I'd fled New York with the stolen mask in my possession.

I'd not realized I was robbing the CIA until I was staring at their reports on my wife's desk. Her division, Section 9 and its Director, had seen through my efforts, but I'd been working with next to no time or preparation and relying almost entirely on a digitally produced set of theatrics orchestrated by a cunning hacker.

It hadn't worked but I'd always put that down to the limited time frame I'd given him to work with. This was a different affair entirely.

Where my last attempt had been digital deep fakes posted all over the internet and social media, this was an actual undertaking with dozens of real vehicles and hundreds of people.

Periodically, vehicles would stop, and security personnel emerged wearing the same jacket and hat I favored. Over the course of an hour, Lynch would be chasing no less than fifteen versions of me as they made their way all over London.

Elsewhere, decoys of my father and Lara were also traipsing all over the city.

The convoy would drop someone off and continue moving before picking another up. It was a carefully planned and executed choreography designed to boggle the minds of the most sophisticated intelligence network in the world.

I just hoped it was enough.

Andrew Lynch was the head of Clandestine Operations, and I had no doubt that at this moment every single one of his analysts were hunting us. They of course would think we were terrorists, or people of interest in some plot against the United States.

The Brotherhood didn't truly control the world, only the narrative. If one was to dig too deep into the cover story, they might start to learn the truth.

That was what we hoped to bring to light today.

After the best part of an hour of misdirection, the security officer who had been driving me in silence turned and pointed to the black duffel resting on the seat beside me.

"Mr. Caldwell, there is a change of clothes in the pack. If you wouldn't mind, we'd like to ensure we give you a sporting chance at making it inside undetected."

"Fair enough," I replied as I unzipped the bag. I wasn't wearing my favorite hat anyway. I hadn't exactly been planning this outing when I'd gotten up this morning.

Inside was a baseball cap. It was worn and faded, a second-hand Yankees cap that had seen better days. I pulled it down tight, keeping the brim low to obscure as much of my face as I could manage. I tossed aside the jacket I'd been wearing on the estate and pulled on a black leather duster. It was a long way from what I would usually wear, even in winter, which I supposed was the point. I pulled the jacket tight around me only to see the driver still staring at me in the mirror.

"Something wrong?" I asked.

"The vest too, sir. Just in case."

I realized there was a bullet-proof vest resting in the bottom of the bag. I hadn't even seen it there.

I undid my seat belt again, pulled off the jacket and my shirt, and strapped on the bullet-proof vest. I put it underneath my shirt in the hope that a lazy marksman might not aim for my face. If I wore it over the top and gave away its presence, I was only encouraging them to make a more ambitious target out of my relatively unprotected skull.

I pulled my shirt over the top. It barely fit, and I looked like an over eager bodybuilder, but it was better than the alternative. The duster went over the top and I pulled it tight around me as we rolled to a stop.

I didn't need to be told we were there. The London Palladium in the heart of West End was one of the most recognizable theaters anywhere in the world, renowned for hosting the Royal Variety Show and headline acts from every artistic discipline. I'd been here a dozen times.

My father had opted for the Palladium as the most conspicuous possible meeting place, and therefore the least likely to be the real destination. We would have been far safer with fifty journalists crammed into a warehouse somewhere. But that sort of traffic in a commercial district might also attract attention. Journalists and foot traffic passing the London Palladium, even on a day when no show was scheduled to take place, wouldn't be noteworthy. The only problem was that the venue was massive, and securing it against unwanted entry would have been a logistics effort in and of itself.

"Thanks, gents, appreciate the ride," I called as I pushed open the door.

"We'll be circling the neighborhood, sir. If you need us, we've texted you the number. Call and we'll be here in minutes. Godspeed."

I tipped my baseball cap, then pulled it low over my eyes and slid out of the car. The air was bracing. but the fortunate part about my father's choice in disguise was the duster was proof even against the cold air blowing through the city streets.

I made it all of fifteen steps before two more security personnel fell into stride beside me.

"Lara and your father are waiting We'll take you the rest of the way, sir."

It didn't matter how old I got, being called sir never felt right to me. But if my father really was preparing to hand the reins over to me, I would accomplish nothing by correcting it now.

I focused on the task at hand.

We were about to walk into a den of journalists, all hunting for their next headline story. If we weren't careful, the story they walked away with would be just as damning for us as it would be for Lynch, and our position was far more precarious.

There was no outing the Brotherhood without confessing the role my family had played in it. That admission gave our evidence credibility, yet it also tarred us with the same brush. I might have never joined them, but the smell of what the Brotherhood was would no doubt rub off on me too.

Even if we managed to take care of Lynch, there would still be a price to be paid. What we were about to do could never be undone.

But I couldn't let that stop me. Not now that I had my father on board. We were about to light a fire and set it at the base of the Brotherhood's very existence.

I was acutely aware that this would have ramifications not only for us, but for those whose names were on my father's list.

Some of them would inevitably die when their true loyalties were revealed. That was the thing about loyalty. You can't serve two masters, and once your loyalty is in question you become expendable.

I wasn't particularly comfortable with sentencing people I'd never met to death, but the Brotherhood's hierarchy was like a vast fortress. Removing a single brick wouldn't be enough to bring it down. We had to shatter its walls, destroy its framework, and erode the very foundations on which it was built.

The security force guided me through the Palladium, empty but for our personnel. I took a deep breath as we reached the stage.

There was no turning back now.

Security personnel flanked the stairs. I slipped between them and made my way up onto a stage I had no business being on.

The first five rows of the center section were full of journalists. They sat, recording devices in hand, notepads and laptops at the ready. Throughout the hall, Caldwell security forces were stationed at entrances and exits. Several snipers perched in the alcoves of the highest level.

My father and fiancée sat on the stage. Not the royals the journalists had been expecting but their curiosity piqued, nonetheless. Frank Caldwell might not have spent much time in public in recent years, but he was still a London elite.

The journalists had no idea of the import of what they were about to discover. The scope of it was going to blow their collective minds.

My father and Lara sat in two leather chairs facing the audience. A third empty chair sat between them.

I made my way over and sank into it. Lara leaned back and let out a sigh of relief at my presence. I rested a hand on her knee.

I'd never enjoyed the limelight, but after today, I would be lucky to ever enjoy peace again. I supposed being hounded by reporters and conspiracy theorists was better than the alternative: certain death at the hands of Andrew Lynch.

My father rose to his feet.

"I'm sure most of you know who I am. But for those who don't, I'm Frank Caldwell. I have not spent a great deal of time in the public eye of late. Doubtless you have all heard the rumors. As you can see from my countenance, there is some substance to them. I am dying."

Hands shot up as the reporters readied questions.

My father shook his head. "I have not brought you here to discuss my health, or other societal nonsense. The reason you're all here is a matter of greater import. Call it a confession if you will."

He glanced sideways at me. I nodded for him to go on.

"Before we proceed, I must warn you. The things I am about to tell you will put your lives in danger. From the moment you hear them, until you publish them widely, you will be in danger. If you wish to leave, that is your prerogative. But if you wish to learn the greatest secret ever kept in modern times, stick around. I'll make it worth your while."

The reporters were silent, waiting on his every word. I had to give it to dad; he knew how to work a room.

"You must swear you will spend every waking breath trying to bring to light that which I am about to share with you."

"Enough with the drama, Frank. Out with it already."

My father peered down into the mass of journalists. "Ellis Kitchener. Glad to see you are still breathing. Steady on, old man, this one will be a darn sight more interesting than the nonsense the BBC has had you covering the last six months."

My father drew a deep breath and held up a remote. He clicked a button and an overhead projector whirred to life. A massive white static filled the screen behind the stage.

"All of you believe you understand the world order. Countries and governments vying for control, as they compromise to share scarce resources for the betterment of their citizens. Economies, ofttimes fragile and easily threatened, are brought into balance through careful collaboration.

"Well, I have brought you here to tell you that behind it all, there is a single overarching agenda. An organization you've never heard of other than in whispers and rumors. They manipulate and control the affairs of the world."

My father paused, letting the journalists teeter on the edge of their chairs.

"Do not fear. I'm not a conspiracy theorist or tin foil hat wearing lunatic. I'm just merely pointing out they weren't wrong. I know. I have been a part of painting them as delusional for decades, to conceal the truth. Which is, for four hundred years, one society has controlled the course of humankind's progress."

There was a smattering of laughter through the Palladium. Several of the journalists started to stand.

"If we'd known we were coming here to listen to the deranged rambling of an old recluse, we would have stayed home," one journalist called.

"You've seen better days, Frank," another said.

My father cleared his throat. "Leave if you will, cowards. You'll note I mentioned this was a confession. I was a part of it. Those who remain and hear me out will be party to re-shaping the world. These moments don't even come around once in a lifetime, so squander it if you will."

The standing journalists paused, and my father continued. "We immortalized the men who signed the Declaration of Independence and history remembers every one of their names. What do you think will happen to those who brought down a shadow government that ruled the world for centuries? You will be heroes."

"Give us something concrete, Frank," Ellis called from the front row. "Or let us go home to our families."

The reporters started to sit down, though I noted those who hadn't moved. Thomas was sitting patiently at the end of the first row. Another in the third row was young, and he watched my father intently.

Skeptical as the others might have been, the younger participants seemed more inclined to give my father the benefit of the doubt.

Thomas had been looking for these answers for most of his life. I knew what it was like to search for something only to have it dance just outside your grip.

My father clicked the remote and Andrew Lynch's face filled the screen.

"Let us start at the top then," my father said. "Andrew Lynch, head of Clandestine Operations for the United States of America. And still, that's only the second most powerful title he holds. The other is Chairman of the Inner Circle of the Brotherhood. He and a handful of other men preside over an organization that has infiltrated every government of consequence, significant industrial interest, and military power structure in the world. They draw their greatest strength from the fact no one knows they exist, and no one is looking for them."

The room was quiet, so my father plowed on. "Some instances of their most recent activities include that mess in the South China Sea last year, the Suez Canal being blocked to bring global shipping to a halt. These were not simple accidents, but were carefully choreographed maneuvers to consolidate power."

The journalists were taking notes now. Even Ellis Kitchener had his pad out once more.

"I know I can't possibly hope to persuade you with words alone. But if you connect to the wireless network in this room, you'll find an open archive. It's unencrypted and it contains a wealth of evidence for your reference. Among the files is a listing of every operative on the Brotherhood's payroll, including but not limited to their entire command hierarchy and the grievous acts they've perpetrated to garner their influence. There are mountains of evidence I've gathered over a lifetime. You might ask how I come to be in possession of it."

My father swallowed. This was it. He was about to undo a lifetime's worth of effort in a heartbeat.

"Well, ladies and gentlemen, until this morning, I was a member of the Inner Circle myself. In fact, my family funded many of their operations. Our intentions had been to improve life for mankind, but when we refused to be a party to the increasingly erratic agenda, they tried to kill my son, and then murdered my wife."

I noted his lie. If Lynch learned of this meeting, at least he would continue to think he'd succeeded.

"So do all the digging you wish. You will find the events I've documented transpired precisely as I have indicated. The modus operandi was always that the ends justified the means, but such excuses play well behind closed doors. I'll let the public be the judge, when the facts are known. You will find complete paper trails, documentation proving the funding of these events, and irrefutable evidence that Andrew Lynch's intention is to rule the world from the safety of obscurity. A tyrant whose name is barely known by those whose lives he spends without remorse."

Thomas raised his voice. "Did they kill my parents?"

My father fixed him with a stare. "Son, I don't even know who your parents were. Be specific."

"They were FBI agents who discovered the existence of this Brotherhood you're talking about."

"I don't know the names of everyone whose lives were taken to preserve their secrets, but I can tell you they'd have killed them without hesitation, FBI agents or not.

"Young man, around this world are countless victims just like you. Victims of decisions made by a group of men the world might never have known. Lives cast aside in the pursuit of a greater good. That's the lie we told ourselves."

"What changed?" Kitchener called. "Are we to believe that the greatest conspiracy of our time has only been bought to light out of petty revenge?"

My father shook his head. "No. Lynch has changed things. He acts to accumulate power and influence. It is not the benevolent and guiding mandate the organization was founded on. It has lost its way and so must be dispersed to the four corners of the earth. The only way that happens is if you publish every detail you have found here. Mind you, the organizations you're a part of will do everything to suppress this story. The Brotherhood's influence is that great."

"You paint a grim picture," Kitchener said.

"That's why you must work together. Corroborate each other's stories, push them out on social media, dump it on the dark web, and shout it into every camera and micro-phone you can find. Only if this evidence finds its way into the public eye will their anonymity be shattered and the power structure of this monolithic evil be undermined forever."

There was a grinding rumble, and the Palladium shook gently. My chair shifted slightly as the entire building trem-bled.

It had to be an earthquake.

"Lord Byron is on this list," an older journalist near the front called.

"Indeed, he is," my father replied. "One of the inner cir-cle, he's had his hand in most of the matters we've already discussed. And dozens that we haven't. Further down the hierarchy you will find a handful of other lords. There are also senators and members of the House of Representatives from both sides of the aisle in the United States government.

"It doesn't end there. There are leaders of industry, political activists, super PACs and more. Influence is the currency of the Brotherhood. Many of you work for organizations that are controlled, influenced, or funded by assets of the Broth-erhood and don't even know it."

My father drew a deep breath.

"But to be clear, there are those who are members of the Brotherhood, and there are those who have served its interests unwittingly. If we are to bring down this evil, it must all be dragged into the light.

"That is the part you must play. I've given you all the ev-idence you could ever need. All you need to do is find the courage to print it. Shout it from the rooftops and spread it any way you can."

"What of your son?" Kitchener called. "What part does he play in all this?"

"He's here to support me," my father replied. "He's never been willing to join their cause. That's why they tried to have him killed."

"If they will kill him, they'll certainly kill us," a blonde woman called from the second row.

"Almost certainly," my father said "Why do you think I warned you? The sooner and wider you spread the message, the safer you all are.

"The Brotherhood strives for secrecy over overt action. Once the message is everywhere, killing you gains nothing and only serves to stir sentiment against them."

A second rumble stirred the Palladium and the journalists looked at each other, their uncertainty growing by the moment.

"Relax, it's just the tube," my father called. "Sometimes these old buildings shake a little."

I shifted uneasily in my chair. I'd been here enough to know it shouldn't be that loud. What was my father thinking? Perhaps he wasn't. It was possible that he was so hellbent on unmasking Andrew Lynch that he was overlooking the fact that something was very wrong.

My father changed the slides until Lynch's face filled the screen again. "But the piece you must all print is that this man, Andrew Lynch, is at the head of it all. He won't surrender his influence easily. You will feel the weight of it as you unmask him. His resources are immense and in the coming days you will likely see him attempt to wipe my family off the face of the earth for betraying their identities to the public. Let our deaths stand as a witness against them.

"My ancestor founded this organisation four centuries ago to try and lead the world to peace and prosperity. Now all we built is being used to accumulate power at the expense of others. It's not what we wanted. It's not what I spent my life building, and I won't have its existence be my legacy."

A grinding rumble shook the Palladium. The twisting sensation in my gut told me we were out of time. After all these years, I knew to trust it.

Rising to my feet, I grabbed dad's arm. "It's time to leave. I don't know how, but they've found us."

"Leave? We've got questions," one of the journalists shouted.

"Thousands of them, I'm sure," I called back. "Take the data and run. You might just live to print it. Go now!"

The journalists bolted for the exits.

As they filed out of the rows, one didn't move. He simply stood still, staring us down. He was the same young man who hadn't moved earlier. He couldn't have been any older than thirty and had a dark complexion. His eyes were fixed on my father.

"Frank Caldwell, you are a traitor and your forsaken vows call down the punishment of the brethren upon you." His thickly accented voice rang with power.

The Palladium shook harder.

Several journalists were thrown off their feet. I barely managed to keep mine beneath me. Thomas reached into his pocket as he moved closer to the stage. The Seeker looked like he was spoiling for a fight.

"You have what you want, Thomas. Now run while you still can. Spread the message far and wide. Ensure the Seekers bring the Brotherhood into the light."

"What about you?" Thomas called.

"I'm going to try and survive the week," I replied.

The rumbling intensified as the man in the third row began to chant.

The security forces opened fire on the man in the third row. The bullets rebounded harmlessly off a transparent arcane barrier that surrounded him.

"Lara, off the stage now," I shouted, as I turned to look for her.

Thomas was already running for the exit, as Lara leaped off the stage. My father and I raced down the stairs.

From the front row, Lara emptied her magazine at the wizard.

The bullets ricocheted harmlessly off the shield as the man reached beneath his robes. He pulled out an amulet that was made of bronze. It glowed an angry amber hue as he resumed his chanting.

We hit the carpeted floor as the stage was obliterated. A massive dark shape surging up through it.

The form splintered right through the center stage with an almighty crash. Timber was cast aside as a jet-black serpentine mass rose from the destroyed stage of the London Palladium.

CHAPTER 6

The serpent opened a chasm fifteen feet wide as it rose toward the ceiling, stalling for a moment before its massive bulk lost momentum and teetered forward.

The scaly mass landed on the stage with a thud. It was ten feet wide and perhaps thirty feet long.

Or at least that was how much of it protruded from the hole it had made through the floor. The serpent hissed, before opening its jaws to reveal massive fangs and a forked tongue that lashed about.

"It's a basilisk," I shouted. "Don't make eye contact with it."

One of the security personnel opened up with his assault rifle, and others followed suit. Heavy weapons fire smashed into the creature's scales. The basilisk whirled its head around, fixing him with a stare.

A throaty rasp filled the air as the creature's cursed sight killed the security officer.

Lara reached into her bag and pulled out a compact. She used the mirror to avoid making direct eye contact with the creature.

"Its gaze will still petrify you," I called as she squeezed off several rounds at the creature's head as it lunged forward into the audience.

"Still better than dead," she said.

Journalists screamed. Most of them were well on their way to the exits as the basilisk slithered off the stage. In total, it was easily forty-five feet long.

"Open fire," my father bellowed. "Kill the beast and its charmers."

One of the Caldwell security teams redoubled their efforts. Snipers in the balcony started firing. Each high-powered bullet sent a report echoing through the excellent acoustics of the Palladium.

On the ground floor, security teams flooded into the room, assault rifles roaring as they engaged the beast.

Scales and great chunks were blown out of the creature's hide as the bullets slammed into it. But there was simply too much bulk between our men and its vital organs.

Two men in robes climbed out of the hole the creature had made in the stage. More of its handlers perhaps. Beasts like basilisks seldom strayed into the mundane realm unless driven by charmers for their nefarious purposes.

"We need to get out of here," I called. "The longer we stay, the more of them we'll have to contend with. Shepherd the reporters to the doors and let's go."

We didn't have to beat them; we just needed to survive.

"Run, you idiots," Lara called.

"Seth, there are more of them." Thomas pointed at the stage.

The two men I'd seen were now four, and other hoods appeared at the rim of the hole.

Above Thomas' open hand, three stones levitated and spun. With a word, he let fly. He was a much better shot than I was.

The first stone smashed into a charmer's forehead and shattered his skull. There was a sickening crack before he fell backward into the pit he'd been climbing out of.

The second charmer conjured a ball of fire and hurled it at Thomas.

Thomas was too close to conjure a shield. He hurled himself onto the ground. I ducked behind the row of seats. The fire soared past us and struck the wall of the theatre. As the flames played across its surface, they caught on the ornamental curtains. The wall was ablaze.

More of the men in black robes climbed out of the pit.

We were in danger of being overwhelmed. The security team was so focused on the terrifying form of the basilisk they were missing the arcane practitioners who would soon turn the tide against us.

Drawing on my own power, I hurled two bolts of ruby red arcana. The missiles slammed right into the midst of the charmers, carving through the chest of one of the black robes before colliding with a second charmer.

I let out a grunt of satisfaction as both of the charmers collapsed.

More of their comrades emerged from the pit.

"We need some suppressing fire on the stage," I yelled to the heavily armed personnel moving to escort us.

Our security forces took up position in the seating and opened fired on the stage. The roar of their weapons was deafening as the massive basilisk wreaked havoc on those undisciplined enough to catch its gaze.

As the fire spread, the building's fire suppression system kicked in, raining water down on the blaze and the rest of us with it.

Most of the journalists had made it to the doors, but my father, Lara and I were only halfway up the aisle. I was starting to wonder if we were going to make it out of here in one piece.

"The convoy is waiting," my father called from farther up the aisle. "Let's go."

Smoke and steam spread, and visibility was declining rapidly. The London Palladium had seen better days.

"Perhaps we should have picked a less historic venue," I called back.

"If we survive, they can send us a bill." My father shrugged as I raced toward him.

"Who are these people?"

"Sapera. They are nomadic mercenaries from northern India. I suspect Lynch is footing the bill. Though how they got into London with one of their monstrosities is beyond me."

"But it's not beyond Lynch, is it?" I replied. Given time, there was little the Brotherhood couldn't manage.

Lynch had given me a month, but as I beheld the chaos unfolding in the Palladium, I realized the truth. He'd never expected me to say yes. Lynch had spent the whole thirty days maneuvering his forces into position for my inevitable refusal.

That was why he'd had a response team at Glastonbury so quickly. It was also why he already had so many forces on the ground in London.

We had underestimated him. I wouldn't make that mistake again.

"He's been operating in bad faith," my father replied, drawing the same conclusion I had. "And he will pay for it."

Rather than focus on those on the stage, I turned my attention on the man who'd started it all. The snake charmer in the third row. I hurled another volley of arcane missiles at him. At the last second, the Basilisk slithered between us, crushing chairs beneath its bulk as it moved to protect its master.

Most of my magic simply glanced off the hide of the titanic beast. Tearing my eyes away from it, lest it turn its head in my direction, I realized the danger was growing.

More than half a dozen paralyzed statues marked where the creature had managed to make indirect eye contact with our personnel, via the mirrored surfaces or pools of water.

Thomas raced for the door, realizing discretion was the better part of valor. I didn't blame him. He'd just learned everything he'd ever wanted to know. Dying now would put his life's work in jeopardy.

"Back to the manor?" I called as I raced up the wet carpet toward my father. "Hopefully we have done enough damage to Lynch for one day."

"Not yet," my father replied, stubborn lines etched in his furrowed brow. "We still have one stop left to make."

"Are you kidding?"

"No. I need to go to The Run and talk to that diviner. I might not get another chance."

The Run was a dangerous place on the best of days, almost exclusively inhabited by those who favored money over morals. The last time I'd gone, I'd been chased out by Thomas and the Seekers. Journeying into The Run with Lynch on our tail seemed tantamount to suicide. But the more I thought about it, the more I saw the opportunity.

The Run was also home to the Panhandle, Levi's bar. After my conversation with Murdoch, I needed to speak with him, and he didn't do phones.

It was risky, but perhaps that might play in our favor. Lynch might expect us to make for home. Perhaps this would throw a wrench in his plans.

Perhaps our security could hold the Sapera and the basilisk here. Their numbers were falling but we'd brought an army.

Gunfire continued to echo through the Palladium. The basilisk let out a defiant hiss. There were now more than a dozen of the black robes hurling spells at the security team, and more than that lying dead on the stage. Our forces had elevation and superior entrenched positions on our side.

There was a crashing racket behind us as we raced for the exit.

"The basilisk, it's coming after us," Lara shouted

I didn't dare look behind me. In my mind's eye, I could see it clearly, plowing through the rows of chairs. The noise was deafening.

Lara shut the mirror. With the creature coming right for us, the risk of inadvertently catching its gaze was too high.

Lara had never seen a basilisk and yet she moved with planned purpose, adapting on the fly, firing behind her as she went.

She was unflappable.

With a surge, the basilisk slithered past us, obliterating the back row of chairs, before positioning its considerable girth to block the exit we were making for.

We needed out of here, so I channeled lightning at the creature. Eldritch energy played up its serpentine body, scales crackling and warping as I lashed at it repeatedly. The creature hissed and began to turn its head toward me. I looked, away racing for the cover of the next row of chairs.

"Take out its eyes," my father called. "Security teams, focus our heavy weapons fire on the creature's head."

As one, the security forces redirected their attention to the massive basilisk. There was a squeal that choked off as one unfortunate soul was turned to stone. He'd made eye contact through the scope of his rifle.

The deafening weight of fire drowned out all other consid-
erations. The creature hissed and the wizard in the third row
screamed in pain.

I looked at the beast's body, then slowly moved my gaze
upward, ensuring that its head was facing away before risk-
ing a look in that direction.

The basilisk hissed in fury, blood and ichor running from
the creature's ruined eye. The lid was closed, but the eye had
been obliterated. Dozens of wounds marked the side of the
snake's head. As it came around, I averted my gaze, just in
time to spot the fireball whistling toward me from the stage.
I ducked, letting the fireball soar through the space I'd just
been occupying.

"That's a hit," my father called, directing our forces. "Now
the other."

The basilisk thrashed about, on the move again.

"Seth!" Lara's voice was pained.

The creature was after me.

"Hit it with everything you can," I shouted, scrambling
through the chairs and heading in the other direction. Unable to look at the creature for prolonged periods, teamwork
and coordination was our best chance of survival. If I could
draw it off, the others might bring it down. Then we could
make a run for it.

The creature was so close, saliva rained down on me as its
rasping hiss echoed overhead. I groaned, shaking saliva off
one arm.

The creature hit me in the back, throwing me against the
wall.

There were bits of broken chair and battered Palladium
everywhere I looked. I snatched up a piece of broken chair
and used the back of the reflective plastic as a guide. It wasn't
much to go on; I could barely make out shapes. Fortunately,

the creature was huge and impossible to mistake for any-thing else.

The creature's body slithered close to me, threatening to crush me against the wall.

I scrambled to my feet and ran. Kicking off the wall, I threw myself back at the snake's body in an effort to climb it rather than be crushed.

I gripped the edges of the ridged scales as the creature moved on. I held on for dear life. When I got used to the motion, I started to climb. The beast was far too big for me to consider transmuting it. The effort of unleashing that much energy in a single spell would likely kill me. I knew from painful experience what happened when I pushed my limits.

Lara shot indiscriminately at the creature as I was dragged along for the ride. Having failed to crush me to death, the snake went after my father.

"Run, Dad," I shouted as my father hobbled toward the next exit.

Three security personnel stood before it, firing back at the basilisk. One by one, they perished as the creature met their stare. One died, the next two were paralyzed. Each gave their all to buy my father precious seconds before the basilisk smashed through the petrified bodies.

To my right, a massive shape swung over the lip of the upper balcony like a gymnast on the high bar. Only it was no gymnast. It was hundreds of pounds of silverback gorilla.

"Dizzy!" I gasped, relief flooding through me.

She threw herself towards the snake's head as it loomed over my father. I watched in slow motion as the basilisk's jaws opened wide, its head plunging toward my father. The creature's wicked sharp fangs were large enough to punch through three people.

Dizzy slammed into the side of the creature's head. Its ruined eye hadn't even seen her coming and she hit the creature like a wrecking ball.

The basilisk hit the wall with a bone-snapping crunch.

"Dizzy," I shouted. I was about to warn her of the creature's stare, when I caught myself. She knew more about animals of the mundane and mythical varieties than most people alive. After all, she was an Alasa; it was her birthright.

The basilisk tried to rise but Dizzy dropped her shoulder and slammed back into the creature's skull, wedging it against the wall.

The basilisk opened its jaw, drawing back in an effort to raise its head out of her range. Dizzy wrapped one gorilla fist around its fang and held tight as the basilisk reared up until it hit the ceiling, or rather the floor of the level above us.

The creature hissed, spitting saliva at Dizzy which I knew would only serve to antagonise her.

With the creature stalled, I climbed to my feet and ran along its back on uneven footing. I had a ways to go and not much time to do it in.

The basilisk's jaws attempted to snap shut on Dizzy. The crushing force was considerable. But Dizzy's massive gorilla feet planted themselves against its bottom jaw. She stood there, her massive frame wedged in place, keeping its mouth open and its one good eye facing uselessly at the wall.

"Dizzy, you're insane," I shouted as I ran.

The gradient grew steeper and steeper, but I needed to get close enough to do real damage. The body of the snake was not the best place to do it. Closer to the skull, I couldn't see past it, but the basilisk's tongue lashed about as it tried to yank Dizzy free.

She held firm against the crushing weight of the creature's jaws.

Lara jammed her pistol between two of the scales and fired round after round into the basilisk's flank.

My father managed to get to his feet and holding both hands before him, bellowed, *"Espada Arcana!"*

A beam of energy stretched from his closed fist like a lightsaber. Raising his hands above his head, he drove the beam of energy into the basilisk's stomach.

The war raged on between the security team and the other sapera.

The creature pitched forward. If it couldn't dislodge Dizzy, it would smash her into the ground.

But the same motion made it far easier for me to climb and as it teetered forward. I leaped and grabbed hold of the scales at the base of the creature's skull.

"Piedra!" I shouted, unleashing my will. I simply hoped I was close enough to its brain to make a difference. I poured power into the base of the creature's skull as I transmuted. I could feel bone and sinew hardening as they turned to stone. The basilisk hissed until its vocal cords turned to rock. I felt faint from the exertion.

But I was close, too close to give in. I could almost feel the creature's will diminishing as its head turned to stone before my unrelenting will. I fed the creature a taste of its own paralyzing medicine.

My vision went dark, and I willed everything I could muster into the beast. The basilisk pitched forward, only now it wasn't intentional. So much of the creature's head was stone that I'd affected the creature's momentum.

Dizzy swung free as the basilisk's half stone, half fleshy head smashed into the carpeted floor of the London Palladium. I was thrown clear, my vision going dark, my brain pounding with pain.

I hit the carpet hard. I tucked and rolled free of the creature's bulk before sprawling to a halt.

Dizzy in her gorilla form pinned the basilisk down as my father drove the blade through its jaws and into its brain.

There was a keening shriek as the wizard in the third row cried out and pitched forward, never to rise again.

"Seth, Seth," Lara shouted.

I pushed myself to my hands and knees, struggling to my feet.

Lara took some of my weight as she threw my arm over her shoulder.

Dizzy shifted back into her human form. "What the hell is a basilisk doing in London?"

"Our new friends bought it," I muttered.

"Charming," Dizzy replied as she drew her bow off her back. She nocked an arrow and sent it flying at the mass of black robed wizards on the stage.

When the arrow lost height, I thought she'd missed. I simply hadn't seen the wizard clambering over the rows of chairs.

Dizzy's arrow caught him in the chest and sent him back the way he'd come.

"Shall we?" My father pointed at the door. "The security teams are mustering out front. It's time to move."

"You're welcome," Dizzy replied, throwing a thumb over her shoulder at the basilisk.

"Your timing, Ms. Alasa is impeccable," my father said. "Thank you for that, but if you don't mind, let's discuss it in the car."

Dizzy grinned. "After you."

We raced through the door, my father reaching for the communication device in his ear.

"We're out, making for the convoy. Terminate any remaining hostiles with extreme prejudice."

I looked back over my shoulder at the black robes scurrying off the stage after us. They had taken their eyes off the security personnel. That was their final mistake.

I smiled as the launched grenades rained down from the upper level. With their employers out of the way, the security team were less concerned with collateral damage. The first few detonations devastated an entire seating section and obliterated a dozen of the black robes with them.

I took off after the others, confident that the remaining sapera had their work cut out for them.

We raced through the lobby, down the stairs, and out onto the street. A dozen of the black SUVs were waiting for us. This time, we all piled into the same vehicle. If the game was up, there was strength in numbers.

"Where to, sir?" the driver called as my father clambered into the front seat.

"The Run. Have all teams converge. Form a beachhead. We need an hour."

I looked at my father. An hour?

With Andrew Lynch on our tail, he was hoping for a lot.

Before I could speak, my father closed his eyes and held up his hand.

"Later, you nagging harpy. Get out of my mind!"

I winced, knowing exactly who he'd been speaking to.

Aleida.

My father was far from being in his right mind, and we were following him into one of the most dangerous places in London while being hunted by the most powerful man alive.

What could possibly go wrong?

CHAPTER 7

The Run was an underground black market in the heart of London. On a good day, you could find just about anything you were looking for. On a bad day, you'd find the pointy end of a gnome's knife, or a vampire looking for an easy feed.

Unfortunately, there were more bad days than good. I'd spent a lot of time there buying and selling arcane relics. Most knew better than to ask where something came from.

We stepped out of the elevators onto the underground cobblestone streets. While London city had come a long way in the last hundred years, no one had passed that message along to The Run. It was lit by old fashioned streetlights, and the cobblestone streets while neat and mostly even, looked like something time had left behind.

Each side of the street featured storefronts, or low-end accommodations. The sorts of places where one wanting to avoid the Arcane Parliament might lay low for a few days.

As we stepped into the street, heads turned.

While I usually traveled a little more incognito, my father was a member of the London elite. His face had been on the cover of magazines and newspaper articles for years. And when he strode into the Run with a dozen armed security, people took notice.

Lara, Dizzy, and I trailed behind. I kept an eye open, looking for anyone whose gaze lingered long enough to signal interest.

Lynch's ambush at the Palladium had been brutal but by its very nature had contained his forces in a firing zone for our security personnel. The sapera, if any survived, would have retreated underground and would be licking their wounds. Lynch had been forced to make his play and failed. Now our journalists would be out there verifying the information they'd been given.

In a world where it was better to be first than right, I expected the stories would come thick and fast.

"You sure this is a good idea?" I asked my father. "Lynch clearly has men in the area."

"We're not going to get a better chance than this," my father replied. "Lynch will have more assets, but I'm willing to bet, he's consolidating his forces between us and the manor. He won't want to risk us getting home in one piece. I have no intention of taking that road."

I hoped he was right.

The Brotherhood had money and influence but now their problems had multiplied. Soon, the sapera would report back what we'd done. We'd leaked the Brotherhood's most private secrets to the world. My father had betrayed his sworn oath.

No doubt Lynch would want us dead, but he now had dozens of threats to track. Every journalist that had been in the building had enough dirt to bury him.

Hopefully, Lynch would be so busy playing defence, we would get in and out of the Run without incident.

My phone dinged. I'd set an alert for the phrase Brother-hood. I pulled out my phone and found a social media post linking to a prominent Channel One news piece.

That was fast. Even quicker than I'd expected.

Others would follow any minute. Lynch would have to start extinguishing and suppressing the reports as best he could.

"Still, we should move quickly," I replied. "He's going to be mad as hell."

"He should have known better than to target your mother," my father said, the indignation ringing in his voice.

I shared his pain, and not for the first time, I wondered how she was doing.

"Right now, Lynch is facing a war on every front. Soon, his phone will start ringing and it won't just be journalists. People like the government he's meant to be serving will have questions. The more they dig, the more curious they will become. Then it will be the other members of the Inner Circle. They'll all be upset that his petty grievance has exposed them. They too will start exerting pressure on him."

"What good does that do us?" Dizzy asked. "Surely that will only increase his desire to want to kill us all."

"Perhaps," my father replied. "But he already wanted that, and the chairman only maintains his power as long as the others vote to keep him in his seat. He will have sold them this agenda on the premise that it will further their own interests but now it's getting messy. And they won't long abide the fallout of Lynch's greed. We have planted a cancer at the very heart of everything they stand for. I expect it will bring them to their knees."

"And then what?" I asked. If it was just a matter of holding out, perhaps we ought to have picked a safer course of action.

"Then they will likely redouble their efforts to destroy us," my father replied. "If they succeed, they will rebuild and rebrand as something else. Try and salvage something of what they once were. When it becomes apparent the extent of the information in the possession of the media, I expect they will try to wipe us out before going into hiding."

"Just the wedding gift I was hoping for." Lara's sarcasm made me chuckle. At least she hadn't lost her humor.

"That's why we're here," my father replied, "to solicit additional manpower and get answers from the Diviner."

"Well, perhaps it's best to split up and cover more ground," I replied. "You go see the Diviner. I'll head to the Panhandle. I want to speak to Levi and some others."

"Levi? The barkeep?" my father asked. "Not sure what he'll be good for."

Clearly, my father had spent less time with him than I had. "I think Levi's capacity might surprise you. Besides, he'll know who else is in town."

My father shrugged. "Do what you will, but let's meet back here in one hour. If you so much as see trouble, raise the alarm."

We parted company at the next intersection. My father took the security personnel with him, which was just fine by me. The three of us would have a far easier time blending in if we weren't flanked by men in body armor and carrying assault rifles.

Lara, Dizzy, and I reached the Panhandle in good time. Music spilled out into the streets, familiar vocals accompanied by an acoustic guitar. From the din, the bar was full to capacity.

I sighed. I'd been hoping to catch it empty or at least on a quieter afternoon so that I had a proper chance to speak with Levi.

If he was focused on serving his patrons, it might be difficult to have the sort of meaningful conversation I was hoping
to have. I needed him to hear me out, and I wasn't confident
he would give me that chance.

Particularly not if he took a look inside my head. One look
inside my mind would tell him I was recruiting him for a
suicide mission.

I tried to think more positive thoughts as I turned to the
others.

"When we go inside, could the two of you find a table while
I speak with Levi privately?"

"Wherever you go, I go," Lara replied, her hands moving to
her hips out of habit.

"Ditto," Dizzy added, "hard to save your skinny ass if I have
to cross half of a crowded pub to do it."

"As long as we are in here, I should be fine," I replied.
"Trouble is rare in the Panhandle. Levi and his men see to
that."

Lara looked less than convinced.

"I need Levi comfortable enough to speak freely, which
he won't do if he's speaking to a crowd," I hastened to add.
"Please. We don't have a lot of time."

"Okay," Lara relented, "but we'll be over at the first sign of
trouble."

Some men would be a little emasculated at that, but Lara
and Dizzy weren't wrong. I had a certain penchant for getting
myself in trouble.

"Fine, we'll have a grand old time. You try not to get yourself
killed while we're having a drink," Dizzy said.

"You ladies have a good time. Try not to burn the place
down."

I pushed open the double doors to the Panhandle and
stepped inside. The music intensified, and a few raucous pa-

trons sang along to the popular tune, as a red-haired guitarist strummed away on his guitar.

He bore a striking resemblance to a certain superstar which I was sure played into his favor when he was busking. That said, he was pretty talented.

Heading for the bar, I did a quick sweep of the tavern for any signs of an ambush. Most of the occupants looked far more interested in the meal in front of them than in Lara, Dizzy and me.

The Panhandle was a safe space, or as safe as things got in the Run. Levi's gifts tended to head off most trouble before it could manifest, but there was always the chance some moron would give in to their baser nature and spontaneously stir trouble.

The ladies broke off and headed for an empty table not too far from the door. Fires roared in pits on opposing sides of the vast room, providing heat to stave off the innate chill that was ever present in The Run.

The room was filled with small round tables set at irregular intervals. Low hanging timber beams ran the length of the roof and lent the feel of a medieval tavern.

A large bar ran down the far wall of the establishment; behind it a set of doors led into a kitchen.

Levi was tending the bar. The golden-haired man stood several inches over six feet tall, and he wore a simple cotton spun shirt and khaki slacks with a leather apron. A dish cloth hung over one broad shoulder. His physique, all muscle, seemed to flex with tension at odds with the relaxed environs of the Panhandle.

As his eyes met mine. He leaned on the counter with one hand. "A little bit busy to chat. You should come back later."

I swung my leg over the stool and sat down. "I'd love to, Levi, but this is all the time I've got. What are the chances you can give me the time of day and let someone else tend the bar for a few minutes?"

Levi raised an eyebrow. "What do you have in mind?"

I smiled. "You know exactly what I've got in mind. It's one of the reasons I'm here."

Mind magic was a dangerous game and one that most people would avoid showcasing. Using it on others tended to be a recipe for execution. The Arcane Parliament, not to mention the Congress, took poorly to meddling in the minds of others.

"Don't talk of such things so openly," Levi growled. "Even these walls have ears."

I leaned back. Perhaps I'd been a little too direct. It did make me wonder why he'd been so open with me in the past. Was it because he already knew my secrets? Or had he deemed me so little a threat as to not care if I knew?

"I saw in you a kindred spirit," Levi answered my unspoken question.

A shiver ran down my spine. I wasn't sure if it was nervousness at him reading my mind, or excitement that he saw something in me.

"How is that?" I wondered aloud.

"You and I both want the same thing." He sighed. "Born of different realms and yet the heart still yearns for the same desire."

I knew he wasn't talking about the curse. That problem was mine alone. I glanced over my shoulder.

"How are things with your fiancé?" Levi asked, nodding toward Lara.

"Pretty good," I replied, and in the scheme of things, they were.

Some days I wasn't sure why she put up with my baggage, but she seemed to love me in spite of it. It was more than a man could ask for.

"We're getting married in a few days," I said, leaning on the bar. "At least I hope so."

"I'm not one to meddle in other's affairs, Seth. This problem you've stirred up with Lynch and his ilk—I cannot afford to interfere."

"Who said anything about interfering?" I asked, holding my hands up. "We're just talking, aren't we?"

"You didn't have to," Levi replied as he reached beneath the bar. He grabbed a tankard and filled it to the brim.

A man in a thick coat sat down two stools from me. Levi set the tankard down in front of him.

"Am I so predictable?" the grizzled man asked in a deep voice.

"I prefer reliable," Levi replied as he took the man's bill from his outstretched hand.

"Keep the change, and keep them coming," the man said.

Levi pocketed the note and returned to me. "You came here looking for allies, but I have no desire to put myself in his cross hairs. The price is simply too great, the payoff too small, and I have not come this far to fail now."

I tried not to smile. He'd mentioned payment, which meant he hadn't rejected me out of hand. We were negotiating.

"Fall short of what exactly?" I replied. "Perhaps I can help."

I was fascinated by his turn of phrase. It intimated that he'd been working on something and for some time. Which didn't make a great deal of sense, given he never seemed to move from his place at the bar.

I suspected that I knew exactly what kind of being he was. Mind magic was rare. Few species had any capacity for it and only one that I knew of could exercise it with anywhere near the talent he had.

"That is not a problem to concern yourself with, Seth. Let me fix you a drink and then you can be on your way. Trouble seems to follow you, and another incident and I'm going to have to ban you for life. The others won't abide special treatment."

"What if I was to make it worth your while?" I reached into my pocket and produced a piece of gold.

It'd been a stone until I'd used my gifts to transmute it. His eyes gleamed as he looked at the small lump of gold. I figured I might need to bargain, so I'd come prepared.

"You'd be wise not to so openly flaunt so valuable a trinket in here," he said. "There are unscrupulous sorts in here, Seth Caldwell. Even I can't keep them all in check."

I set the gold down on the bar between us, ignoring his warning. I'd come too far to stop now. I was willing to risk the display of wealth, particularly with the way Levi's eyes seemed to focus on it.

I was dealing in the right currency.

"It's yours, whether or not you agree. All you have to do is hear me out."

Levi picked up the piece of gold. Both his eyes and the gold gleamed.

"A potent bribe, Seth," he replied as he tucked the gold into his apron. "I can spare a moment."

"I'd rather we went somewhere private. What I'm about to share, I would rather not become common knowledge."

"We can talk here," Levi replied as he scanned the tavern. "We'll be safe here."

"There are people everywhere."

Levi smiled, as he pressed the note into the register and grabbed some change. "Just a moment."

He handed the change to the man who'd told him to keep it, and before the man could remind him of his earlier instruction there was a grinding of stools against the floor.

The grizzled patron and almost the entire population of the Panhandle rose and headed for the door simultaneously.

"Thanks, Ed," Levi called to the musician, who'd hung his guitar over one shoulder. "Now we're even."

"Until next time." The singer winked at the barkeep and followed the others out the door.

"You better make this worth my while, Seth. That particular favor was one I had been sitting on for a year."

"Was that...?" I couldn't bring myself to say his name out loud.

"He was on tour," Levi replied. "So you can imagine the tips this little private viewing was bringing in."

The pub was empty, save for Lara, Dizzy, and a smattering of others scattered throughout the bar.

"They're mine." Levi gestured at the others. "They're my security and they won't talk. Your secrets are safe with us. Would you rather yours stay or go?"

"It's safer in here than out there," I said, motioning for them to relax.

Levi nodded and his security team went back to pretending to eat while Lara and Dizzy exchanged awkward glances and watched the now empty pub.

"How did you do that?" I asked. "Even for you, that was impressive."

"That secret would get you in considerable trouble, Seth. Suffice it to say, each of them felt they had somewhere else they needed to be. And I encouraged them to pursue that feeling."

I smiled. I had certainly come to the right place.

"Look, Seth. I have nothing against you. In fact, I kinda like you. But you've picked a fight with the wrong dog."

"What do you know about Lynch?" I asked.

Levi folded his arms. "Everything you've thought about him since you've walked in. And everything I have mined from the heads of my patrons over the years. In my realm, I'm an apex predator. But here, Lynch would have to kick down to find me. To pick a fight with him is to court extinction. Even you believe you're recruiting to a doomed cause."

It was one thing to view my own prospects as dim, another to hear them come out of someone else's mouth.

"Lynch's time is limited," I said. "We have just torn the shroud off the Brotherhood. The anonymity is gone and their most heinous deeds are a matter of public record. In the hours, days, and weeks that come, everything Lynch has built will come apart. All I need is help to survive that long."

Levi buffed at the bar with his dishrag.

"It would put everything I have built in jeopardy," he said. "I've spent my entire life building to this point. What you're suggesting could cost me everything."

"I know." I ran both hands through my hair in frustration. "That's what I'm up against. But you didn't clear the bar to tell me you couldn't help me. You are standing there wanting something from me and if you didn't think I could help you, you would have sent me packing with the rest of them. So rather than beating around the bush, out with it."

Levi reached into his pocket and pulled out the lump of gold. He set it out on the bar between us.

"This interests me, Seth. Most other people would think this was gold."

"It is gold."

Levi nodded. "It is, but it's also more. Until your last visit, I didn't even know it was possible."

"What is?" I asked, giving him room to make his ask.

"Alchemy," Levi replied. "Turning substances into gold. I can still feel the magic that went into its creation."

"And that diminishes its value?" I was a little confused. "What are you? A gold connoisseur?"

"Quite the contrary," Levi replied his eyes fixated on the lump of gold. "I want to know more about it."

"Oh, let's stop with the foreplay. You can read my mind," I replied. "You tell me."

"A deal cannot be struck with deception," he said. "I can't jeopardize the validity of our compact by tampering with your mind. I stopped probing it the minute you sat in that seat."

His words told me everything. Levi was just as eager to see me as I was to see him. He'd been waiting for me. The fact he was considering that a bargain might be struck gave me the courage I needed.

"It's not alchemy," I replied. "It's a gift. The bloodline power of my people and my family might be the only ones on earth who can do it."

I reached over the counter and grabbed an empty glass out of the rack. "*Oro!*"

Magic flowed from my palm into the glass until the entire glass was solid gold. I set it on the counter beside the rock.

"Do you have any idea how valuable your talent is?" Levi asked.

I nodded. "My family have used it to shape the world for four centuries. Money makes the world go round and until only decades ago, gold was the premium measure of value."

"It still is," he replied. "Certainly is among my people."

"Well, that talent is about to be wiped off the face of the Earth. The real question is, why do you care?"

Levi let out a long sigh. "I was exiled from my people. Cast out because of my father. He drew the wrath of a being even my kind don't deign to cross. He paid with his life, and I was exiled lest I should remind that being of his ire."

"So you decided to tend bar?" I asked, leaning on my fist.

"I needed somewhere that would be a confluence of knowledge. The things I learn here bring considerable profit, and I have been accumulating wealth for decades. If I ever want to return to my people, I'm going to have to buy my way back in, one ounce of gold at a time. The bounty they set was so considerable they deemed it impossible. They doubt my resolve."

"And how is that going for you?" I asked.

Levi groaned. "I'm less than halfway there, and I'm still decades from buying my way back in to my own lands. Even then, I would be broke and if I would have Jakira to be my wife, I would need more. She's been waiting this long, but even her patience has limits."

"Jakira?" I leaned back and held my tongue, giving him ample opportunity to fill the silence.

"She was my soulmate," he said. "It is a bond between the spirits of our kind. Her father would never allow her to live in exile, and the dowry would be unthinkable. It's likely one of the reasons she remains unbonded."

"So you need gold?" I was starting to understand what Murdoch had been guiding me toward him.

"An unthinkable quantity," Levi answered forlornly.

"Well, I can help you with that. Given time and rest, I can produce all that you require in a fraction of the time it might take you to earn it. More importantly, at our estate we have a strong room. My father calls it the cavern because it's deep beneath the grounds of the estate. It's where he keeps an emergency stockpile of Caldwell gold. Several tons of it."

"Several tons?"

"One might almost call it a mountain," I replied. "It's our golden parachute, our get out of jail free card. If the financial institutions of the world turn their back on the Caldwells, gold still has value. I'll make you a deal, Levi. Throw in your lot with me. Come to my wedding and you can call the cavern your new home."

"It's on the estate?" he asked.

"Indeed." I'd dangled the carrot, but I needed him to understand the consequences of what we faced. "And if Lynch comes for us, he will find it and take it with him. Or help us and it can be yours."

"And if I were to accept your offer, I would be welcome there? On the estate?"

"It would be your new home. For as long as you need it, if it's enough to return to your people, I'll be happy to have helped." I answered. I could think of worse guests to have around.

"And I would be bound to protect it and all who resided on its lands. You have been studying, Seth."

"Everything I can," I replied "but your kind aren't particularly known for recording their customs and traditions. I had to connect a few dots myself."

"And you would give all that gold to me?" Levi asked.

"More gold than you've seen in your life," I replied. "And if you manage to keep me alive, we can always make more. Sure, it could get us both killed, or it could buy us both the lives we want. Are you a gambler, Levi?"

I held out my hand, ready to seal the deal.

"The cavern for my patronage. It is a deal."

Levi gripped my hand. A pulse of magic ran from my wrist, up my arm, and into my soul. The intensity of it all set my entire being ablaze. Levi's eyes glowed gold and I saw for the first time the true nature of the ancient being I had bargained with.

"I will gather my things and meet you at the estate," he said. "Try not to get yourself killed between now and then."

I'd hoped he would come with me, but if he'd been accumulating wealth like he'd said, I was sure it would take him some time to organise the logistics of moving it to the manor.

"When should I expect you?"

"Give me a day, perhaps two." Levi looked around. "I will have no more need of this place, but I should see it handed to another."

He folded the dishrag neatly in four and set it on the counter. Without a word, his security rose.

"Where are they going?" I asked as they filed out the door.

"They are preparing my things for transportation. You should make for the manor, Seth, while you still can."

My pulse quickened. "Know something that I don't?"

"The Run is quiet. It's never this quiet. Something is amiss."

CHAPTER 8

My stomach twisted itself in knots. Levi was right. The Panhandle was quiet and the din from the Run outside should have been making its way through the saloon doors.

There should have been the sound of foot traffic, buyers arguing and haggling with vendors, and the inevitable disagreement. Bloodshed wasn't unusual.

Silence was.

My hands trembled in anticipation. My nerves were wearing thin. Living on high alert these past few weeks was causing them to fray. I felt like I was laying on the executioner's block, just waiting for the axe to drop. Only I had no idea how or in what form Lynch's next strike might come.

But the silence in The Run told me I wouldn't be waiting long. We needed to get back to the relative safety of the manor.

I rose from my stool.

"I'll see you soon, Levi. Don't linger longer than you need to," I said as I headed for the table where Dizzy and Lara sat watching.

"Head right," Levi called after me. "I'll have my boys try to slow them down."

Them.

There was more than one. Heading right would take us deeper into The Run, away from the entrance we had entered through. While I knew there were other ways to get back to the surface, I wasn't particularly familiar with them and wasn't ready to test that knowledge with all our lives depending on it.

"Trouble?" Lara asked as I reached the table.

"Seems like it. Let's get out of here while we still can."

I was in full stride by the time I reached the saloon doors. Shoving them both outward, I stepped into the street, Levi's warning still ringing in my ears.

I took stock of the situation. The entire street was closed. Every door and window that had been open when we had entered The Run was now sealed shut. Which could only mean one thing.

Danger.

Someone or something hostile was in The Run. Something dangerous enough to make its criminal elements go to ground in fear.

Looking down the street to my left, I tried to get a sense of what we were dealing with. Fleeing in a blind panic seemed to be a great way to get ourselves killed.

A dense mass of people were making their way up the street toward us. They were still two intersections away and trudging forward at a steady pace. Even at this distance, I could make out their distinct features, or lack thereof.

They were all dressed in black robes, with silver featureless masks intended to obscure their identities.

There was only one group of people I knew that dressed like that and could inspire fear of this magnitude amongst the denizens of The Run.

"Sentinels," I breathed. "We need to move."

The sentinels were the enforcers of the Arcane Congress, ruthless and capable battle wizards who enforced the governing laws of magic throughout the mortal world. Accountable only to the Congress, they hunted warlocks and supernatural lawbreakers alike. And unlike most normal law enforcement agencies, if the Congress thought you were a danger to society, they were far more likely to bring you in dead than alive.

Prisoners needed to be housed. That took manpower. Manpower they would rather devote to keeping society safe from things that went bump in the night.

Judge, jury, and executioner. If you lived long enough to see a trial. Those that did saw a silver mask one last time as the sentence was carried out.

Even those who had done no wrong rightly feared the sentinels.

And it wasn't hard to work out what they might want with me.

For one thing, we had just laid waste to the London Palladium. We'd also killed dozens of sapera who were accepted members of the magical community. If we couldn't prove we were acting in self-defence, that had the potential to draw the Congress' ire.

More importantly, we'd pissed off Andrew Lynch. And that cardinal sin, more than any other, seemed the likely cause of their presence here. I doubted they would need much of a reason to come after us.

We were a powerful presence in the wizarding community. The opportunity to brings us down a peg or two would appeal to some of the more contentious parties in the congress.

Unfortunately, with no one in the street to distract them, they spotted us almost immediately.

I took off down the street, heading right as Levi had suggested.

Of course, it was always possible that he was in on it, but I doubted that. I'd given him too much reason to want me alive. I was one of few people who could get him what he actually needed: an unfathomable amount of gold.

If I lived to use my gifts, that was. I trusted in his self-interest.

Levi's security piled out of the pub and headed left, making a beeline for the sentinels.

The sentinels shouted after us, but I didn't pay it any heed. We reached the next intersection and turned right. With any luck, we could head into the back streets, double-back, and slip past them.

In The Run, the further one gets from the central thoroughfare, the more maze-like the underground lair becomes until eventually the narrow streets and alleys become entrances to the city's sewer network and tube tunnels. Those fringes were where all manner of dangers lurked. If you weren't careful, man or beast might drag you into the dark, prey to be consumed at their leisure.

Right now, though, I would take my chances with any of them, rather than bet on the sentinel's goodwill.

The optimist in me hoped the sentinels weren't after us at all. There was certainly an abundance of other activities that could be potentially interesting to them down here. Not the least of which was Levi and his obvious use of mind magic.

But the cynic in me, the voice that had kept me alive for most of my life, told me they were gunning for me. The commotion over Levi's security getting in their way wouldn't buy us more than a minute or two.

We rounded another corner, heading deeper into The Run.

My father was at the diviners. I knew from my last visit that it was inconveniently located at the end of a dead-end street. Thomas and the Seekers had forced us to fight our way free. We could not afford to do that with the sentinels.

Neither could I leave my father here. Our only hope was to reach him and his escort, and get them out of that street before the sentinels found us. We hurried for the diviner as fast as our feet could carry us.

The Run was a rabbit warren of side streets, alleyways, and underground establishments we might hide in. The sentinels weren't yet here in sufficient numbers to search them all thoroughly. If we played our cards right, we might be able to slip past them. I just had to warn my father first.

We turned right and then left, in quick succession, heading for the diviner. If I'd charted the correct course, she ought to be at the end of the lane way. Unfortunately, there were already two black-robed sentinels coming towards us from the other direction. They had already been to the store.

And come up empty.

My father wasn't there.

I screeched to a halt, my boots squeaking on the cobble-stone road. If my father had already made a run for it, we needed to do the same. Our best chance was rendezvousing back at the convoy on the surface.

"There they are," one of the sentinels shouted, pointing at us.

Well, at least the cynic in me was on point today.

A narrow alley off to our right seemed to be our best chance of not running into the larger group of sentinels that were likely already closing in from the rear.

"In here," I shouted, leading Dizzy and Lara into the alley-way.

Waving them past, I placed myself between them and the sentinels. At least if I was taken, the sentinels might not bother pursuing them.

The sentinel barked something in Latin. I raced into the alley and was about six steps into the narrow passage when a spell struck the wall behind me. It cratered the stone wall and sent dust and chips of rock flying in every direction.

Racing through the cluttered alley, we leaped over old crates and discarded garbage. I felt like Aladdin trying to escape the palace guards, only my palace guards were armed with magic and trying to kill me.

Any hope I had of losing them in the alley was dashed. Twice I checked over my shoulder and caught sight of them as they moved inexorably after us. They were doggedly determined, and seemingly unafraid of ambush in the narrow confines of the alley.

Perhaps we could use that to our advantage.

We did outnumber them, but I didn't particularly want to assault standing members of the Arcane Congress if it could be helped. That was the sort of action that you couldn't talk your way out of. The sentinels were best avoided until we sorted out Lynch.

"*Interitus!*" one of the sentinels bellowed.

The crates beside me exploded outward. Flying timber struck me hard, my ribs taking the brunt of the blow. I slammed into the stone wall and toppled to the ground, hard. Rolling onto my back, I tried to catch my breath and draw on my power.

The two black clad sentinels picked their way through the alley toward me.

"I wouldn't recommend it," the first called to me. He raised his hands, power playing across his fingertips.

"Right now, we have orders to take you alive," the second sentinel added. "Don't give us any reason to do otherwise."

"Take me for what?" I grumbled. "You've just attacked me without provocation. Here I was thinking sentinels are meant to protect the community, not cripple it."

The two of them glanced at each other. My feigned ignorance was not what they had expected. So I pressed my luck, anything to buy time to think and get my breath back.

"Here I am, minding my own business, and you pair run me down and assault me. My family are going to have something to say about this. My mother went before the Parliament this morning. You think we don't have friends at Congress? It'll be both your jobs, this will."

I wasn't in the habit of hiding behind the Caldwell name but even in the Congress it still meant something. Money and influence were currency even wizards respected.

"I imagine they will," the man replied, his silver mask showing no emotion. "And the Watchman will have the same questions for them in due course. You and your father just torched the better part of the London Palladium and left a score of bodies in your wake. You are wanted for questioning in connection with the reckless use of magic and endangering the public. You're both to surrender yourselves to the Congress for questioning, during which time a thorough investigation of your conduct will be carried out."

"You can't possibly have any evidence of that, so why don't you just send the charges to our lawyers?" I replied. "Why bother with the questioning at all? It would seem we are already guilty in your eyes, and I have plenty still to do this afternoon. We'll see you at trial."

"Mr. Caldwell, you'll submit for questioning and tell us the location of your father."

The sentinel advanced, leaving the rest of the threat unspoken.

They didn't have my father yet, which was a relief. It meant he was still around here somewhere with his escort, though. I just needed enough time to slip these two overzealous enforcers.

I shook my head. "My mother was called before the arcane parliament this morning and assassinated on her way home. Whoever you think is handing down these orders, you're wrong. This is a concentrated attack on our household and I'm not going to be assassinated under the guise of protecting the peace. So I'll pass, thank you very much."

I let go of my power so as to convey the impression I had no intention of attacking them and started to my feet.

One of the sentinels produced a set of iron cuffs from beneath the folds of his robe.

"You'll stay on the ground and roll onto your stomach. I don't know what you're banging on about, nor do I care, but these orders have come straight from the Watchman. Any resistance will be seen as further evidence of the accusations that we've already outlined."

"You'll want to hold right there," Lara called. Her voice carried down the alley, but with all the junk stacked against the walls, it wasn't particularly clear where she it was coming from. "Unless those masks are bullet-proof."

The sentinels glanced at each other, their power building as they readied to strike. "You would dare threaten us? We are the Congress."

"And I have a loaded Glock and an award in marksmanship issued at the Farm. If your lips so much as form a single word syllable, I'll put a bullet in both of your skulls. Try me. I dare you."

The two sentinels shifted awkwardly. They couldn't be sure where she was, but she was close. If I had to hazard a guess, they were weighing their options and wondering if they laid out enough power if it might catch her in the blast.

They were so busy, they didn't notice the tiny black form soar through the darkness over their heads. If I wasn't on one knee, looking up, I doubted I would have seen it myself.

The sentinels opened their mouths to start a spell. Dizzy shifted into her human form, dropping behind them like a cat. Her boots struck stone, startling both of them, interrupting their spell.

Dizzy lunged at them, grabbing both by their heads, and smashed them together hard enough to knock their brains into next week. The sentinels plunged to the ground.

I scrambled to my feet, grabbing the iron handcuffs as they clattered across the ground. I fastened them around the wrists of the first sentinel, before grabbing the cuffs from the second and repeating the process. The manacles were designed to dampen the powers of any who wore them. And while I'd never worn these particular cuffs, the Inquisition had used a similar device on me in Panama.

"Nice work." I nodded to Dizzy, before looking over my shoulder. "You weren't really going to shoot them, were you dear?"

Lara stepped out of the shadows, tucking her pistol back in its holster. "If they tried to take you, dear, I'd have shot them both without a second thought. With everything we've seen from Lynch, I'm not letting you out of my sight for a minute. Fortunately, Dizzy had a less terminal solution."

"Let's try to avoid executing sentinels if we can avoid it," I said. "The Watchman answers blood for blood."

Armando Flint was the current Watchman and led the sentinels with ruthless efficiency.

"Then they best keep their hands to themselves," Lara replied.

I didn't have the time to press the point, with the rest of the sentinels hunting us.

"We need to move," I said. "If they haven't found Dad, he'll be heading for the surface. We need to get out of here too."

The three of us pressed on down the alleyway. If my sense of direction was intact, we were running parallel to the main thoroughfare and slipping past the main body of the sentinel's search party.

At the next intersection, I bore right. The debris thinned as we passed by a series of heavily reinforced doors. The store owners in the Run took ample precautions with their security. Not that I would risk breaking into one of them, unless we had to. There was no telling who or what might be waiting inside.

We couldn't be that far from the elevators. All we had to do was get there without being accosted by an army of sentinels.

Nearing the end of the alley, I slowed my pace and peered around the corner. I was right; we were almost at the elevators.

Only there were eight more sentinels guarding the one route I knew of that led back to the surface.

Far too many to risk trying to force our way through.

"Sentinels," I whispered as I ducked back into the alley. "Too many of them."

A steady cadence of footsteps carried through the alley behind us. Dizzy raced back to the intersection.

"More of them behind us," she hissed.

We were trapped.

My heart pounded in time with the boots. I turned, sweat running down my brow, and came face to face with a heavily reinforced steel door.

I let out a long, low breath.

It wouldn't be the first time I'd done a little B&E. Drawing on my power, I focused my mind on the lock. I needed something that wouldn't leave a discernible trail.

"Ab-"

The door ground open, revealing a man in a sharp three-piece suit and fedora. One I'd hoped to never see again.

"No need for that, Seth. We've been waiting for you."

"Edward Knight," I groaned. "Could my day get any worse?"

CHAPTER 9

My heart raced. What was Knight doing here?

"What are you waiting for, Seth? Get in here before those zealots throw you in a cell," Knight said, beckoning with one hand.

In spite of the fact that he was one of the most wanted men in the world and currently being encircled by the Congress' most dangerous enforcers, Knight seemed almost completely unconcerned. His presence here only heightened my concern. He was one more deadly variable.

Accepting his help was akin to stepping out of the frying pan and into the fire. I'd bargained with him before and in return, I had been extorted into kidnapping the Oracle of Delphi. The whole debacle had made me a pawn in a fight between Hera and Apollo. And when I had failed to deliver the Oracle, I'd been kidnapped myself and press-ganged into acting as Knight's champion in Ares' Grand Trial. I'd barely escaped with my life and had nothing to show for it but a gold coin Ares had given me.

I could only imagine the price he would extract for this little deliverance.

"Your father is already upstairs. Let's go." Knight beckoned. "In three seconds, I'm closing this door. So take your chances with me or you can spend some quality time with those clowns in the masks, and I very much doubt that they'll let you out in time for your wedding. I know which I'd choose."

"Of course you do. You always choose you," I grumbled as I stepped inside.

Knight smiled. "What can I say? I've always been a big fan of me."

Dizzy and Lara followed me into the small store, my soon-to-be wife glaring at Knight the whole way. She was less forgiving than I was and had taken my kidnapping hard.

"You lay one hand on him, and I'll put a bullet between your eyes."

"Don't worry, my dear," Knight replied as Tan slid the heavy steel door shut and locked the deadbolt. "I'm on your side this time."

That particular concept was so hard to swallow I tried not to choke. "Oh, I'm sure you are. You help me out of this little pickle and all you'll want from me is to topple a tyrant, or destabilize a democracy."

"Seth, you're being melodramatic." Knight waved his hand.

"Melodramatic? You've kidnapped me, forced me to fight for you. I know this dance. We've been here before, Knight. You're not fooling me with this old routine again."

Knight stuck his hands on his hips. "You really can be a bit of a wet blanket, Seth. I am not the one trying to kill you—they are. If you have another way out of The Run, then by all means take it. I'll open the door and you can give it your best shot."

He had me at a disadvantage. I had no other plan. I'd been flying by the seat of my pants since the attack at the Palladium and my bag of tricks was running on empty.

"That won't be necessary," I muttered as I rested my hands on my knees and caught my breath.

"Excellent. I believe the words you are looking for are *thank you*." Knight gave that smug little smile of a man who knew you might want to wipe it off his face but were in no position to do so.

The prospect of thanking Knight for anything irked me, but he was a stickler for protocol and manners. It wouldn't serve to agitate him when he held our continued well-being in the palm of his hand.

I couldn't afford to take chances, not with an army of sentinels outside.

"Thank you," I managed through teeth that were so close to grinding against each other it was barely audible.

Knight stared at me, weighing my response. There was so much friction between us that any wrong move might light the fire that would consume us all.

Slowly, Knight broke into a smile. "My pleasure. After all, what are friends for?"

He slapped me on the back. "We can linger and catch up if you like, but I think we'd all be better served if we leave this place and your new friends behind. Any objections?"

I was about to reply, but Knight cut me off. "Good, come with me. I'll take you to your father."

Knight turned on his heel and led the way through a small warehouse lined with long steel shelves and endless boxes of unlabeled inventory. There could be anything in them. Knowing Knight, it was almost certainly all illegal. A warehouse this deep in The Run would be great for avoiding normal law enforcement agencies. Even the Sentinels' visit was out of character.

"What are you doing down here?" I asked, quickening my pace to keep stride with him. If I was going to be forced to endure his company, I might as well learn more about how he operated. Call it opposition research but if I survived Lynch, there was every chance Knight and I might cross paths again.

"I maintain facilities in most cities of consequence around the globe," Knight replied. "This one is a particularly popular black market and I was this very day engaged in procuring some rather difficult to come by components when the sentinels made their appearance. My vendor fled like a coward. Imagine my surprise when I discovered it was you they were after and not me." He laughed. "I'm not used to being overlooked, Seth."

"I'm sure you were thrilled," I replied. "No one likes to be the last pick at the dance."

"When it means not being hunted by wizards with a penchant for execution, I'll learn to live with my disappointment."

We passed through the warehouse and into a small office set against the rearmost stone wall.

Knight held the door handle. "Power is the currency that matters, not popularity. Even politicians would rather the former than the latter. Never forget that."

He ushered everyone into the tiny office and then locked the door behind us.

"Knight, I thought we were leaving?" I asked, shifting my weight from one foot to the other. I didn't like being backed into a corner.

"We are," he replied, as he crossed the office.

He opened a closet. A short filing cabinet sat inside it, but not much else.

Knight stepped onto the filing cabinet and started feeling about in the top of the closet, looking for something.

"There it is," he muttered as he caught hold of something in the darkness and pulled. A retractable ladder rolled into view.

"Follow me, everyone. Don't be shy. It's a little dark, so watch your step."

The retractable ladder descended into place and locked with a steady click.

Knight placed his foot on the bottom rung and tested his weight. When the ladder didn't move, he proceeded to climb.

As he entered the narrow hole in the ceiling, a series of dim lights flickered to life. They seemed to be coming from the wall opposite the ladder and cast a faint illumination on what was a narrow crawlspace carved through the stone roof of The Run.

I motioned for Dizzy to go first. I knew Tan would bring up the rear and if anything went wrong, I wanted to be close enough to Edward Knight's bodyguard to put him out of commission.

Between Lara and Dizzy, I was pretty sure they could account for Knight.

It never hurt to exercise caution, and where Knight was concerned, an abundance of caution was warranted.

I still had no idea what we were getting ourselves into. The only assurance we had was Knight's word that my father was waiting for us upstairs. His word was usually good, but the same could be said of most criminals. Their word was good until it wasn't and then they usually tried to murder you.

Dizzy disappeared up the ladder, followed by Lara.

Tan motioned to the closet. "After you, Seth. I'll ensure the ladder is back in place, so that we cannot be followed."

I climbed up onto the filing cabinet and gave the ladder a little bit of a rattle, just to be sure. It didn't even budge.

I had to give it to Knight. He knew how to make a reliable getaway tunnel. I started to climb, slowly. My ribs were still a little tender and I took the opportunity to regather my thoughts. I marveled at Knight's information gathering and reconnaissance efforts. Sure, my father and I hadn't exactly been traveling incognito when we had entered The Run, but when the sentinels had appeared, Knight not only went to ground, but was soon able to discern who the real target was and how he might intervene.

How had he worked out who the sentinels were hunting? Surely, he didn't have ears in that particular organization. The sentinels were notoriously insular and their anonymity would make placing a spy in their ranks difficult.

I wondered how many others Knight had swooped in to save over the years. I knew why he did it. Saving someone's life engendered almost limitless goodwill. I was sure that, as he had spared his fellow criminals from the wrath of governments and bounty hunters alike, he curried favors across the world.

It was almost as noteworthy as his own efforts to evade law enforcement organizations. Doubtless he had boltholes and safe houses just like this that allowed him to lay low or move so effortlessly across continents.

If it weren't for the sentinels, I was sure one might hide down here for days, perhaps weeks at a time.

I'd likely only seen the tip of the iceberg when it came to Knight's criminal organization. Where most wanted men traveled with an entire coterie of muscle and advisers, Knight moved light and without ceremony or pomp. Usually just he and Tan conducted business, while beneath the surface, his minions moved in the shadows, carrying out his will.

There was an efficiency to it all that was impressive. It also made it difficult to determine just how large the organization actually was.

I couldn't even be sure that this was his building. For all I knew, we were trespassing in someone else's location and Knight was taking credit for our deliverance.

I climbed for what felt like forever. Normally, the trip to and from The Run was made in an elevator, a fact I would be far more grateful for the next time I rode in it.

We were heading for the surface, and the closer we got, the more brightly lit the crawlspace became.

The others climbed out of the crawlspace ahead of me.

On reaching the surface, I found myself in a carpeted office room. The trapdoor concealing the exit was hidden beneath a desk, which made climbing out of it a little awkward.

Shimmying out from underneath the desk, I found Lara and Dizzy waiting, as was Knight. Tan scrambled out from under the desk and closed the trapdoor behind him. Once it was shut, the carpet rested perfectly flush, the grain concealing any hint of the tunnel's existence.

Standing, I looked around. There was no trace of my father.

"Knight, I seem to recall you mentioning my father would be here."

"Don't worry, he's waiting for us in the conference room. There's a little more space there. We'll be joining them momentarily."

I didn't let my guard down. I subtly exchanged a glance with Lara. She slid her hand to her pocket, only inches from the holster at her waist.

"Well, then lead the way," I said. "I'm anxious to be sure he's still on his feet. He isn't as young as he once was."

Knight laughed. "Your father is no shrinking violet, Seth. Don't worry, he's in good hands."

Knight straightened his suit and vest as Tan opened the door for him.

I knew we were still underground, on account of the fact that there were no windows anywhere. Only walls and stale recycled air. Try as they might to conceal it, there was no hiding the fact these rooms hadn't seen fresh air in years.

Still the offices were tidy and well-maintained, not a speck of dust to be seen.

The logos on the office doors announced the business as *Efficient Logistics,* transportation and moving specialists.

How appropriate.

As we headed through the office corridors, workers hustled past us. They paid us no heed. It was almost as if we weren't here. The workers came and went with stacks of files and archive boxes.

Knight's employees clearly knew the score.

We slipped through the office and into a large boardroom. My father rose from his seat at the table. His security force was stationed around the room, and it seemed their numbers were undiminished.

"Seth, you made it." My father's lips creased upward into a rare smile.

I could hear the relief in his voice, and it surprised me. Frank Caldwell wasn't one for showing much emotion.

"The sentinels jumped us as we left the Panhandle. We managed to take them down and make a run for it. Knight found us before the others could close the noose."

"And a good thing I did," Knight said, setting his fedora on the table. "It would seem that you two have drawn the undivided attention of Lynch and his cronies. A little internal strife in the Brotherhood, I take it?"

My father stroked his chin. "Knight, we both know your informants are better than that. Would you do us the courtesy of not lying to our faces. Level with us and we'll do the same."

Knight smiled. "Very well. Only a matter of hours ago, the two of you spilled the innermost workings of the Brotherhood to members of the world press. Stories are already being publicized about the existence of a clandestine organization that pulls the strings behind the world stage. Conspiracy theorists are having a field day, even the major news outlets of the world are starting to pay attention. An hour and a half ago, Lynch terminated your status at an emergency session of the Inner Circle. He declared you persona non grata. He also mobilized his considerable resources in an effort to destroy you.

"It appears he's even called in a favor with the Watchman to drag you before Congress. Anywhere he can bog you down, separate you from your resources, and crush you like a bug. I suppose my only question is why turn on the organization you spent your entire life building?" Knight asked as he sat down. The Brotherhood, four centuries in the making, is burning itself to the waterline."

"The Brotherhood once stood for something," my father said. "Now it is merely the muscle Lynch would use to ensure the world marches to his tune. If he'd gained the Grail, the Earth might be facing its first immortal tyrant. Recent events have only illustrated the danger its existence poses to the world at large. He would eliminate us to consolidate power, so we cast him out of the shadows and into the light."

"So you went nuclear?" Knight replied. "The fallout from what you've set in motion is going to shake the world to its core."

"Perhaps, but when it collapses, it will take the puppeteers with it. You think I overreacted?" My father rested his palm on the table.

Edward Knight paused, his eyes never leaving my father's. It was like watching two lions circle a carcass.

"No, just feeling reassured that I have always had the right measure of you, Frank. We never crossed paths and for good reason. The world is big enough for both of us to exist."

"A wisdom that Lynch doesn't seem to possess," my father replied. "Otherwise, this morning he would not have dared..."

His voice caught in his throat.

"He tried to kill my mother," I said, sparing my father the need to finish his sentence. I didn't feel the need to lie to Knight about her survival. He considered himself in competition with Lynch. Otherwise, we would all have a bullet in the back of our heads.

I continued. "He had my mother summoned before the Arcane Parliament, and then when she returned home, he waited and attacked her convoy in our driveway. He wanted us to watch as my mother burned to death before our eyes."

Knight closed his hand into a tight fist. "That is cold, even for Lynch."

"Lynch," my father spat. "Has clearly lost all semblance of reason. He's a bully and a coward, and now he is a cancer that must be excised."

Knight nodded. "I gathered as much, though not the unfortunate business with Jillian. My best wishes for her recovery. If there is anything I can do, please let me know."

"And become more indebted to you than we already are?" I asked, leaning back in my chair. "You still haven't told us what you want in exchange for this little favor."

"Little favor?" Knight laughed. "Don't sell yourself short, Seth. This is a gargantuan favor. Right now, the pair of you are perhaps the most valuable commodities in the country. Lynch would pay handsomely for you."

The security team bristled.

"But rest assured, in spite of our differences in the past, I have no intention of helping Lynch. Moreover, I'm sure you'll be delighted to know that I require nothing of you."

I almost fell off my chair. "Don't toy with me Knight. I'm not in the mood."

He placed a hand on his chest. "What? A man can't just spring his friends from a spot of bother and expect nothing in return?"

I shook my head. My memory wasn't that short. "You expect me to believe you would put yourself in the Congress' cross hairs for nothing? I don't believe that for a moment.

"Rest assured, today I don't want you to do anything you weren't already planning to do."

"Which is?" I prompted.

I'd made enough deals with Knight to be wary of terms.

Knight brushed at an imagined blemish on the conference table. "I'll see you all safely to a destination of your choice within the city. I'll use my resources so that those monitoring that convoy choreography on the surface miss you entirely. You'll return home safely. Then all I ask of you is that the pair of you fight like hell and try not to die."

"Mutually assured destruction," Lara muttered.

"What was that, dear?" Knight asked, his gaze shifting to my fiancée.

"You're only sparing us so that Lynch will have to commit more resources to wiping us out." Lara looked up from the table. "The more effort he has to expend, the more likely he is to expose and compromise himself and the Brotherhood. You want us to take him down with us."

Knight nodded. "I suppose that is how the CIA would see it. I prefer to think of it as the devil I know and trust, against the tyrant I could do neither with. Lynch sees none as his equal, only as his subjects. So yes, that is my condition—bleed him down to the bone. Will that be a problem?"

"I intend to do considerably more than that," my father replied. "He tried to kill my wife. Lynch is a weed in the garden of the world, and I will tear him out root and stem."

I nodded. "I can live with that."

"I imagined that you would." Knight clasped his hands together. "I seldom have to work very hard to convince people to live, but from time to time people surprise me, or steal from me, but that's another matter entirely."

His gaze drifted off and left me wondering which of his poor employees had been caught with their hand in the cookie jar.

"So I propose an accord," Knight continued. "I will absent myself from Lynch's efforts to extinguish you, and you will do your best to carry through on what you started this morning. The Brotherhood is a relic of the past. Let it burn."

Knight let that linger before adding, "Do we have an agreement?"

It was less than I'd expected, in the sense that it didn't involve anything I wasn't already intending on doing. That was the cold, calculating genius in Knight's suggestion.

On the surface, it was just so easy to agree to his terms. After all, he didn't want me to kidnap an Oracle, or win him a god's favor all over again. He merely wanted me to survive long enough to topple the greatest rival his criminal organization had in its bid for global supremacy.

Therein lay the rub.

The question was, could I live with winning if I knew it would advance Knight's agenda?

I looked at Lara and knew the answer. I'd come this far, and I would do anything I could to last another day. Another day with her was a day worth fighting for.

"We have a deal," I replied.

The sooner we got home, the safer I would feel.

"We have an understanding," my father replied. "If you can get us to Battersea, we have a helicopter fuelled and ready to take us back to the estate. Once we're there, nothing short of an army can reach us."

Knight got to his feet. "I'll see to it. In the meantime, signal your convoy to continue the circus they are putting on up there. We have an underground garage and vehicles of our own that you can use to reach the heliport. Might I recommend you maintain the highest possible cruising altitude? Lynch's forces are heavily armed, and a low-flying vehicle is more vulnerable than you might expect."

My father tilted his head to the side.

"You wouldn't happen to be referring to a certain low-flying military transport vessel?" he asked. "I always wondered if someone else was pulling those strings. There was no chance those random rebels just happened to be sporting surface-to-air missiles and be waiting along the routes his plane was scheduled to take."

Knight picked up his hat. "If I'd known then what I know now, it might have saved me a small fortune and the lives of dozens of men. I knew there was hardware on that plane. I just didn't realize he was it."

Murdoch. They were talking about Murdoch. They had to be.

He'd been shot down while flying a military mission during the Iraq War and been stranded in the desert for three days.

It was his remarkable survival that had attracted my father's attention. Or so I had thought. It seemed there was more to that particular flight that I realized.

If Knight had taken an interest in the flight, there had to be something of value on board. Perhaps that was why Murdoch had been there in the first place. He seemed to intervene in mortal affairs at key junctions. Or at least, that was what I had gathered from our limited discussion.

Was that why my father had summoned him to the manor? Perhaps that was why Knight had been in position at Glastonbury. His bid for the Grail wasn't a casual bout of opportunism. He'd been planning it for decades.

"The Grail is gone," I volunteered, eager to ensure Knight wasn't holding out hope of recovering it from us. "And so is he. You'd do well to let that particular dog lie."

Knight smiled, and it was all teeth. "On that we can agree. I have no interest in tangling with the divine. Now if you ladies and gentlemen will excuse me, I'll have Barbara show you to the garage. Tan and I still have some business in The Run. Don't worry, we'll see that the sentinels chase their tails a while longer."

The two of them slipped out of the meeting room.

A woman in her early fifties with dyed blonde hair, wearing a blazer and pantsuit, appeared in the conference room doorway.

"Gentlemen, if you will follow me, I will see to your transportation."

Her calm and casual demeanor made me wonder if she had any idea who she was truly working for. Did she know her boss was one of the most wanted men in the world? Or did she simply not care?

I stood and stretched. As I did, a realization dawned on me. Edward Knight had had me and my father over a barrel, and still not bothered to extract so much as a favor from us. No matter what he said about the Brotherhood, I couldn't help but think there was another reason for his generosity.

More than anything, it spoke volumes as to what he thought our chance of survival was.

In a fight between us and Andrew Lynch, he didn't expect us to last the week, and he certainly wasn't planning on us surviving long enough to repay the favor.

CHAPTER 10

I never thought I would see the day when I was grateful for Edward Knight's interference. Thanks to his timely intervention, extensive network, and unmarked transportation, we were soon safely aboard the helicopter my father had chartered to take us back to the estate.

The rotors whirred overhead, and I glanced down. My stomach lurched. I closed my eyes and took a deep breath. When I opened them, I made sure I was facing anything but the window.

"I was never going home by car," my father called through the headset. "Not after that ambush this morning. I just didn't count on the Sentinels moving so quickly."

I nodded. "I heard them talking in The Run. Their orders came from the Watchman himself. Lynch must have dug deep for that favor."

"He's relentless," my father said. "But that single-minded determination will be his undoing. Even now, his cover is starting to fray. He's going to need to survive the retribution of those who can now put a name and face to their suffering."

"It's exactly what he deserves," I muttered.

I wondered just how many Seekers there were out there. How many lives had the Brotherhood run over in their quest for the greater good?

"Making it to The Run was a gamble, but worthwhile," I said.

I smiled as I thought of Levi and his promise to relocate to the manor. I wasn't quite ready to tell my father the price I had paid to secure Levi's assistance, but in time, I hoped my father would see it as a worthwhile investment.

"How did things go with the Diviner?" I asked.

My father's grin broadened. "It was most productive. The Blind Lady remembers your mother fondly. She was very willing to answer a few questions."

The Blind Lady, or Matilda as I knew her, had the useful talent of being able to detect, interpret, and understand arcane residue. Any practitioner could feel the aftermath of magic that had been unleashed. That was part and parcel of being a practitioner. Being able to detect that residue on a thousand-year-old sacrificial blade was an art only a diviner could manage.

We sailed over the city as our convoy continued the carefully choreographed routine on the streets below. Every five minutes, a different set of vehicles would strike for home. It gave those tracking them and trying to ambush us on our way home a never-ending source of targets. None of which contained the prize.

Lynch was going to have a migraine trying to stop them all, while all the while we were passing safely overhead.

"What did Matilda have to say?" I asked.

It wasn't a long trip home, but I didn't feel like being left alone with my thoughts right now.

My father looked at Lara and Dizzy, and hesitated. He didn't want to talk about the curse in front of them, but I waved off his concern.

"Both of them know all about it," I said. "And I doubt we'd have made it this far without their help. No more secrets, Dad. At least if something happens to one of us, the rest of us will be able to continue the fight."

"Very well," my father said. "I have had a theory. Ever since I first experienced the curse and her voice, I have been trying to understand the different degrees of torture Aleida has subjected me too."

"You mean it isn't uniform?" Lara asked. "I always figured it was constant."

"What has Seth told you about the curse?" my father asked.

"That it kills all Caldwells eventually," Lara replied, "but he's only spoken of it broadly. I know it drives you mad, but I'm a little fuzzy on the details."

"Well, let me explain," my father said. "The reason that it is so potent is that its true nature is the perpetual, enduring presence of a spiteful four-hundred-year-old witch. She haunts your every waking moment, speaking poison to your mind. Sure, you can silence her for a time, but doing so requires exertion. It is a perpetual struggle: your will against hers. And that is the problem. We are mortal."

"You get tired," Lara chimed in. "She's a spirit. She doesn't have a body to grow weary."

"Precisely." My father nodded. "And so she nags, a ceaseless teasing torment that she is sure will eventually break us. No one can endure it forever."

Dizzy leaned forward to look across at my father. "But you said that her attacks were inconsistent. What did you mean?"

My father cleared his throat. "What I was never able to understand was why her attacks intensified at certain points of my life. She certainly has no reason to let up, or so I thought. At times, she was relentless. Others, she seemed content to just nag at the edges of my mind. The most discernible difference came three decades ago. I remember the day precisely because it was both the happiest, and most painful day of my life."

"What happened?" I asked.

My father looked out the window. "You were born, Seth. And when you were, Aleida's voice went from nagging torment to brazen banshee. It was as if she could sense my happiness and was determined to destroy it. I always assumed that it was your very existence that offended her."

I swallowed. He'd never shared that with me before. I thought of what I knew of Aleida and her daughter, my forebear.

"That makes sense," I replied. "She was abandoned by her child, who fled to the new world while her own people were massacred by the conquistadors. It makes sense that she would rage at others enjoying the happiness that had been taken from her."

The helicopter whirred effortlessly through the cloudy skies as it headed for the manor.

"I too had always figured that change in her demeanor was a reflection of her own daughter's betrayal," my father replied, "but as we've worked together these last few weeks, I have had a new theory."

That must have been what he wanted to check with the Diviner. I leaned forward in my seat. He had my undivided attention now. "And what theory was that exactly?"

"That her attack intensified not because she was enraged at your birth, but because I was no longer her only living descendant. There were two of us, and the value of my presence diminished."

"I'm not sure that I follow," I replied. Why would my birth diminish his existence?

"I remembered my father saying something similar to me when I came of age. He had fathered me quite late in life. My mother often reflected that he had changed in his advancing years. I suspect Aleida only intensified her efforts against your grandfather when I was born. Much as she tortured me after yours."

It was certainly an interesting phenomenon. Why did having children make us so much more vulnerable to her influence? It didn't make sense.

My father smiled. It was almost as if he could hear my unspoken question. "But why relent in those early years? Why give us peaceful youth? If it was her objective to torment us, why not start sooner? That is the question that's been troubling me for weeks."

My mind raced as I thought back to my own visit to Matilda. There were several elements she determined that played a part in the curse. As I raced through them, I couldn't believe I hadn't seen it sooner.

"It's your blood," I gasped. "Our blood really. I always thought the curse was in us, but it's not."

"Exactly," my father replied, pointing at me. "She was a constant presence after my father's death, but she didn't torture me until your birth for the same reason she hasn't said a word all day. The same reason she's praying this helicopter makes it safely back to the manor."

I knew exactly what he was saying. "Because this helicopter is carrying every living Caldwell heir. The sum total of her bloodline still present on the earth. She didn't curse her progeny's bloodline. She bound herself to it."

My father clapped his hands together. "That cunning little witch. For four-hundred-years she might have tortured our bloodline but she also needed to see to its survival. While we were in The Run, she warned me the sentinels were coming.

The realization brought hundreds of thoughts crashing together in my mind.

"Because if we both die, her spirit has no anchor in this realm, and she is finally sucked into the after-world where she belongs."

I couldn't believe it. That was it. It had to be. Aleida might be a wicked wretch who wanted us all dead, but if my father was right, she wanted it on her terms. Her tenuous grip on the mortal realm relied on one of us surviving the mess we faced with Lynch.

For years, I'd felt helpless in the face of my curse, but that wasn't exactly true. If my father died, Aleida actually had a vested interest in keeping me alive.

If we could outlive Lynch, Aleida and I were going to have a heart to heart.

"Unsurprisingly, she's been rather quiet since I left the diviner." My father chuckled. "I think we both know the score now."

I couldn't believe what I was hearing. My father had done it. He'd found the answer. Albeit one that was rather unpalatable. We could take care of Aleida any time we wanted to. All that required was for the pair of us to stop breathing.

Not exactly the solution I was looking for. And if anything happened to my father and I was stuck with the wicked priestesses as my constant undying companion, at least I would know that she needed me as much as I wanted to get rid of her. If she wanted to avoid whatever torment the gods had in store for her in the next world, then she needed to play nice. More than that, she needed to ensure I survived. It was like having your own insane guardian angel. She could only linger here as long as I did. As long as I had no children of my own, she was stuck with me.

The thought sent a pang of sadness through me. I had not really had the luxury of dreaming about my future, but I'd always hoped it would include a family of my own.

But that was contingent on curing the curse. The day I had learned of my curse, I had made a promise: I wasn't going to bring another soul into the world if they were going to be subject to it. I didn't want my son or daughter feeling like I had every day since I turned eighteen. Perhaps now that I knew how she was binding herself to us, I could find a way to sever that connection.

The possibility raised my spirits.

I looked out the window. We were too high to make out any details below. But I knew we couldn't be far from the manor, now. In the aftermath of my father's revelation, the helicopter grew quiet.

I couldn't believe just how simple yet effective Aleida's plan had been. Many practitioners had taken a shot at immortality, but she had practically ensured hers by binding herself to a bloodline with no material limitation. With her bloodline talents, they were bound to have the means to ensure their own survival.

If anything, her aggressive haunting of her posterity had limited her potential. If she wasn't such a conniving, malicious excuse of a creature, she might have a far broader posterity, and no risk of being cut free. She would have assured her immortality.

I shook my head. She was her own worst enemy.

The bitterness of her daughter's betrayal was still raw enough that four hundred years later she still wanted nothing but to extinguish the lives that betrayal had brought into being. Torturing them to the brink, relenting only long enough to ensure another was born to anchor her existence to the mortal realm.

She was mad, clearly, but it was a cold calculating madness.

Between my father and I, we had made more progress in months than any past generation of our family had in their lifetime. The smile on my father's face said it all. He'd always expected the curse to be the end of him. Now if we were lucky, we might just save his life.

Lara reached into my lap and took my hand. "What are you thinking?"

I glanced sideways at her and smiled. "Just trying to sort my way through this mess. Things are starting to look up."

She squeezed my hand. "Lynch is on the run. Compromised loyalties aren't exactly something the government is going to turn a blind eye to. Everyone is going to want a piece of him, from the president to past enemies, just you watch. They'll all come crawling out of the woodwork. He is going to be scrambling for cover. So you and I have more important things to attend to."

I smiled. "The wedding?"

"You ask that like it's a question. Seth, it's three days away. It's high time we took a moment's respite and plan some memories of our own."

It was more than fair. I'd been so absorbed with Lynch I'd barely participated in the planning. I justified it, of course. Not in the way that many men might. I figured I had a far better excuse in Andrew Lynch.

I told myself that if we couldn't survive Lynch, there wasn't much point in having a wedding. But that single-minded focus had also threatened to drive me insane. The seeming inevitability of our demise had weighed me down so thoroughly I'd lost sight of the future. If anything, today had taught me how quickly everything could change. This morning my father and I had been at odds about the Brotherhood, and my mother had been her usual regal, cheery self.

Now she was at death's door, and my father and I had set fire to the Brotherhood's entire command structure.

This morning, I'd had no notion that we would ever cure my curse. Now there was light at the end of the tunnel and a chance we might even reach it.

I was in danger of having hope once more. All it had taken was an angel to drag me out of the self-pity party I had been wallowing in.

"I can do that," I replied. "How did the RSVPs go? Is anyone bold or foolish enough to show up?"

Lara smiled. "Very well, actually. The RSVPs are coming in thick and fast, though I dare say a few might cancel when they see the news tonight."

"Yes, marrying into our family doesn't really have the prestigious social status it once did," I joked. "I'm surprised you're still willing to risk it."

She slapped my leg. "Enough of that. I'm lucky to have met you, Seth. Of all the museums in Manhattan, you wandered into mine. I wouldn't have it any other way."

I squeezed her hand. "You're the best thing that's ever happened to me. So, who's on the list? I know some of my mother's family were planning on coming. Are any of yours crossing the pond?"

Lara had been raised by her father, and I was curious because I was yet to meet him. He didn't live in New York, and his work had precluded him from ever coming to see us while we'd been living together.

"Just the one," Lara replied softly.

"Your father's coming?"

Lara nodded. "He said he wouldn't miss it for the world."

"Marvelous." I squeezed her hand. "I'm looking forward to meeting him."

Lara swallowed. "Just make sure you remember saying that, when he gets here. He can be a hard man."

Was that her way of telling me I hadn't yet earned his approval? Well, we were going to have to see about that.

The helicopter started its descent.

Weybridge Manor came into view as the helicopter pilot aimed for the pad beside the west wing. I thanked my lucky stars the trip had passed without incident. I felt like I hadn't been able to catch my breath since Murdoch had visited me this morning.

Now safely back on the manor grounds, we at least had the buffer of our security team to filter out any unwanted aggressions.

No sooner had we landed and the pilot shut off the rotors, than Dizzy took off out the door. She took a deep breath, as her feet got back on solid ground.

"Geez, I hate flying," she muttered, "at least when I'm not the one doing it."

"You can shapeshift and can fly. What are you worried about?" I asked.

"It's not the flying I'm worried about, it's the falling," Dizzy replied. "Haven't you ever worried what might happen the day you go to draw on your gifts and your body says no?"

I hadn't but it was an unsettling thought. My powers didn't let me fly, but they were a fundamental part of who I was. What would I be without them?

Dizzy headed for the house, and I climbed down out of the helicopter.

"Don't you go anywhere, Seth!" Lara called as she climbed out of the chopper. "We have a wedding to plan."

I was just about to reassure her when my phone started to ring. I reached into my pocket and drew it out.

Saved by the bell, I mouthed, knowing I would pay for that later.

Lara's face twisted to show her displeasure. "Don't you dare."

I looked down at the screen, wondering who I might have to ignore to avoid my wife-to-be's ire.

Unfortunately, the number flashing on the screen belonged to someone I'd been trying to reach all day.

"I have to take this, dear. It's one of the guests. I think she's looking to RSVP."

Lara bit back whatever retort she was considering as I picked up my ringing phone. I was going to need to do double time on my wedding planning efforts to make it up to her later.

Stepping away from the chopper, I held my phone up to my ear.

"You're a hard woman to get a hold of, Kasey. Where have you been?"

CHAPTER 11

Kasey Chase was one of the most well-known witches in the world, a notoriety caused in no small part because of her connection to the chaos in New York City: a rampaging wizard whose actions resulted in the world of magic being dragged out of secret and into the public eye.

Kasey had put an end to him, and some teenager with a smart phone had sold the story to cable news. She was a hero.

A real one. The sort they made movies about. She didn't do it for the glory. She did it because she felt she could save lives.

I just hoped she would be as interested in saving mine.

"I've, uh, had my hands full," Kasey said, breathing heavily. "Sorry I missed your call."

I made my way across the lawn toward the house. Something wasn't right. She didn't sound like her usual sassy self. I'd only spent a few days with her in New York, but even I knew something was wrong.

"Everything alright in New York?" I asked. "Or are those vampires giving you trouble again?"

"I wouldn't know," Kasey answered, the sound of boots against gravel carrying down the phone line. "I'm a lot closer to London than LaGuardia."

"Wait, what?" I held the phone closer to my ear.

I couldn't have heard her properly.

"You're in London?" I asked, not knowing what stroke of luck or fate had brought her here, but if it was true, things were really starting to go my way. "What are you doing here?"

"Not quite London," Kasey replied, her boots flicking up gravel as she ran. "I'm in Wales, uh, sightseeing."

A likely story. Kasey didn't strike me as a tourist. She was, however, a druid of Welsh heritage, and I imagined her presence here had something to do with her roots.

"Sounds like you're having a real time of it." I paused. "Have I caught you at a bad time?"

Kasey's breathing carried down the line. It took her a few moments before she answered. "Not at all. Just seeing some sites and taking care of some business. I would have called but things have been a little crazy of late."

I got the distinct impression that I was disturbing her, but she'd called me. Maybe she'd wandered into some trouble and needed a hand.

"Are you ok, Kasey?"

"I'm just out for a run," Kasey replied, her tone growing more and more distressed by the moment. I wasn't buying it for a second.

"Oi, get back here," a voice shouted down the line.

"It sounds like you're running for your life," I prompted.

"To-mae-to, to-mah-to," Kasey replied. "Gotta tell you, Seth. The more of it I do, the less it bothers me.

"Can I ask what you did to upset them?" I glanced over my shoulder to ensure I was alone. Lara was loitering by the chopper waiting for me. But for the time being she seemed content to wait.

"Something between gardening and grave robbing," Kasey muttered. "Or at least that's what they think I did. It's a long story."

Kasey wasn't a thief. There had to be more to it than that. I wanted to ask, but the sirens carrying down the line crushed my curiosity. If Kasey was in a cell, she wasn't going to be able to join me in the fight against Lynch. "Kasey, if you're in trouble, I can help. I have resources."

"Unless you have somewhere to lay low in Cardiff, you might have to bring some of those Caldwell lawyers with you. Hope you have some good ones."

"An army of them," I replied. But I didn't have time for that. "But if you're open to the idea of not spending a few nights in lockup, I have a safe house in Cardiff. All you've gotta do is get there and keep your head down. We'll do the rest."

"Of course you do." Kasey chuckled. "I'll take it."

"Hang on," I called as I popped the phone on speaker. "I'm texting you the address. It's on Talbot Street near St. Mary of the Angels."

Even as I said it, I couldn't help but smile. Murdoch had picked the location. He'd said that he'd always liked the neighborhood.

"There is a key stashed under a loose brick near the shed in the backyard. It'll get you inside. You'll find food, clothes, and some cash in a slip behind the fireplace. Help yourself if you need it."

"You're a lifesaver," Kasey breathed. "Heading there now."

"Excellent. I'll send a team to get you safely out of town. They'll be there in less than three hours. Hang tight."

"On it. Now what can I do for you?" Kasey asked.

"Pardon?"

"I highly doubt that you left that message on the off chance I was in town and needed to be bailed out of trouble. What can I do for you?" Kasey asked. "Still having trouble with your inheritance?"

By inheritance I expected she was talking about my curse. I had asked her for some help while I was in New York City. It turned out that was much easier than trying to steal from her.

Kasey wasn't a stranger to familial burden. She was descended from a line of Welsh druids and when it came to blood magic, there was no one better anywhere in the world. But speaking with her gave me the distinct impression that her gifts brought both strength and sorrow.

It was Kasey's help that had set us on our current course. Without her insight, I would still be thinking of my curse as some sort of arcane malady rather than the presence of a malicious spirit. I'd spent a decade searching for the wrong solution before I'd met her.

"Actually, things are going quite well on that front. The real reason I am calling is to invite you to a wedding."

"A wedding?" Her surprise carried down the line. "You and Lara? Congratulations."

It was a strange conversation to have while she was running from what I assumed to be an angry groundsman, but timing had never really been my strong suit.

"It's this weekend and if you don't have anything else on, we'd love to have you here."

Silence.

What I figured was Kasey taking a moment to catch her breath lingered into an uncomfortable pause.

"I can hear the hesitation in your voice, Seth," Kasey eventually replied. "Normally, it's the bride that's a nervous wreck. What is it you haven't told me?"

Yeah. I hadn't expected to sneak it past her, but even as I'd contemplated this moment, I still wasn't sure how to put it into words. How did you ask someone you'd barely met to risk their life for you?

I just hoped she was as interested in the Brotherhood today, as she had been the night she'd strapped me to a chair and interrogated me about them.

"When I was in New York, you wanted information about a certain group of people. Suffice it to say that we've had something of a falling out. You may not have seen the news yet but the information you were looking for is now being shared across the world. In the next few hours, the veil of secrecy the Brotherhood has been hiding behind is going to be torn to shreds. I've made a lot of very powerful people very unhappy. Lynch, their current Chairman, wants me dead."

"One of those types of weddings," Kasey replied. "I guess I should have seen that coming."

"Hopefully not," I answered, but even I wasn't convinced. "If he shows up, things could get hairy. Madison Square Garden hairy, but if it's any consolation, they should all be focused on me this time."

Kasey let out a long low breath.

"So, you're telling me that if I come to your wedding, there is a very real chance that the man responsible for allowing Akihiro to run rampant through my life, will show up and try to kill you?"

"That's a very glass half-full way of looking at it," I replied as I paced the lawn nervously.

"And you'll have no issue with me intervening?"

I'd seen her work. Intervene was far too subtle a verb for Kasey Chase.

"Frankly, I'd be delighted if you did, but I don't want you to be under any illusions. Lynch is wily and dangerous, and has no qualms about killing those who are in his way."

"Not a worry. Once we're done, we can get on with the party. I could use a break."

I scratched the nagging itch at the nape of my neck. It didn't feel like Kasey was taking me seriously.

"That's a very optimistic outlook," I answered. "I'm just worried you might be underestimating him."

"Which part?" she asked. "He's human, right?"

I shrugged, not that she could see the gesture. "Well, yeah, but he's also one of the most influential men in the world, and he's about to try and crush me like a bug. If you come, you'll have the singular opportunity and pleasure of standing with us as we try to break down the world order."

"He's not an undying vampire or an immortal Sidhe monarch. Let's just say I like our chances."

A Sidhe monarch? What had Kasey been up to since I saw her last? Was that why she was here?

I didn't want to talk her out of helping, so instead I opened the invitation.

"I could use all the help I can get. I don't suppose Sanders is with you?"

There was a long awkward pause.

"No," she whispered. "He is otherwise detained."

If that relationship status was viewed on social media, I was pretty sure it would be marked as, 'it's complicated.'

It was a shame. The current head of the Arcane Council being in attendance might have given the Congress and others pause.

"Sorry to hear that," I replied. "I'd have been more than happy for you to have a plus one."

"You and me both," Kasey replied.

Clearly there was something going on, but it wouldn't pay to pry. If she wanted to talk about it, she would have.

"Tell you what, Kasey. Get to the safe house. I'm sending a security team that will escort you safely to the manor. You're welcome to lay low here until things blow over."

"Or until we all get ourselves killed?" Kasey countered, her usual sass creeping back in.

I chuckled. "Or that. But between you and me, I'm kind of hoping it will be a peaceful, uneventful wedding."

Kasey's laugh carried down the phone. "The last time we were in the same place, New York was almost destroyed. Why would this glowing dumpster fire be any different?"

"Hey, that's my wedding you're talking about."

"And a glorious wedding it's going to be. Count me in," Kasey replied.

I punched the air jubilantly. Having Kasey in my corner changed things considerably.

"I don't suppose I could push my luck and ask for another favor?" I asked, striking while the iron was hot.

"That depends what it is," Kasey replied as her heavy boot falls slowed "Anything past the weekend is going to have a pretty big question mark hanging over it. Might want to cash it in quick."

Gallows humor. What else should I expect from a coroner?

"No, this one is much easier. I was hoping you would be able to put me in touch with someone."

"Oh yeah?" Kasey puffed. "Who?"

I stared at the wall of Weybridge Manor, unsure if I was making a terrible decision. But an idea was forming in my mind and I needed to speak to the only other person I knew who had ever been where I wanted to go.

"I need you to put me in touch with your Hades. I have something I'd like to discuss with him."

Kasey's feet pounded the pavement, but she didn't answer me. Had she not heard me?

I waited before asking, "Kasey, are you there?"

"I am. I also remember watching the two of you butt heads when you met in New York. I'm not sure that's a good idea."

"Nonsense." I tried to brush off her concern. "Just a rough first impression. I'm sure it will be fine, but I could use an introduction."

"Hmm, I can't really give out his number. Maybe it's better if I ask him to call you, leave things in his hands."

It was less than I'd hoped for, but it would have to do.

"Sure thing, whatever you can do would be greatly appreciated. You've got my number. Tell him I'll take the call night or day. He could be the answer to a problem I've been trying to solve."

"That's what worries me, Seth. He might be, but whether that's any good for you is another matter entirely."

I wasn't sure what to make of her warning. Before I could respond, sirens filtered down the line, threatening to drown out the phone call.

"Get to the safe house, Kasey. Keep your head down."

"Always. See you soon." She hung up the call.

I slid my phone into my pocket. The discussion could have gone better, but it also could have gone much worse. I was expecting to have to persuade her to leave New York. The fact that she was already on my side of the world seemed almost too good to be true. Maybe that was what Murdoch had been hinting at. In any event, things were falling into place. If Lynch had to go through Kasey, he would have his work cut out for him.

As I made my way back to the house, Lara met me halfway.

"If that call is your attempt to weasel your way out of helping set up for the wedding..." She left the threat unspoken but

I was fairly sure it involved sleeping somewhere other than our bed.

"Easy," I said. "That was Kasey. I've been waiting for her to call me back for days."

Lara stopped in her tracks.

"Kasey? What did you want from her?" There was an edge in her voice. Being a normal and a native of New York, she was a little skeptical of the young witch in spite of what she'd witnessed. Or perhaps because of it.

"Well, I figured Lynch is going to do his very best to interrupt our celebration. So I wanted to be sure we had as much muscle as was humanly possible on our side. Kasey qualifies. You saw her in New York City."

Lara held my gaze. "I did. I'm just surprised that you invited another woman to our wedding without asking."

I hadn't considered inviting Kasey from that angle. I was more focused on survival than how it might be perceived.

"I'm really sorry about not speaking with you first. I didn't mean to upset you. I'm just trying to gather as much help as we can get."

"And what did she say?" Lara asked. "Is she able to get away from New York? She seemed to have her hands full when we were there."

Lara wasn't wrong. When we'd been there, Kasey had been fighting off an invasion of vampires, and their allies.

I nodded, trying not to seem excited as I didn't want it misinterpreted. "She's actually in Wales right now. I'm going to send a team to pick her up."

Lara shifted her wait from one foot to the other.

"Is everything alright, hun?"

"Yeah, I just didn't realize she'd be coming to the wedding. She's a little odd and definitely dangerous."

I took her hand in mine and headed for the door. "I know. I was in Madison Square Garden too. But I would do anything to give *us* a chance."

I emphasized the us. I wanted her to know what was driving me.

"Dad thinks Lynch is gonna roll over and die," I said. "I'm not half so confident. Levi, Kasey, I'm hunting down every bit of muscle I can find. We have less than three days to ensure we have an army big enough to repel whatever Lynch throws at us. Kasey gives us a fighting chance."

"You make it sound like our wedding is going to be a blood-bath."

I swallowed the lump that was in my throat. This felt like one of the times that lying ought to be acceptable, but I'd made her a promise.

"Personally, I hope I'm wrong, but just in case, I want to be prepared. Kasey hates the Brotherhood as much as we do. One of their assassins tried to kill her last year. Then Akihiro tried to level the city. She stopped him but now gets hounded by the rest of the city. They've made her life miserable. She is one of the few people we can trust that Lynch can't get to. We need her on our side."

We strode up the steps and into the manor's lobby. Almost on autopilot, I headed for my father's study. But it was empty.

"He'll be with your mother," Lara said. "We should give them some time together."

She was probably right. The matters I wanted to speak to him about could wait until tomorrow.

"Well, let me just take a minute to get a team sent out after Kasey."

With so much manpower deployed in the convoy, I was going to have to go to the source to get what I needed. I headed for the manor's security center.

It was a solid concrete bunker in the cellar. My father had constructed it somewhere intruders would have trouble getting to in a hurry.

We slipped through the kitchen and into the larder. Taking a set of stairs down into the basement, we entered a wine cellar. At the far end stood a reinforced steel door. It would take a small mountain of C4 to move it.

"What is this place?" Lara asked.

"The beating heart of the estate's security." I knocked on the door and looked up at a small security camera situated off to our right. Its occupant was a particularly cautious sort. There was little chance he would open the door without being able to see our faces.

"Who is it?" a voice called.

"It's Seth, Lucky. Open the door. I need a team."

There was a series of footsteps, and a creak as the heavy door swung inward. On the other side stood a five-foot-five man with sandy blond hair, an open collared white shirt, and dark slacks. He was lean and wiry, with a thick set of glasses that rested low on his nose.

"Seth, what can I do for you?" Lucky leaned on the door with one hand.

"Lucky, I need a team prepped for dispatch at once."

He scratched at his scalp. "We're a little thin on the ground right now. Many of the teams have pulled a double shift just to execute that show your father ordered today. Others are out recovering the bodies of the fallen. I don't have a team, not one I can send without compromising the estate security."

"Lucky, this task is of the utmost importance. We have a VIP at my safe house in Cardiff. I need her picked up and escorted safely here."

"Seth, your father's instructions are quite clear."

"Lucky, the rest of the men will trickle back in. I need three or four men, and I need them now."

Lucky growled in nervous anxiety. "Okay, come on in. I'll see what I can find."

He waved us inside the small concrete bunker. One entire wall of the bunker was occupied by a digital display featuring a map of the estate. Red dots moved in synchronized patterns around the estate's perimeter.

Five more dots seemed to be positioned in the manor itself, though I suspected they were the snipers my father had stationed on the roof. A handful of other dots moved about and a large glowing pile of them rested in the barracks. Others were arriving steadily as the convoy trickled back in.

On the adjoining wall was a communications panel. The room also featured a square table in the middle, on one corner of which a chessboard sat. From the look of it, Lucky was part-way through a game.

"Who's winning?" I asked.

"I am," Lucky replied, managing a faint smile.

"One of these days, you ought to let him win," I replied. "My father doesn't like to lose."

Lucky shook his head. "He told me the day he beats me, he'll fire me."

He shifted his weight from one foot to the other.

"What's up, Lucky? Is everything okay?"

"I haven't seen your father since this morning," he whispered. "Not since the attack."

Lucky ran both hands through his hair. "I'm the head of security. Who else's fault could it be? I didn't think they'd hike for half a day through the forest to pull that off. I should have accounted for that. I won't let it happen again, but I suspect the next time I see your dad, he'll be firing me. I wouldn't blame him."

I put my hand on his shoulder. "Right now, we need you more than ever, Lucky. So shake it off, get your head back in the game, and find me someone we can send to Cardiff."

"On it," Lucky replied, sinking into his seat. He opened a small bar fridge under his desk, grabbed an energy drink, and cracked it open. He chugged half of it.

"When was the last time you slept?" I asked, leaning on the back of his chair.

Lucky looked at the clock in the corner of the screen in front of him. "Ah, yesterday some time."

"You need to get some rest," I replied. "If you don't, you won't be able to function. We need you at your best right now.

"I normally sleep during the day," he replied. "The night is the most commonly exploited opportunity to attack, but today I haven't had the chance. This visit to the Palladium has kept me going all day."

He started typing on the laptop and flicking between different readouts.

"Look, if I take one man from a few of the current perimeter teams, I can cobble together a four-man team for the extraction. Please tell me your guest is coming willingly."

"Yes, Lucky..." My voice dropped an octave in warning.

"Because there was that one time..."

I put my hand on his shoulder to stop him in his tracks.

"As I told you back then, the daughter of Lord Byron had been kidnapped by those men. She just didn't realize it."

Lara's eyes narrowed, and I looked back to Lucky to avoid the judgment in them. "We don't need to relive the past now. I just need the team."

Lucky swallowed. "Got it, boss. Who are we picking up?"

"A wedding guest. She'll be the only occupant in the safe house. You can't miss her."

"I need a name," Lucky replied. "To run the background checks."

"She'll be fine. I'll vouch for her when she arrives," I replied. I didn't want Kasey's visit to become common knowledge, or to be leaked before she was safely ensconced within the estate.

"Got it, boss. They'll be ready to go in minutes."

"Excellent. I'll get you coordinates." I started pulling up the address on my phone.

"I already have them," Lucky replied. "You said Cardiff, right?"

"Yes, but she's in my..." I was going to say safe house and then I realised who I was talking to. My father had probably had Lucky keeping tabs on me for years.

"Then it'll be the one on Talbot Street, won't it?" Lucky called without looking over his shoulder. "You seem to favor that one."

"That's the one," I replied, a little taken aback. I was glad he was on our side. "Send the team, would you?"

"Consider it done."

I turned to head for the door.

"Oh, uh, Seth?" he called after me.

"I'll put in a good word for you with my father," I called back, guessing at what was on his mind. "Don't worry about your job. Just keep doing it. We have VIPs and guests pouring into the estate for the next three days. We need your protocols and focus to keep them safe. Keep your eyes peeled. Lynch will be looking to get his people inside."

"I'm on it," Lucky answered, before downing the rest of his energy drink.

"Don't have too many more of those." I grabbed the door. "Once the team is dispatched, you ought to get a couple of hours sleep. We need you sharp, not sleep deprived."

Lucky nodded and pushed his glasses back up his nose. "I'll see what I can do."

Lara followed me out and I pulled the door shut behind us. She gave me a funny look.

"That's an unusual choice for head of security." She glanced at the door. "I expected someone a little more ex-military like the rest of your father's detail."

I smiled. "The rest of the team are, but every security force needs comms and coordination. Lucky is the beating heart of ours. He was the two-time chess world champion when Dad offered him the post. He is young but incredibly intelligent, and his pattern recognition is off the charts. It's outside the box, but he has proved utterly ruthless in his defense of the family. This morning's attack is the first time anyone's landed a blow on Weybridge Manor since he was appointed."

"Second," Lara corrected.

I raised an eyebrow.

"Your car," Lara replied. "They've tried to kill us before."

She was right. Someone had blown up my Aston Martin, Here in the heart of the estate.

Still, I sincerely doubted there was a better man for the job. He was also the last person anyone might suspect to be working for us. And that was what made him so much more difficult for others to bribe or compromise.

If everyone in the world considered him a recluse that played hundreds of online games of chess a week, no one would really give him a second thought.

"Your father has an unusual way of doing things," Lara replied as we headed back through the cellar. "I'm starting to see where you get it."

"Me?" I stepped onto the first stair to take us back to the larder.

"Yeah, you." She grinned. "The man who thought his best move was to steal from the CIA."

She had me there.

"If I hadn't taken that mask, we might not be where we are today." I climbed the stairs two at a time. I didn't particularly like reliving that memory. It certainly wasn't me at my best.

She laughed. "No. I'd still be sitting in a museum in New York City studying relics and hoping to meet a wizard, all the while being oblivious to the one I'd been dating."

"Oh, I would have told you eventually," I replied. "You have no idea how hard it is to live with a secret like that. I just figured you would think I was a freak."

"You're my freak, now," she replied, clapping me on the back. "Now get upstairs and let's talk about these wedding preparations."

I caught the sigh before it escaped my lips. One way or another, this wedding was going to be the death of me.

CHAPTER 12

F or the first time, I devoted my undivided attention to planning our wedding. Deciding on napkins and table covers bored me to tears, but seeing the excitement in Lara's eyes made the whole undertaking worthwhile.

The only part of the wedding I was particularly concerned about was having her there. As long as Lara and I were together at the altar, I could take or leave the rest, but the longer I spent working on it with her, the more I realized it mattered to her.

We wolfed down a lamb roast that the kitchen had whipped up as a taste test for the reception and like most meals coming out of the Caldwell kitchens, it was spectacular. It met even Lara's exacting standards, which meant one less problem to worry about.

Lara crossed the wedding menu off the list as we headed to our bedroom. She scanned down the rest of the items.

I stole a look over her shoulder, right as she was turning the page only to reveal another almost full page of dot points.

"That thing has multiple pages?" I blurted.

Lara looked at me and raised an eyebrow.

"There are a lot of moving parts, Seth. Weddings don't just plan themselves. Some people spend a year planning their weddings."

I shook my head in disbelief. Thanks to my curse, time had always been a treasured commodity. The notion that people would devote that much of their life to a day was something I struggled to fathom.

"Isn't this what we have Millicent for?" I asked.

Lara scoffed. "She was your father's choice."

That would be about right. My father wouldn't trust just anyone to plan a function at the manor.

"She has thrown galas, balls, and state dinners. There should be precious little she needs us for apart from our preferences."

"If only," Lara muttered. "It seems for everything I give her, she gives me three chores back."

That didn't sound right, but Millicent was a tough old bird on the best of days. She listened to my father's every instruction, but that was Frank. No one gave chores back to Frank Caldwell. If Lara wasn't getting the same response out of her, it was likely due to the staff's perception of my father and my priorities.

I mentally etched Millicent's name into the top of my priorities list.

"Not anymore," I replied. "I'll see her first thing in the morning and iron things out. I imagine we'll find her much more cooperative."

Lara let out a sigh of relief. "That would be wonderful. I feel like she's fighting me the whole way."

"If I promise to get her on board, can we take the rest of the night off? I'm wrecked."

"If you can wrangle Millicent into line, I think we can arrange that."

"Done. I'll tackle her first thing in the morning." I pushed open the door to our room and held it for Lara. "I could really use some rest."

As I pushed the door closed, my phone played a message alert.

I lifted it out of my pocket, wondering who it could be.

"Hades," I breathed, the words slipping out before I could stop them.

Lara's head whipped around so fast, I was surprised it didn't snap her neck. "Wait, what. You gave that felon your phone number?"

"I've been trying to get in touch with him, dear. He's an unusual character. You never know when his skills might come in handy."

"Kasey I can understand." Lara paused. "Unusual. I think you mean dangerous. I'm not a fool, Seth. Don't take me for one. What do you want with him?"

I hesitated, not because I didn't have an answer, but because I wasn't sure how Lara would take it. When I had asked Kasey to put me in touch with Hades, I'd had a very particular idea in mind, but it was the sort of mad plan only a desperate fool would chance. Unfortunately, I was no stranger to desperation.

That said, there wasn't a snowflake's chance in hell that Lara would sign off on this particular gambit so I needed to tread carefully.

The timing of his call had put me in a difficult predicament. I'd promised I would never lie to her again. At the same time, I was also sure if I told exactly what was on my mind, she would be livid. I might well be sleeping on the couch, rather than in the honeymoon suite.

"Seth, the CIA are no strangers to interrogation. Don't make me pry it out of you."

I held up my hand to slow the onslaught. Lara's all or nothing nature was something I loved about her. She operated at speed and didn't do half-measures. But this wasn't her call; it was mine.

"We are dealing with the spirit of a soul that has not departed," I replied. "It's not an area of magic that I have any expertise with. It isn't knowledge that is easy to find. In fact, it borders on necromancy and the Forbidden and there won't be anyone who advertises this sort of skill set. So we're going to be looking for someone, and I figured better to talk to the devil I know."

"And you really think Hades can?"

I sat down on the end of the bed. "I think that he might. He's definitely far more than a street criminal. All of that is a façade, Lara. He walks around openly assuming the identity of Hades, Lord of the Underworld. I have met Hades, the real one. The very sight of that Olympian chilled me to the bone."

"So he's using his name. What difference does that make?" Lara asked.

"In the supernatural world, there is power in a name. I saw his master in him. When I mentioned meeting his master, he didn't bat an eyelid. He doesn't fear him, because he's operating with his blessing. For this Hades to be, there has to be some sort of agreement between them. Gods don't just let others leach off their name and reputation like parasites."

"What are you saying?" Lara asked. "That he works for the real Hades?"

"Something like that," I replied, leaning back on the bed. "That's how I know there is more to Hades than meets the eye. I need to plumb the depths of that relationship. I need answers. We need answers."

"Why?" she asked, raising both hands. "Why are you so determined to court chaos so close to our wedding. Why now?"

My father's visit with the diviner changed everything.

"You heard what my father said. There's never been a better time than this for putting an end to this curse. Aleida knows we're onto her. She'll be scheming for her survival. If we give her too much time, we might lose this opportunity."

"I get that," Lara replied. "But your father still seems pretty able. He was able to drive her out of his mind today, wasn't he? We've got time."

She took off her jacket and threw it over the chair.

"That's true. If she kills him, she'll be back to square one. She can't kill me without severing the ties that bind her to this world. But we'll be stuck too. We can't bring a child into this world without signing my death warrant. Tell me that thought hasn't run through your head a hundred times since you got off the chopper."

I put my head in my hands. I couldn't hold her gaze. "Because it's certainly gone through mine."

Lara went to speak but her voice caught in her throat.

I looked up from the bed. She bit her lip, her eyes glistening.

"Of course I've thought about it. It's all I have been able to think about. Why do you think I want this all so badly?"

"I want it too." My voice grew louder. "A life, and future, and family with you. But for that to happen, we need to be rid of her. That's why we need Hades. To help before it's too late."

"It already is." Lara choked up. "That's what I've been trying to tell you. It's already too late, Seth."

Tears ran down her face, and my heart hammered in my chest.

"What do you mean?" My voice faded with every word.

She stared deep into my eyes. "You know exactly what I mean. You're going to be a father."

I heard the words, but my brain just wouldn't process them.

"We're going to be parents."

I simply couldn't speak. A thousand thoughts rampaged through my mind, but none of them were making it to my mouth.

On the one hand, there was the profound joy and excitement at the imminent realization of my dream of having a family. It was already here. I just hadn't been expecting it.

On the other hand was the harrowing reality that the next generation of Aleida's unwilling anchor had already been maneuvered into position, and my own life expectancy diminished by the moment.

How had this happened? I knew the answer, of course. I just thought we'd been more careful than that. My mind raced. I wasn't ready for my child to bear my burden. I wanted them to be born free in a world where they could do anything they wished without the weight of four centuries of Caldwell baggage grinding them beneath it.

"When you got back from Ares' Trial, we got carried away. I was so happy to see you. I wasn't really thinking about it, and you clearly weren't either."

She was right. I had just survived three rounds of Ares' Grand Trial, with my death being an ever-present threat Future planning hadn't been at the forefront of my mind.

Lara stood there, tears running down her cheeks, and I realized she was waiting for something more substantial than a gawking goldfish.

Pushing aside my own internal conflict, I shoved to my feet and threw my arms around her.

"That's the greatest news anyone's ever given me," I whispered as I held her tight, her cheek pressed against my chest, her tears seeping through my shirt. "I love you."

She pulled me tight, sobbing into my chest. There was a bittersweet feel to the entire announcement, and I cursed Aleida for tarnishing what should have been the greatest day of our lives.

Instead, her bloody-minded hatred cast a shadow over it. She was destroying our lives, and our happiness. I'd had just about enough of it.

You thought you had me, the voice hissed inside my mind.

I recognized the tone the second I heard it.

It was the airy haunting words of Aleida, high priestess of the Brujas de Sangre. My bitter belligerent forebear.

I hadn't heard her since Panama, and I wasn't going to let her taint this moment. Remembering the words Kasey had shared with me, I let out an effort of will and a whispered an almost silent command.

"Out." It was so faint, it was barely audible, but the effort of will was fueled by a tsunami of emotion that drove her from my mind. I felt the priestess try to resist, but the inexorable pain and weight of my will drove her out.

As the voice faded to nothing, Lara wiped her eyes. "What was that?"

"Nothing important, dear," I said. "I just want you to know that we are going to get through all this. There's nothing I won't do to keep you both safe."

And I meant it. There was only one place I had ever witnessed the disembodied soul of the departed and done battle with them.

And that was in the underground arena of Hades, Lord of the Underworld. If I had to pass through hell to rid myself of this wretched ancestor, that was precisely what I intended to do.

"You're not upset?" Lara whispered.

"No," I answered. "I mean it. This is all I ever wanted."

"I could feel the hesitation, Seth." Lara looked up at me.

"It's not hesitation," I answered quickly. "I just never wanted my child to feel the way I do. I wasn't ready. But screw being ready. We can do this. We're so close."

Lara wiped the tears from her face. In all the time we'd been together, I'd never seen her this vulnerable. It was in that moment that I understood the weight she had been carrying these last few weeks. And she'd been doing it without me knowing, or sharing the burden.

"How long have you known?" I asked, still playing catch up.

"Weeks," Lara whispered. "I've been too scared to tell you. I worried what you would think. I know how you feel about your parents, and the curse. I didn't want you to hate yourself or me."

She swallowed. "But I couldn't not tell you. You've been so down of late. Every day I've wanted to tell you. I wanted to show you all the reasons we have to fight, and to live. Screw Lynch. Screw the Brotherhood. Let it all burn. You and me, this is what matters. We're going to be free, free of it all, Seth."

In that moment, I gained more clarity than I'd had in months. I rubbed her back.

"Yes, we will," I replied soberly. "Yes, we will."

We stood there in silence, just holding each other. As we did, I realized just how mistaken I'd been about everything. Lara wasn't fixated on the wedding for some superficial reason; she was looking to the future. To the start of our family. She was determined to bring our child into the world in a family.

"I also knew if I told you, you'd be reluctant to let me come along with you and there was no chance I was letting you out of my sight after the Trial."

She knew me well. I certainly wouldn't have taken her to The Run. I wouldn't have put both their lives in jeopardy.

"Very sneaky." I laughed. "But that's behind us now. The wedding is almost here. You have me, and I'm going to make sure everything goes smoothly. Remember every day we live, Lynch gets one step closer to the abyss."

The announcement also made the talk with Hades all the more pressing.

I let go of Lara and she slipped into our ensuite to freshen up.

I knew what I had to do.

In the back of my mind, I'd thought I could procrastinate dealing with the curse by stalling before having our first child. That was no longer a luxury I could afford.

Lynch needed the axe, and Aleida had an exorcism in her future.

Both of which made responding to Hades' text all the more important.

I drew out my phone and pressed the video call icon. I wanted to look into the eyes of the man whose hands I was placing my life in.

Hades answered on the fifth ring. The screen flickered to life as his face appeared, the smooth olive skin complexion, the dark hair, and the ready smile. I'd met enough criminals to know the danger that lurked behind those smiling eyes.

"Master Caldwell, I must say I was surprised to hear you wanted to talk. Our mutual friend reached out to me."

I looked down at my phone, noting both the time and the fact that Hades hadn't mentioned her by name. Intriguing.

"It must be a slow day over there," I replied. "I wasn't expecting to hear back from you so soon."

"Speedy service, that's my motto." Hades chuckled. "No, Seth. Given the news making headlines around the world, I wasn't entirely sure if I waited any longer that I would actually be speaking with you. You've angered a lot of people. Powerful people."

"They were already angry," I said with a laugh. "So no great loss."

"I hope you're not looking for allies." Hades' grin was anything but reassuring.

"Why is that?" I asked. I had an idea, but I felt it prudent to let him speak so as to better understand his position.

"I've always been one to seize on an opportunity, but I'm not a martyr, Seth. If you're looking for someone to die on the hill beside you, you're barking up the wrong tree. We aren't that good of friends."

"You didn't have any qualms about your life when you walked into Madison Square Garden with us," I replied.

"The stakes were different. That was for my city, my home. Those creatures ransacked my empire. And I was asked by a friend to help. In my life friends are rare. You, on the other hand, are more of an acquaintance. One with power, influence, and connections. But one who's pissed on the pant leg of one of the most influential men on earth. You have the life expectancy of a fly sailing into oncoming traffic, and much as I want to see the show, I think it's best that I stay out of it."

"Thanks for putting it so bluntly," I said. "I was starting to think I might survive."

"You and I both know that's unlikely," Hades replied flatly. "So, is that why you've called? Or is there something else?"

"I'm not looking to enlist your help against them." I wasn't quite willing to say Lynch's name into an open phone line. "It was more your employer I was interested in. But it's not the sort of matter that can be discussed over the phone for so many reasons."

"Then we might have to wait a week and see if it's still worth discussing, perhaps when the heat dies down. You can come to New York. I'd love to talk about it, for a price of course."

"Price I can pay," I replied, eager to grab any momentum I could get. "Caldwells have deep pockets, and I know the favor I'm asking is unusual. But I can't wait."

I paused.

I couldn't tell Hades the exact nature of my issue. But if I died in Lynch's assault and Lara managed to survive, my child was going to be born into exactly the same problem I had been.

This needed solving and it needed solving now. I had an answer, but I needed Hades' help and I needed him here to do it.

"I imagine you're on the no-fly list, but do you have the means of getting to London?"

"Difficult," Hades replied icily. "I seldom travel, and I have extensive business to conduct here."

"I could make it worth your while," I replied, hoping I could bait him into making the journey.

"Why the urgency?" Hades asked. "I thought you were getting married? You might have your priorities mixed up."

Word traveled quickly; he certainly hadn't been on the invite list.

"I am, but this needs to be seen to as a matter of urgency. Come to London, enjoy a drink at the wedding if you like, not an obligation, but our friend will be here and her plus one isn't. Perhaps she could use some company."

The words just spilled out of my mouth. I suppose I'd seen the way he looked at her. I'd watched the unrequited love in his eyes. He was a lovesick puppy following a heroine into the heat of battle, hoping she would see his sacrifice for what it was.

"You're quite sure of that?" Hades asked, leaning toward the screen.

"Positive. No plus one. Don't ask me why, but she'll be here. You know what that means, though."

His voice dropped to an angry rasp. "You've invited her to a slaughter, Seth. When your enemies come for you, they won't care who else is in the way. You're putting her life in jeopardy."

"She does the same thing every day. They've tried to kill her before. She believes in this fight. No one's making her do anything she doesn't want to do. You know that."

"If you ever use her to leverage me again, I will end everything you hold dear. Do you understand me?"

Hades' voice sent a shiver down my spine.

Lara appeared at the door of the bathroom, a towel wrapped around her. It was a most distracting view.

"As I said, it wasn't my intention, but it is the way things turned out. I only thought to tell you so you'd be aware, as one man who knows what it means to care, to another."

"This is going to cost you, Seth Caldwell."

"I expected as much. Don't worry, I'm good for it."

"Now I just need to work out how to cross that many jurisdictions in such a short time frame."

"Don't bother," Lara called. "Kendra is coming as Dizzy's plus one. She'll be wheel's up in three hours. I suggest you be on her plane."

"An arrangement I'm sure she'll be delighted about," Hades said with a smirk.

"She'll bear it for our sake, and so will you," Lara replied. "I don't expect a present, but I do expect peace. Be sure to bring it with you and get on the damned plane."

"I will do my level best to be a well-behaved guest, Ms. Stiel. I cannot speak for your other guests."

Hades looked me in the eye. There was amusement there. "See you soon."

The screen went dead. I breathed a sigh of relief.

That went better than expected.

I looked to my wife-to-be. Her tears were gone, and her head was cocked to the side, a cheeky grin on her face.

"Is he gone?"

I nodded and set down the phone on the nightstand.

"Good," she replied. "I hope you're not too tired."

With that, she slowly undid her towel and let it drop to the floor.

CHAPTER 13

When I woke, I did so with a clarity of purpose I hadn't felt in weeks.

Learning that I was going to be a father refocused both my mind and my priorities. It was as if the fog that had been smothering me in fear, anxiety, and doubt had been driven away by the light of a new day.

In truth, it was so much more than that. I was going to be a dad. It wasn't the timing I had in mind, but life seldom seemed to have any regard for my plans. Still, the thought thrilled me. It was what I had always wanted, but perhaps had never believed might actually be possible. That was the power of the curse: smothering my dreams since the day I'd learned of it.

Lara's revelation had shattered all of that. She loved me in spite of my shortcomings, and for reasons I couldn't fathom, had a faith in me that seemed unshakable. And I was determined to prove her right.

There would be no more wallowing, only preparation. Lara had shouldered the burden of planning our wedding alone, but that changed today. It must have been hard, wondering how I would react to the pregnancy whilst pushing forward toward a wedding that I must have seemed almost indifferent to.

I kicked myself. My inattention must have hurt and still she had put on a brave face. She deserved so much more.

Well, she would have it.

I grabbed an early breakfast and was making the rounds, checking in on the workers erecting a massive marquee on the lawn to shelter the ceremony.

We couldn't really go anywhere, but fortunately the expansive estate offered an excellent substitute venue.

Only two days remained, and there was still plenty to do. I expected most of the day would be taken organizing the estate and welcoming the first of our guests. The locals would show up on Sunday, but those coming from overseas would likely start arriving today and tomorrow in the lead up to the rehearsal dinner.

Hopefully, Levi would make his way here too. The sooner he arrived, the better I would feel.

As I circled the estate, it became apparent that my father had further increased the number of mercenaries he had hired. Trusting such sellswords was a difficult prospect, which was why most of them were set up in camps beyond the walls. Only those who had passed more rigorous security protocols and had a history with the family were permitted on the estate.

Lynch had eyes and ears everywhere, and we weren't inviting potential wolves into the fold.

Every person who set foot on the grounds needed to be vetted, construction crews and wedding staff alike. Security protocols had been tripled since the assassination attempt, and Lucky was doing his level best to ensure no one was able to make a repeat performance.

Once was a stain on his reputation; twice was unforgivable in his eyes.

Apart from the trouble with Millicent, preparations seemed to be moving forward. Tomorrow would feature last-minute arrangements and a rehearsal dinner, and then Sunday would be the big day. If Lynch made his move, we would be ready for him, at least as ready as we could be.

I watched the news on my phone as I walked a lap of the estate. The stories were coming thick and fast but in spite of the amount of evidence we'd provided, there was still speculation. The fact that conspiracy theorists seized on the Brotherhood's existence so eagerly meant that others had a tendency to dismiss it a little too quickly.

Perhaps we had overestimated the public's willingness to believe that unbeknown to them, they had been controlled by a small group of puppeteers for centuries. It wasn't an easy truth to hear, or to buy into. But those with resources would soon know the truth. The deeper they dug, the more irrefutable proof they would find.

I suspected it had been a very rough night for Andrew Lynch and that thought brought a broad smile to my face.

Sprawled out on the lawn was the massive marquee, and within it was the object of my wife's frustrations. I pushed aside one of the clear panels that would serve as a window and slipped inside.

On the far side stood a woman. She was impeccably dressed in a black blazer, white skirt, and flat shoes. Her hair was worn up in a tight bun. In one hand she brandished a clipboard, which she waved like a weapon as she shouted orders to her team.

"The rear of the marquee needs to be open. Get those walls bundled up like the curtains on stage. It would just be criminal to hide that view of the lake."

Two men rushed to comply with her request as she shouted after them. "We want the guests to look to our bride and groom, and beyond them see the beauty and splendor of the estate. Let's move, people. Contrary to popular belief. we don't have all day."

"Millicent," I called, sparing her team her wrath. "How are preparations this morning?"

She turned, one eyebrow arching as she took me in.

"Mr. Caldwell, I was beginning to think you might never surface. I trust your wife is well?"

Her words were a painful reminder that I'd been dropping the ball.

"She's perfectly fine. I just thought I'd come and check on progress. I understand we're falling behind schedule. That's not like you, Millicent."

Millicent reacted like she'd caught a raw tuna with her face. "But, sir, I assure—"

"No excuses, Millicent." I stopped her dead in her tracks. "My father assured me you'd be up to the task, but my wife tells me differently. If there's one thing I won't have, Millicent, it's my wife being under stress when we've hired a *professional*."

I stressed the word intentionally so as to redirect the pressure she'd been channeling into my wife.

"I assure you, we're doing everything we can, with the time we've been given." Millicent gestured at the marquee. "It's no small undertaking to prepare all this on a moment's notice."

"Then tell me what you need to ensure my wife's expectations are met, without giving her any more chores."

Millicent looked down at her clipboard, and as she raised her head, her countenance had regained its composure. "Another dozen hands, more furniture settings for these unexpected guests your wife has sprung on me, and don't even get me started on the budget. I'm going to need your wife's signature on these variations."

It was never a good sign when your wedding planner discussed pricing increases using the same terminology builders might use when constructing a house.

Millicent turned the clipboard so that I could see the quote. It was certainly generous. As I considered the extortionate sum, I wondered if Millicent had orchestrated the entire ordeal, tormenting my wife until I came to her aid. If there was one thing that could be said for the shrewd old wedding planner, it was that she knew an opportunity when she saw it. And a rush wedding for the Caldwell dynasty was an opportunity for her to bolster her retirement, or take a small holiday around the world. Both perhaps.

But it was too early in the morning and my mood too good to bicker about money.

"Let me see to that, Millicent." I took the clipboard and her pen and scrawled my signature across the bottom line. "The Caldwells never come up short."

She tried and failed to hide her triumphant grin, but as I set the pen back on the clipboard, I fixed the wily old bird with a look. "Don't for a minute believe I am unaware of the considerable markup in those figures. You'll make this the finest wedding you've ever planned, and you'll do it without adding any stress to my wife. Am I clear?"

She stared at her carefully manicured nails. ""I'll be needing those extra hands."

"A dozen," I replied. "I heard you earlier. Do you understand me, Millicent? In three day's time, one of two things will happen. My delighted and relaxed wife will walk down this aisle in your greatest triumph to date, take my hand, and smile as we start the next chapter of our lives. Or you will fall short of our expectations, tarnish your reputation, and incur the enduring frustration of the next generation of Caldwells. Am I making myself clear?"

Millicent noted my signature and nodded once. "I never disappoint a client."

"And I don't expect you to start today. See to it that my wife manages to relax." I headed for the exit.

"I'm a wedding planner not a spa attendant," Millicent called after me.

I waved my hand dismissively. "Millicent, for that much money, you could build a spa. See to it."

She muttered under her breath, but I was content she was back on task. The cheeky opportunist.

Now that I'd restored the natural order of things, I set out to finish my morning walk.

I wandered past the lake and into the grove of trees. It was one of the few areas I didn't feel like I was under constant observation.

Part of me that hoped Murdoch might reveal himself to me again. If nothing else, I wanted to thank him. I'd been an ungrateful brat when all he'd been doing was watching out for me. I could do better, be better, and my old friend deserved that courtesy.

The day was on the colder side and a gentle breeze stirred the manor grounds. I sunk my hands into my pockets to keep them warm.

My right hand struck something small and round, and cool to the touch. I closed my fingers around it and drew it out.

It was a small gold coin on a leather thong. I'd been carrying it since the day Ares gifted it to me.

My lucky coin. Or at least that was how I saw it.

It was hard to consider it as anything else when it was the sole prize I had won from surviving Ares' Grand Trial. It was an unusual coin in that it didn't bear any indication of its value.

On the back it featured the likeness of a boat with a shrouded figure standing in it. I recalled Charon and a shiver ran down my spine. It was impossible not to shudder at the thought of the haunting visage of the ferryman that bore souls across the river Styx. It was he who had come for the priestess of Hera that had tormented me at Delphi.

The coin was an unusual sort of gift, though Ares himself had worn it. I supposed there was some significance to that. In ancient times, the deceased would have a single coin, known as an obol, placed in their mouth to pay the ferryman.

Ares' injunction had been never to be without it. I had figured it best to follow his instruction and fastened the thong around my neck as he had.

Ares had given the real prize, his gauntlets and the power they possessed, to Edward Knight for a week. What I wouldn't have given to have those right about now. Lynch and his allies would have had their work cut out for them then.

I glanced down at the coin and sighed. It wasn't much of a consolation prize but perhaps I would find a use for it. Something other than paying the ferryman.

Perhaps it wasn't really a gift at all. Maybe it was just a taunting reminder from the God of War of the certainty of my own demise.

I could almost hear his taunting tone. "Congratulations on surviving the Trial, Seth. Here, let me prepay the ferryman on your behalf."

If that really was the consideration he had given it, then I hoped to disappoint him.

Thus far, it had manifested the opposite effect. Since receiving it, I had managed to navigate a dozen life-threatening exchanges, including New York City, the ritual Rhaine had instigated in Madison Square Garden, and the events at

Glastonbury. Not to mention the ambush, and attack of the sapera at the Palladium.

I rubbed my hand over the coin. It was cold to the touch and even my fingers brought it no warmth.

"Interesting gift," a melodious voice called from the forest to my flank. The tone carried and was at once sweet and sultry, but demanded obedience. I turned to find a stunning woman with blonde hair, piercing blue eyes, and a toga that was several centuries out of place, yet she made it not only work, but look good.

I dropped the obol and bowed my head in deference. I took the opportunity to ensure we were alone, and no one else was lurking nearby.

"Now what's a god like you doing in a place like this?" I said.

Weybridge Manor was a long way from Olympus, and Hera wasn't exactly on our guest list.

"I just stopped by to see if you'd thought through my proposal," Hera replied as she glided onto the path. "Normally, I don't have to wait for men to get back to me."

Her voice had an allure to it that I was sure enticed men to do precisely what she wished. Men that spent more time staring at her inviting figure, than they did thinking about the fact that her husband was the jealous god of the skies. I kept my gaze above the shoulder to avoid temptation.

"I wasn't aware I was keeping you waiting." I ensured my tone was neutral, not wanting to give any offense. I'd been in her good graces of late, but had been pitted against her interests at Delphi. I had no desire to return to that state of affairs. I had more than enough enemies to contend with.

"At the trial I made you an offer. One I reminded you of in New York City. Don't pretend it's slipped your mind. I'd like an answer."

I laughed. I couldn't help it. In my present circumstances, there was just something amusing about her interest in my service.

"What's so funny?" Hera cocked her head.

"I'm sorry, I always just assumed you were omniscient. Are you somehow unaware of my current predicament?"

Hera placed one hand on her hip. "Your circumstances were fairly dire when I made you the offer. The smart money was certainly on you losing at the Trial, and yet I made it anyway."

"Is that your way of telling me you are omniscient?" I goaded. "Or is the staffing shortage getting that grim?"

"I've always had an eye for unusual opportunities." She flicked her hair as she ignored both my questions. "And you are many things, Seth. All of them unusual."

Flattery. At least, I hoped it was flattery.

I scratched an itch behind my ear which also gave me a good excuse to break eye contact. "I would love to tell you I have thought about it. But for the last few weeks I've been so busy trying to save my own skin, I really haven't had the chance."

When she was silent, I was forced to meet her stare.

"Haven't even considered it. You wound me." She placed her hand over her heart, her fingertips catching her toga, causing it to slip off her shoulder just a little.

I stared at those blue eyes and held her gaze.

"Before you get your toga in a twist, my lady, the oversight was not intended as a slight." I had no intention of provoking her and figured a little groveling might be in order. "Merely a necessity of trying to survive."

"Well, I'm here now," Hera answered. "I'm certainly willing to accept your response now."

"And how might I do that?" I countered. "You haven't been particularly forthcoming with the details."

"Walk with me, Seth. We can discuss it."

She ambled down the path, and I set off after her.

"It seems you want an agent, that much is clear. But I still have no idea what that entails, or why you want me? I understand at least on a surface level why my family's means might be appealing to you, but there are many wealthy families. What I don't understand is why of all the families in all the earth, you and your husband both want me and mine. Why have we become the rope in the millennia old tug-of-war with your husband?"

Hera laughed. "Tug-of-war? Dear, that implies we're both playing the game. My husband has been distracted for decades. If he wasn't such an absentee patriarch, I doubt we'd have half the troubles we're facing now."

"Distracted?" I couldn't help but indulge my curiosity. "With what?"

I wondered what could be of sufficient import as to attract Zeus's unwavering attention.

"The Internet, dear," Hera replied matter-of-factly. "That old horn dog has been distracted since its creation. He doesn't have to charm maidens to get them naked now. He can stream it. He hasn't spent more than one day in seven seeing to his duties since they made Onlyfans."

I held my tongue. Because that was what someone who wanted to keep it does in the presence of a woman who, while oft scorned, had a well-documented track record of gaining vindication.

"So if it's attracting my husband's displeasure that is preventing you accepting my offer, understand that he probably doesn't care. If he did, he'd be here. Granted, he'd probably be trying to seduce your wife to be first, but that's neither here nor there.

That wasn't exactly a thought I wanted to dwell on, so I changed the topic. "You're still overly light on details. What is it exactly you're doing, and how can I help?"

"I'm trying to preserve the order of things, Seth. Power is shifting in the world. The seasons turn against each other. The hearts and minds of humanity turn from the gods they once sought to other more idle pursuits. And as the attention wanes, so does our influence, and ability to protect them. The gods..."

Her voice trailed off.

"You mean to tell me the gods are losing their grip?" My jaw drooped open like an idiot.

"I guess that's one way to put it," she replied. "An unsettling shift and not necessarily one for the better."

I wasn't so sure about that. The gods had largely meddled in my life, taking without giving anything in return. Like Ares had for his amusement, or Apollo manipulating me into protecting his oracle at Delphi. "And why should that bother me?"

"Because, Seth, not all of us are the same. Not all of us care for the protection and prospering of the human race. There are those who would just as happily rule over the ashes as the masses. A battered populace can be compelled into obeisance."

My pace slowed. "What are you trying to say?"

"In days past, when attention was less of a battleground than it is today, and the children of men built temples by the dozens and gathered to them, there was plenty of power and influence to divide between us. As that scarce resource dwindles, like all other shortages, it breeds conflict."

"You mean war?" I said.

"Yes, and for the first time, I'm unsure of exactly what that will entail. Such things have always reshaped the world, seldom for the better. Peace is good for everyone, Seth."

I didn't trust Hera as far as I could throw her, but the thought of Olympians at war with each other gave me reason to pause. That sort of conflict would spill over into, or be fought in, our world. While I wasn't of the mind to trade the Brotherhood for another master, I also didn't know that I could stand by and do nothing.

"Prove it to me," I replied. "I've heard nothing of the sort. Not even whispers of such a war."

"Oh, you dally frequently with deity, do you? Have a source in the rumor mongers of Olympus? The gods don't bandy this before the masses, Seth. They move against each other in secret."

I thought of Murdoch, but I didn't want to play my hand.

"From time to time," I replied, "and I think he might have mentioned it. So speak plainly, Hera. I have never been one for politics."

"I don't do dumb, Seth. Open your mind," she hissed.

I stopped moving, worried I'd pushed her too far.

She turned. "When you were at the Grand Trial, did you not find it fascinating? There was friction even there. Think of the choice of battlefields."

I played through each of them in my mind. It was hard not to. Those harrowing days were etched into my soul. "I am."

"When our pantheon took power, three brothers divided the world and its respective domains between themselves. Hades took the realm of spirits and the gateway to beyond. His brother Poseidon took the oceans. Vast and unsearchable are their depths and the treasures they contain. Ever ambitious, my husband took the endless skies, a vantage point from which he can look down on all mankind."

She waved a hand. "But when Ares chose three arenas for the Trials, he chose the Underworld, the watery graves of Poseidon, and his own Areopagus. Three battlefields needed but instead of honoring his father, he elevated himself among the others. It was a slight that did not go unnoticed, and the friction has only grown."

My mind reeled. I had considered it odd at the time. Mentally, I'd prepared myself to do battle in a different arena for the third challenge. I'd noticed the pattern and been waiting for some insane sky challenge. Instead, it had been settled on the sands of Ares' own arena.

My mind replayed the events of that day. I recalled Ares banishing his own sons as if it was nothing. They had been aspiring to take his power for their own, but I'd figured that was just ambition. Now Hera was trying to assert that it was symptomatic of a larger problem.

If Ares, Poseidon, and Hades were consorting with each other, what did that even mean? I wanted to know more, but I wasn't ready to sign my life to her cause. I had no idea if she was even on the right side of the situation. What if she were the danger, and the others merely trying to counter her growing influence? She'd tried to seize the Oracle. She wasn't an uninterested bystander. She too was playing the game.

"An interesting point," I said at length. "I'm inclined to consider your offer."

"That sure as sin isn't a yes," Hera replied. "Don't toy with me, mortal."

"I wouldn't dream of it," I replied. "And try as you might to ignore the present, I'm a man on the very brink of annihilation. You can see that we're preparing for a war of our own. The Brotherhood will come. I have to survive them and thwart my own wretched curse before I can even consider wading into another conflict."

Hera twirled a ring of curls around her finger. "And how has that been going for you?"

"Well, we've actually made a lot of progress. So there's a chance I might survive to be of assistance to you." I paused, just long enough to plant the seed in her mind. "You know, you could always expedite the matter. Give me a hand with things. I wouldn't tell, you know. I can keep a secret."

She laughed. "Nice try, Seth, but if you're good at something, never do it for free. I prosper my own, not those dabbling in indecision."

I sighed. It was worth a shot.

"You have all the pieces, Seth. Don't bother me with petty curses and ancient wretches. The weight of the world and the well-being of your species hangs in the balance."

"Yours too, I presume. Otherwise, you wouldn't be here."

"Precisely," she replied. "So my interests are in alignment with yours. Why won't you help me?"

It was a good question, and I was confident she wasn't going to think much of my answer. But when I'd rolled out of bed this morning, I'd been intent on one thing. My resolution wasn't going to waver the second a Goddess batted her eyes at me.

"Because I need my whole attention focused on the fight in front of me. I have commitments here first. A war to win, a wife to wed, and neither of them would be served by taking my eye off the ball now. So if you want to talk again, might I suggest you render any assistance you can that would help me survive the next three days? Otherwise, you might have to brave Hades' realm to find me."

"That's not how it works, Seth," she replied. "You can only serve me while you remain here. So best you keep both your wits and that coin about you."

She pulled me in for an embrace and I held my breath as the mother of Olympus pressed her cheek to mine. The entire time, only one thought raced through my mind.

I was confident that this was a smite-able offense and prayed her husband was busy on a stable broadband connection.

"Keep it close, Seth. I suspect you'll need it."

She let me go, but I reached out.

"Wait, what do you mean by that?" I called.

Her lips rose into a smile as she faded from view. "Talk soon, Seth. At least, I hope we can."

CHAPTER 14

With Hera gone as abruptly as she had arrived, I was left walking the same circuit I had yesterday. I hoped Murdoch would show up again. But as I cleared the woods and made my way along the inner wall, heading for the manor's driveway, I let go of that hope.

Clearly, he had given me all the help he could.

Murdoch was also one of the reasons I wasn't just running to throw in with Hera and her lot. Seeing him in his true form had been like staring at divinity. You couldn't help but be changed by the experience.

He had viewed the Olympians with disdain. Whatever the truth behind their existence was, it was clear to me that he viewed them differently from the world at large. They might purport to be gods, but he didn't believe that for a second, and the longer I dealt with them the more convinced I was that he might be right.

Powerful, yes. Omnipotent...seemed unlikely given what I'd witnessed.

As I headed for the gate, I noted the cluster of security gathered behind it, their weapons raised. More men streamed down from the house, converging on the gate.

Trouble was brewing there. My boots kicked up gravel as I raced to see what was amiss. On reaching the gate, I found a large eighteen-wheeler truck parked in front of it, the truck was flanked by two smaller vans.

Our security eyed them skeptically, waiting for any excuse to blow them away.

None of the vehicles moved, their occupants content to wait out the conflict from inside their vehicles.

"What's going on?" I called, my chest heaving from my run.

The nearest officer turned, his face relaxing as he recognized me. "Unauthorized shipments, sir. His name isn't on the manifest for the wedding, or the approved personnel. He refuses to allow us to search the vehicle, just keeps insisting we send for you. We didn't want to in case it was another trap, sir."

"Well, I'm here now. Let's see what we're dealing with." I stepped closer to the vehicles.

Smiling down from the passenger seat of the eighteen-wheeler was Levi. His golden eyes regarded me with interest as he sat unmoving in the truck.

I waved for the team to stand down. "It's okay. He's with me. Lower your weapons!"

"We can't do that. We're under strict orders from your father. Every vehicle is to be searched."

I looked up at the truck. "Levi, would you mind stepping down for a minute so that we might introduce you to the team?"

"Very well." The door swung open, and the big barkeep leaped down from the truck, his boots striking the driveway with a heavy thud. He rounded the truck as the gates swung open to meet him.

"This is Levi, one of my invited guests. He'll be staying with us here at the manor for the foreseeable future. He, his trucks, and his people are here at my request. He's a member of the supernatural world and ought not to be subjected to this degree of scrutiny. Please, accord him the respect he deserves.

The team exchanged looks with each other.

"Not exactly the warm welcome I was expecting, Master Caldwell," Levi said.

"Things have been a little uneasy since the ambush yesterday," I replied. "But rest assured, they will protect you and your own as keenly as they do the rest of the estate."

"I understand." Levi bowed his head. "What can I do to smooth over this misunderstanding?"

"You can submit to a basic search of your effects," security replied. "Seth, your father does not want any weapons or explosives smuggled into the estate. We've been trying to reach him to confirm his wishes, but he's been out of contact for the last twenty minutes."

"I am the weapon," Levi replied. "The trucks simply hold my personal effects. I would prefer they remain undisturbed."

"I'll see to my father," I intervened before the security could get any more worked up. "Levi, here, is a creature of magic. His oath should be sufficient to allay your concerns."

The security officer looked at his team as if searching for a way out of his current predicament.

"Levi, do you swear with an oath that as long as you're here, you, and all who serve under you, will bring no harm to the members of this house and those who serve here?" I asked.

Levi lifted his head. "No."

The air turned stiff. The security team raised their rifles once more, eager fingers hovering near the trigger.

"I will do one better," Levi said. "As long as I live here, Weybridge Manor will be under my protection. Both I and those who serve me will exert our whole being in its defense. That I swear on my life."

The air was electric, the tingle of arcane energy absolutely tangible as Levi's oath was infused with the magic that would bind him to it.

The strength of will I felt in that moment reassured me. Not only of his intention and loyalty, but that I'd made the right choice in bringing him here. There was a power to him that even I had underestimated.

I turned to the security team. "He cannot break his oath. That will be enough. Stand aside and open the gates."

The security team hesitated.

"My father has ceded the estate, the company, and everything in the Caldwell empire into my hands. You best get used to following my direction as if it were his."

The man cleared his throat. "Very well, sir. I didn't mean any offense by it."

"None taken. Your diligence is appreciated. Now open the gates."

The gates swung inward, and Levi climbed back into his truck. I stepped up onto the sideboard of the vehicle so that I could direct him to his new home.

"Your people are welcome to stay with you if they wish. There are suitable facilities at the vault. Or if you prefer, they are welcome in our guest quarters."

"They will stay with me," Levi replied. "It is the way of things."

"Very well. I'll show you to the vault."

Holding onto the outside of the truck, I leaned in the open window and directed Levi's driver toward the house. But rather than pull up in front of the garage, we carried right on past it. The big truck rolled off the drive and over the verdant green lawns, leaving a trail I was sure the groundskeepers

would be thrilled with. But there was no paved surface leading to the vault. Such would have been a dead giveaway of
its location.

The truck and its two supporting vans rolled down the
western side of the estate where sloping grasslands gradu-
ally grew into a hill.

"Pull up here," I said, pointing to the hill that dominated
this section of the estate.

Terraced gardens covered the sides of the hill, making
the whole area quite picturesque. In reality, it was a clever
disguise for its true purpose.

"Levi, come with me. Leave the others here for now."

Levi turned to his driver. "Ready our things for transport.
I'd like my effects secured as soon as possible."

"We'll have plenty of time for that once I've shown you
around," I said.

I led Levi along the path that ran over the hill. The path led
to a fountain that had a stone unicorn rising from its heart.
Water poured from the creature's horn. Stepping up onto the
ledge, I dropped into the fountain.

"It's quite shallow," I said as the water lapped at my boots.
Striding across the fountain, I pressed a stone at the base of
the creature's feet. There was a whir, and the entire sculpture
started to rise.

"It's certainly well hidden." Levi nodded approvingly.

"You'll soon understand why," I said.

A small alcove formed beneath the statue. On one wall was
a biometric keypad. I placed my hand over it and the ground
beneath our feet shook.

Levi reached out to steady himself.

"Easy, it's the front door." I pointed behind him where an
eight-foot section of the fountain slid apart. Water ran down

each side as a massive tunnel appeared sloping down into the hill.

Levi smiled. "You store it in a hill? Was that for my benefit?"

"Nope, it's always been here," I replied. "Put that one down to my father's strange sense of humor."

"Most convenient. I think I could come to feel at home here."

I laughed. "Wait until you see the inside."

The tunnel bore down at a forty-five degree angle. The construction of the artificial hill had been necessary to hide the underground facility with its extensive quarters, storage, and ventilation. In truth, the original purpose of the facility had been to protect a series of interconnected bunkers my forebears had built and expanded during the world wars.

"Just how deep does it go?" Levi asked.

"A good few hundred feet," I replied. "This is where my family planned to wait out any apocalypse. They would have more than enough wealth and resources to rebuild, if it ever came to that."

"For a family expecting to die young, you certainly plan to the contrary."

"We've always been empire builders," I replied. "At least my forebears were. The things I value cannot be bought with gold."

"Does your father know you're moving me into this bunker?"

I shook my head. "Don't worry about him. He's given me authority over our assets. He will see in time the merit of having you as our guest."

"Our people have seldom lived in harmony, Seth," Levi replied. "If he learns of my true nature, I fear he will want me gone. Most people are quick to fear, and fast to wrath."

"Then it is good for us both that we are not most people," I replied.

Lights flickered to life as we continued down the path. The deeper we went, the more rooms branched off to either side of the tunnel.

"You'll find extensive stores of food and supplies. There is accommodation, kitchen facilities, and everything you could need. Of course, you're welcome in the manor any time you please. But should you wish to have your privacy, you can enjoy it here, free from the prying eyes of the world. The staff don't come here."

"Good, I will see to its maintenance," Levi replied. "Or at least my team will."

"How does it work?" I asked, thinking of his team and their unquestioned obedience. "Do you control them, or is there more to it?"

Levi placed his hand on my shoulder. "They serve willingly, each for their own reasons. I don't judge. All I require is their loyalty. As long as they give it, I protect, shelter, support, and prosper them. They have a home and a family and for most of them, that is all they really want."

"Do they know what you are?"

Levi smiled. "Those who have been with me the longest know the truth. The others know I'm not human. They have witnessed my talents enough to be aware of that much. But I let them learn in their own time."

We reached a set of steel reinforced doors with another keypad. I placed my hand on it and the doors parted on well-oiled rollers. The moment we passed through them, they slid shut behind us.

The steel doors concealed a small chamber that was fifty-foot square. It was furnished as an office, with a hardwood desk, fine carpets, leather seats, and wood paneled walls. The Monet hanging on the opposing wall was real. San Giorgio Maggiore at Dusk was one of my father's favorite paintings.

On the far side of the room was a series of three biometric locks, beside another door. I placed my hand on the first. It scanned and the light above it flashed green.

At the second, I scanned my retina and the indicator above it also flashed green. Moving into the third, I placed my finger over a small circle. I winced, more in surprise than out of pain as a tiny pin pricked my finger. I'd had my blood tested here before, but it always managed to surprise me. Two drops of blood ran down into the sensor.

"This will only take a moment," I said to Levi. "Of course, we will get all of this reconfigured to your particular biological markers. But for the time being, I just want to ensure we are on the same page."

The third light flashed green. I strode to the massive steel wheel that would open the vault.

I grabbed it and started to turn.

"I thought we were already on the same page," Levi offered. "I have given both my word, and my oath."

Spinning the wheel, I nodded. "You are now a guest on the estate. I suspect Lynch and his allies will come for us. The world might be hunting him, but he is the sort of egomaniac to go down swinging. If we die, Lynch will pass the accusations against him off as the ramblings of a crazy recluse. If we live, he loses everything. The stakes are too high. He has to come for us. When that happens, I expect you to fight alongside us to defeat him and whoever he brings with him. More importantly, I want you to protect my wife and child, in exchange for everything you're about to see."

"Child?" Levi found my gaze and held it.

"My wife is pregnant," I said. "It changes everything. No matter the cost, they are to survive, and I expect you to see to that when everything goes to hell. Do you understand me?"

Levi nodded. "Unequivocally."

"Good, because those are the conditions on which I gift you this."

The spinning wheel locked into place and I pulled open the vault door.

"Four hundred years of Caldwell wealth. A singular prize for you and your posterity in exchange for securing my posterity's continued existence."

The vault door swung wide, and I watched Levi's eyes for his reaction. They grew wide as he took in the vault.

"My word," he breathed.

"Shall we take a closer look?"

I led him into the vault. It was the size of a basketball court. Set in neat rows, stacked to the steel rafters, were hundreds of pallets of gold. Each was shaped into one-pound bricks and stamped with the Caldwell family crest.

"I'm not sure the price of your exile, but this ought to make a dent. How you use it is up to you. Just know this. Each brick has been formed of Caldwell sweat and the power that runs in our blood. If you need more, we can make it with time."

Levi's eyes glowed gold as he scanned row upon row. In an age where wealth was measured in ones and zeros on a computer screen, it was a display of wealth few would ever lay eyes on in their lifetime.

"Is it enough?" I asked.

"This changes everything." Levi's eyes watered. "You have no idea."

On the contrary, I recognized in him much of the pain I'd felt myself. "So we have an accord?"

"You have honored your word, and I will honor mine. I will stay, and I will fight. If they would have your wife and your heir, they will have to come through me. When the battle is won, and I've gathered all I need, I will return to my people. You would serve your child better by ensuring you survive to guide them. The world is not kind to orphans."

"Oh, I'm not planning on dying, Levi, but I may have little say in the matter."

The bartender cocked his head to the side, but I didn't care to explain. I didn't want anyone knowing what I had planned.

Leaving the vault, I fired up the computer on the desk and loaded the scanning software for the vault's door. Within a minute, I had configured it to accept its new master.

I motioned for him to scan his hand, his retina, and his blood.

He did each in turn, not even registering the needle that pierced his finger.

"The system will now recognize you, Levi. See that you and your men are moved safely in. If you need anything, you can find me at the house."

"What role would you have us play in the wedding preparations?" Levi asked.

"There is a rehearsal dinner tomorrow night. It will be the first official function. I would like to have you present. The amount Lynch knows concerns me, I fear there is a traitor among the staff. If you encounter anyone whose intentions run contrary to ours, I expect you to make it known."

Levi pondered that, the notion of being a human lie detector unpalatable to him.

"Their duplicity compromises us all," I added.

Levi nodded. "I will be unobtrusive in my investigations."

"That's all I ask. In the meantime, I'll leave you to get yourself settled."

I reached the door of the office.

"Seth." Levi's voice wavered.

I turned.

"This is generous beyond measure. I won't forget it."

He was giving me too much credit. What was all this wealth to me? I could make more. What I was asking of him was far more valuable.

"I suspect we both have the same dreams, my friend," I said. "I hope we both live to see them."

I strode out of the vault and back through the underground complex. Emerging from the fountain, I made the hike back to Weybridge Manor.

It was a brisk walk, and I was halfway across the expansive lawn when the sound of helicopter blades whirring overhead drowned everything else out.

It was still a little early for Kendra and Hades to be arriving, and the helicopter wasn't one I recognized. Pulling out my phone, I dialed the security team.

"Seth, here. I'm on the lawn. Are we expecting any guests by chopper?"

There was a brief pause, before the operator replied. "We have some listed, sir. Single flight, ten people cleared to land on the south lawn."

"Who is it?" I asked eagerly.

"Our note says bride's family, sir."

My heart skipped a beat. He'd come. Lara's father had actually shown up. But who were the others? Cousins? Maybe they were here to surprise Lara.

I felt my nerves setting in. I'd turned his daughter's life inside out and gotten her pregnant before the wedding. Not to mention, I'd managed to anger one of the most powerful organizations on earth. As far as son-in-laws went, I hadn't done a great deal to endear myself to him.

"We'll send a team to meet them," the comms centre replied, "and we'll send word to Lara."

"I'll greet them myself," I replied. "I'm almost there. Have my wife join us when she's able."

"Roger that, sir. We'll call the house."

I studied the helicopter. It was a heavy-duty craft, not a lightweight conveyance like the one we'd traveled in on from Battersea yesterday. The body was a dull green with a series of black stenciled markers down one flank.

The helicopter reminded me of a military transport, but if the security team had vetted it, I could relax.

I patted myself down, smoothing my dusty shirt as I picked up my pace and headed for the south lawn. By the time I got there, the helicopter was touching down. Its rotor blades slowed to a halt as a cargo door on the side of its body slid open.

There, standing in the breach, was a barrel-chested man in a white suit and a Stetson. He stepped out of the helicopter, greeting me with a big grin and knowing smile.

He called to me with that dragging Texan drawl. "Why, Seth, it's good to see you again."

I'd been preparing for this day since I'd met Lara, and yet I couldn't find a single coherent word to say to her father.

Not because I didn't want to, but because the man standing before me was none other than the Director—the head of Section 9 and the man who had almost shot me down when I'd fled New York City.

CHAPTER 15

A hurricane of emotions formed inside of me, and I was having trouble trying to decide on one.

Anger at his presence here, betrayal at the truth that had been kept from me, concern that this man had tried to have me killed. Once on purpose, and then at Ares' trial, he'd entered his own champion, indirectly reducing my chance of making it out alive.

Not to mention that he was the head of section 9, the tip of the spear when it came to the CIA's attempt to garner intelligence on the magical community.

Could he really be my wife's father, or was this all some elaborate ruse?

In that moment, a great many things suddenly made sense. Like why my wife had been under such close observation at the museum. It was just a father looking out for his daughter. Why he'd been so ruthless in his pursuit of me. I'd robbed him and strapped his daughter to a chair.

While I'd never intended to harm her, he certainly wouldn't have known that.

It also explained why losing such an important relic hadn't scuttled her career. The person in charge of its advancement had placed that blame at my feet and let her off the hook.

That was how Lara had gone from being in a research assignment in New York City to leading a strike team in Panama. It also explained why Section 9 was willing to give her seemingly unlimited leave to pursue her own ambitions.

Her father was the one signing off on everything.

My heart beat faster and faster,

Amid it all, Lara's plea from yesterday echoed in my mind.

"Remember that when you meet my father, he can be a hard man."

I almost laughed. Almost.

Talk about the understatement of the decade. Not that I had much ground to argue when it came to stretching the truth. At the start of our relationship, I'd lied about my identity, the fact I was a wizard, and why I was so interested in her work.

But we'd also promised no more secrets, a promise I'd striven to honor since the day I'd made it. This glaring omission was clearly intentional.

"Don't just stand there gawking like a goldfish, boy," the Director called. "Come over here and shake me by the hand."

Power resonated within me. I hadn't even noticed that I'd drawn on it, but that didn't bother me. I could think of a host of ways I might use it and do the world a favor. Not that my wife would see it that way.

I eyed the outstretched hand. I didn't trust him any further than I could throw him. And looking at the big Texan, I knew that wasn't going to be particularly far. Add a little magic though, and I was suddenly feeling the overwhelming urge to try.

Slowly approaching the chopper, I reached out my hand and took his. He shook it firmly. As he did, I stole a glance inside the chopper. Nine Section 9 strike troops waited, dressed for battle, helmets buckled, assault rifles at the ready.

It was a trap. As I went to open my mouth, Lara's dad gripped my hand firmly.

"Relax, they're here to help. Lara told me the score. This is all I could bring without alerting Lynch of my intentions."

Well, that was a sentence I'd never expected to hear from him.

"So you do realize I could reduce you, and everyone on this chopper, to ash in seconds, right?"

"I watched you at the Trial, Seth. I'm very aware. It's the only reason I've consented to this madness."

Well, at least I knew where I stood.

"You best refer to it as a wedding when your daughter arrives. She has rather strong feelings on the matter."

"No doubt," the Director answered. "She always does. I know that we have a, uh, complicated history, and little in the way of common ground. But we both care for Lara. And in that vein, I hope you will do me the same courtesy that she insisted I extend to you?"

I took a breath to calm my racing nerves and nodded.

"How about we start over?" The Director offered.

It was like being force fed my medicine, and while every part of my ego wanted to fight it, I thought better of it. So I shook his hand.

"I can do that, if you give me your word that you will behave yourself as a guest ought while you are in my house."

"Of course." He let go of my hand and straightened his suit coat. "I'd never intended to do otherwise."

"Then it is my honor to welcome you to Weybridge Manor, Mr. Stiel."

"Call me, Jonas. Please."

"Jonas, it is, sir. Let's get you safely inside. I'm sure you could use some refreshment and Lara will be excited to see you,"

"Dad!" Lara's voice carried across the lawn.

I turned to find Lara racing across the lawn. She looked from her father to me and the moment she had clearly orchestrated. It was a feat. The kind of perfectly crafted lie only a well-practiced agent of the CIA could have executed with a straight face.

That guile failed her now, and the countenance she was wearing was guilty as sin.

"You might have mentioned that I'd already met your dad at the trial," I said. I let my stern expression stew before smiling so that she knew I was joking. I didn't want to put her under any more stress than she was already.

Jonas clapped me on the back. "Well, I did tell you, Seth. When we spoke at the Trial. I told you it was time we started over. You didn't seem overly interested at the time, though."

I laughed. "You might have, but I'm pretty sure you skipped over the reason for your sudden change of heart."

"Well, you didn't really give me the chance to elaborate, now did you?"

He was right there. Though at the time, I'd been in a room with Ares, his father and mother, and a handful of other deities, their retainers, and eleven other champions who wanted me dead. I'd had a bit on my mind, and in that particular room, the CIA had been featherweights.

"Well, let us start here," I replied, pointing to the manor. "With a drink and a new outlook on our relationship."

Lara slipped her hand into mine and whispered, "Thank you."

It was quiet enough that her father couldn't overhear.

Hand in hand, we headed for the manor with my new father-in-law, and a contingent of crack troops from Section 9 to bolster the manor's defences. I could have been irritated at her deception, but it was no worse than anything I'd done.

All in all, things were turning out better than I'd hoped.

Inside the house, we were met by Charles, my father's body man. At six-six he was a mountain of manpower and my father's most trusted staff member.

"Seth, Lara, your father is in his study. He is waiting for you both."

I looked at Jonas. "I guess it's time you met the man of the house."

"I'm told your father hasn't been outside in years. Is he unwell? I mean, there's always been speculation, but even my agents have found little concrete information on him or his movements."

"You can thank Andrew Lynch for that," I replied as I led the way to his study. "The chairman has been curating and sterilizing what information is gathered on its members for decades. Why do you think I never crossed your radar until the museum?"

Jonas stroked his chin. "I saw the story on last night's news. It was fascinating. Word on the street is that your family had something to do with that."

I felt the unspoken accusation behind the statement. By attacking Lynch, we'd put his daughter in greater danger. He would know the truth soon enough, so I leveled with him.

"We had everything to do with that." I jammed my hands in my pockets. "Lynch is a cancer, and so is the Brotherhood. If we don't cut it out, they'll come after us. We didn't want to start a new life on the run from our old one."

We strode down the hallway that led to my father's study.

"The number of complications in my life has certainly increased dramatically since you came crashing into it," Jonas said.

"Oh, that's the nicest thing anyone has ever said to me," I replied.

"I certainly hope not," he answered. "For your sake."

Lara looked over her shoulder, shooting her dad a warning look.

"Play nice, you two. I'm sure when you get to know each other a little better, you'll see the side of you that I do. In the meantime, I refuse to have you at each other's throats at my wedding. Am I understood?"

Lara glared back and forth between us.

"Of course, my dear," I replied. "I wouldn't dream of it."

"I continue to keep an open mind," Lara's father replied in a voice that wasn't particularly reassuring. But he wasn't having me shot down, so as far as I could see, our relationship was on the mend already.

I pushed open the door to my father's study.

He was sitting in his usual place behind his desk. In one of the leather chairs opposite it sat a familiar witch. Her dark hair reached her shoulders and on one wrist she wore a bracelet fashioned from what could only be fangs. Given what I knew of her, I suspected I knew exactly who the previous owner might have been.

She smiled as we came through the door.

"Kasey, it's good to see you again. Thanks for coming." My grin broadened as our prospects of survival increased considerably.

"What can I say? I was in the area and thought it might be nice to swing by the manor and steal a few family heirlooms. You know, return the favor."

"Ha, ha. The wedding presents are in the marquee. You can take your pick as long as we can call it even."

My father looked as if he had something to say. I wondered just how long the two of them had been talking, and about what?

"So, what are you two up to?" I raised an eyebrow.

My father leaned back in his chair. "I was just quizzing Miss Chase, here, on a few matters of family history. She's been most insightful."

"Just trying to help where I can," Kasey replied.

My father noticed Jonas. It was hard not to. The man was a giant, and Stetson's weren't particularly common in these parts.

"Dad, this is Jonas, Lara's father."

"Welcome, Jonas," my father said rising to shake his hand. "Your timing is impeccable. We all have much to discuss."

"Oh?" Jonas took the offered hand. "And what might that be?"

"What is it?" I asked as Lara and I left the other leather chair for him and sat down on the window ledge. "Is Mum okay?"

My father took his seat once more. "She continues to recover well, and she'll be back on her feet soon. But for the time being, we are continuing the charade that Lynch succeeded in his attempt. I don't want to encourage him to take another shot at her, and I've closed off the medical wing to all but her physicians. I don't want word getting out that she survived."

"You're saying there are agents in your household?" Jonas growled. "This gets worse by the minute."

"There may be," my father replied. "Do not underestimate Lynch's pull and influence. We're best off taking precautions, just in case."

"You lot need to get your house in order," Jonas said. "This is madness."

"No, it's war," I countered. "And you'll remember Lynch had agents at every level of your government too. So this isn't just our problem. Lynch is everyone's problem."

"I didn't gather you all so we could cast blame." My father slapped his hand on the desk. "We have other problems to discuss."

"The Arcane Congress?" I asked. I was only guessing, but given we'd given them the slip yesterday, I was fairly sure we'd earned their ire. I considered it unlikely they would give up on us after the mess we'd left at the Palladium.

"Correct," my father replied. "We're still wanted for questioning in connection with the events at the Palladium. Our lawyers are running interference and attempting to build our case. They've also lodged an injunction with the Congress in an attempt to discourage the Sentinels from stepping foot on the property. Citing the two attacks on our household in the last twenty-four hours, they have been informed in no uncertain terms, that if the sentinels enter manor grounds they will be met with extreme prejudice."

"You can just threaten the Congress?" Kasey asked, sitting up in her chair. "Wish I'd known that months ago. Might have come in handy."

"It's not a wise course, Ms. Chase, but we have considerable influence at court. Besides, the sentinels were out of line in the Run. We've also filed a formal complaint against them and named the Watchman personally. There will be mounting pressure for him to disclose his motives for pursuing us."

"In doing so, you will have made an enemy of him," I replied. "That sort of mark will tarnish his career."

"If he's barking at Lynch's bidding, we need to cripple his reach. By applying pressure at court, he'll be unable to move against us without grounds. It ought to discourage a direct assault on the manor, and the more time we buy, the more likely it is that Lynch and his false agenda will be seen for exactly what it is—lies designed to shift the blame on us and discredit us as whistle blowers against their conspiracy."

My father looked exhausted, and I suspected he'd been up much of the night arranging affairs.

"So what's the problem?" Lara asked. "It sounds like you have them on the ropes."

"Well, we're trying our best, but Armando Flint is a particular stubborn bastard who cares little for those who get in his way or question his authority. It's no guarantee that he won't make another move. So for the time being, no one is to leave the safety of the manor."

"I find it hard to believe Flint has any bandwidth for this right now," Kasey interrupted. "He has more than a few problems of his own."

My father zeroed in on Kasey. "What do you know of Flint?"

Kasey threw one leg over the other. "Well, for starters, he tried to have me executed in New York, so I have a PhD on exactly the sort of zealot he is."

"What makes you think he's got his hands full now, though?" I replied.

What did she know that we didn't?

"Well... I have it on good authority that another matter is causing him considerable angst."

"Care to share with the class?" my father pressed. "You are among friends here."

Her face tensed. "I am going to have to plead the fifth on this one. You're better off not knowing."

"We're on the same side, Kasey, come on," I said.

"I appreciate that, Seth. Let's just say that I am aware that one of the Congress' most protected installations suffered a recent breach of security. The resulting mess is both considerable and dangerous. Frankly, I'm surprised the Watchman can spare a single Sentinel right now."

"Then someone has assumed Flint's authority," my father replied. "In any event, they are just as dangerous, more so for not knowing who is actually pulling the strings. We've also been summoned before Parliament. The House of Lords wishes to speak with us about the Brotherhood."

"Not on your life," I replied. "At least six of them are members of it."

"I agree," my father answered. "They will have already been back-channeling with the others. Our fate will be sealed before we enter the chamber. We have our lawyers postponing the summons. But we won't be able to refuse it forever. It's scheduled for the twenty-eighth of the month. If we can survive until then, we'll be making a trip to Westminster."

I let out a sigh. When both magical and mundane governments wanted you for questioning, it was a sign that you'd played fast and loose with the rules a little too long and a little too hard.

"In good news, the story is starting to play quite well in the press. Take a gander at this." My father lifted a remote and the TV on the wall switched on.

On the screen was Cleon Driver of the BBC News. The footer running along the bottom of the screen read: *Government Official Vanished Without a Trace.*

Cleon, leaning on the table with one elbow, spoke straight into the camera.

"Troubling news in the United States. A senior government official wanted in connection with the leaked documents pertaining to a clandestine organisation known as the Brotherhood vanishes during the night. Andrew Lynch was taken into custody and was in the process of being transported to

Washington DC, when he, and the convoy he was riding in, vanished entirely. Officials are still unaware of exactly what transpired. But no trace of Lynch or the convoy has turned up."

Driver paused for dramatic effect. "It's difficult to draw any other conclusion than that the alleged head of the Brotherhood has escaped custody and is now at large. Other government officials have also been reported missing. In every instance, each of the officials in question were also wanted for their alleged membership or services to this cabal. While we don't want to subscribe to the conspiracy theories being reported by other major outlets, it is difficult to ignore the mounting pile of evidence before us. It would seem that Andrew Lynch, former director of clandestine operations for the United States government, may actually be a criminal mastermind responsible for some of the greatest acts of evil to have occurred in the past three decades—genocide in the name of the greater good. A haunting reminder that someone must watch the watchers. This is Cleon Driver for the BBC News."

"The former director of clandestine operations," I breathed. "He got the sack?"

My father's grin broadened. "Indeed. It appears the current administration views compromised loyalties with no tolerance. Even now, his access and influence is drying up. With his disappearance, the others are going underground. I have reports of military officials, intelligence assets, and military hardware disappearing. All vanishing like Lynch as every trace of his network and existence are being wiped from the earth."

"They are clearing house," Jonas added. "The government doesn't like scandal."

"They might be," my father answered, "or Lynch could be gathering his strength. Both are dangerous options we must prepare for."

"We can hope for the former, while preparing for the latter," I added. "Every day, life gets harder for him. Fewer resources, more opposition. The other members of the Inner Circle are going to be cutting ties and going to ground themselves. It is very likely that we have succeeded in crippling their power structure indefinitely."

"And no doubt we have made an enemy of all of them," Lara replied. "Only now, we're dealing with a scattered group rather than a united front."

"Almost certainly, but as they were already against us," my father said. "We can only have increased our chances."

Dad was certainly a little more glass half-full today. I guess that made two of us.

"So what are we planning?" I asked.

"Nothing," my father replied. "I just wanted to bring you all up to speed. The garrison here at the manor has been increased. We're on the lookout for any traffic heading for the manor and will endeavor to ensure things go smoothly."

"Sounds like a plan," Lara answered. "We might just pull off this wedding after all."

My father smoothed the top of his desk with his hand. "But don't let your guard down, and for no reason should any of you step foot outside the manor grounds. If we are dragged before the Congress, or the Council of Lords, we will likely end up with a knife in the back."

I leaned back against the window. My father might be expecting a smooth weekend, but I couldn't shake the feeling Lynch was out there, right now, gathering his strength and preparing to crush us like a bug.

The only question was, when?

CHAPTER 16

Lynch hung over our heads like the sword of Damocles, but in spite of the shadow he cast, we pressed on, determined to make the most of Lara's and my special day.

Between wedding preparations and organizing for our guests who were yet to arrive, the day and night passed swiftly. While the threat of Andrew Lynch was never far from my mind, the growing attention he seemed to be attracting from the world press gave me encouragement.

His portrait and story played on every news program. Hysteria was mounting as the documents we'd provided to the press corps were slowly verified and the true extent of the Brotherhood's influence began to become apparent. My father had been ruthless in his disclosure. The Brotherhood had done a great deal of evil in the name of the greater good. Now society was demanding answers.

It wouldn't surprise me if Lynch had taken what resources he could muster and fled from the ever-increasing attention.

The day of the rehearsal dinner blessed us with beautiful weather. Spring was in the air, and I hoped that it would hold for our wedding the next day.

While Lara ran through her last-minute checklists, I spent the day revisiting the manor's defenses, ensuring everything was in order. I didn't want a single blind spot for Lynch to exploit. Overlapping fields of fire with heavy weapons emplacements threatened to turn the area outside the manor's walls into a killing field if the need arose.

Inside the walls, wedding preparations were in their final stages. With Millicent suitably taken to task, it appeared that everyone else was being held to schedule.

The needed furniture and fixtures had been sourced, and extra staff manpower devoted to the construction efforts. The manor had been transformed.

The driveway was lined with white and gold decorations. A glorious marquee stood looking out over the lake and the sprawling lawn beyond. The gardens and hedgerows had received another trim from the gardeners.

The whole affair was rather picturesque. As I stood on the rear balcony of the manor, looking out over the yard, I felt my own excitement building. Tomorrow, Lara would walk down that aisle to find me waiting for her.

We would be married. Something I'd never allowed myself to believe might actually happen, and yet the day was here. I leaned on the stone rail of the manor's balcony, waiting for our guests to arrive. We were only expecting one more lot before tomorrow morning. According to Lara and Dizzy, Kendra's contingent had landed safely and were now en route from the Battersea Heliport. Either Lynch was too busy running, or he simply didn't care, because since the attack on the manor and ambush at the Palladium, there had been nothing from him.

The afternoon sun was slowly setting, and the rehearsal dinner was soon to begin. With it, the need for me to deliver a toast I was still wrestling with. I wasn't a gifted linguist or a natural orator. How was I meant to adequately convey the depth of my love in a handful of words?

"What's eatin' you, son?" The words rolled together in a long Texan drawl.

I didn't need to turn to know it was my soon-to-be father-in-law. I wasn't going to confide my toast struggles to him, and I was fairly sure that wasn't what the director of a department of the CIA was thinking of right about now.

"It's quiet," I replied, "and while I'd like to think it will remain that way, I don't believe it will. You know Lynch. Does he strike you as one who fades quietly into the night?"

"Not in the slightest," Jonas said without hesitation. "Though he has got most of the intelligence and law enforcement agencies in the world on his tail. FBI, CIA, NSA, FSB, MI6. Hell, even the Mossad have him on their watch list. If Andrew Lynch isn't undergoing an identity change, I'd eat my hat."

"And a full meal it would be," I chuckled, eying the Stetson.

"You got a problem with how I dress?" Jonas leaned over the balcony beside me.

"Not at all," I replied. "I like a good hat myself."

"I feel a *but* coming," He looked at me with an impassive stare that made clear he wasn't asking for my approval.

"I guess you're just not what I expected, that's all."

"That makes two of us," he replied. "I've spent my life fending off the useless suitors that have pursued my daughter. Turns out there isn't a great deal you can say to deter a woman from marrying a billionaire wizard."

I tried not to smile as I waited for the boot to drop.

"Even if he is a liar, thief, and attracts more trouble than a Porsche with the keys left in the ignition."

There it was. "Please, tell me how you really feel, Jonas."

"I've been trying to." He took off his hat. "Are you not listening, boy? Ever since my daughter begged me to put her on that chopper to Panama, I've been asking myself why I said yes."

"And why is that?" I stared out at the marquee. I didn't need his approval, but it meant something to Lara so I tried to hear him out.

"You are dangerous, Seth. Heart of a hero, but principles are dangerous things in our world. They turn men into martyrs every day. Why couldn't you have just played nice with Lynch?"

"You'd rather live under a tyrant you didn't know existed?" I asked, catching his eye.

"I'd like to put my head on my pillow at night without wondering if assassins are going to kill my child in her sleep." Pain crept into his voice. I didn't imagine fear was a feeling Jonas Stiel spent a lot of time dealing with.

"If it's any consolation, I'm spending all the energy of my soul to try and ensure that doesn't happen."

"You might be," Jonas said, "but in case your attention wavers, understand this. If any harm comes to my little girl, you better be dead, because if you aren't, I'll kill you myself."

I stared at the marquee where I knew Lara was waiting for me. "You won't have to, Jonas. The only way they are getting to her is over my dead body."

"I hope you have a better plan than that. Otherwise, you seem more confident than you have any business being."

"I've called in every favor I can. Just because you can't see their potential doesn't mean you should doubt them."

Jonas stood up and placed his hand on my shoulder. "You and your dad play things close to the chest. I get it. No wizard trusts Section 9. You have good reason, given your history. But I wonder if it's enough. I read those documents you released. Lynch has an army. What are you going to do if he brings it here?"

"We're going to fight. We might not look like much, but appearances can be deceiving."

"You really think that your friend the shifter, a witch from New York, and some private security is going to do the trick?"

"Jonas, you're going to have to trust me at some point. Outnumbered, perhaps, but we have quality over quantity. Of that I have no doubt. We're also fighting for the better cause. It's our lives, our freedom, and a better world for our children. That's why we took on Lynch. Surely you can appreciate that."

"I was an idealist once too," Jonas answered. "Then a bunch of wizards trashed New York City and I knew life would never be the same again."

"Well, in case you're not aware, Lynch is a wizard. So if you do see him, put a bullet in him before he has a chance to open his mouth."

A fleet of choppers descended over the south lawn.

"Jonas, I've got to see to our guests. But in the unlikely event things do go poorly, you have my permission to take your daughter, and your escort, and get her to safety. Lynch will want me, not her. I'll lead them away."

Jonas glanced over his shoulder.

"You heard me. I'll draw their attention. You get your daughter to safety. Don't turn back, no matter what happens."

I left Jonas on the balcony, mulling over my instruction. I hoped that if nothing else, it conveyed to him the depth of my desire to protect his daughter. At least if anything happened, I could rely on him and his Section 9 commandos to extract Lara. And that was something.

Four light choppers settled down on the south lawn. I descended the stone stairs and made my way out to meet them. The rotors slowed as the engines powered down.

The last of our guests had arrived.

Two of the helicopters disgorged a task force of Harrington security personnel. They wore full body armor and carried the high-powered rifles I'd seen in New York City. They were a nightmare I was glad to have on my side.

Kendra Harrington disembarked from the third chopper, wearing a stunning silver dress that hugged her frame and a pair of heels that wasn't the least bit practical. They sank an inch into the lawn, but she caught herself.

She was as stunning as she had always been. It was easy to see what had attracted Dizzy to her in the first place. But beyond her obvious charms, she was shrewd and cunning. Somehow, she alone had survived the tragedy that had consumed the rest of the Harrington dynasty.

Only a year ago, Lester and his five children had been some of America's wealthiest and most influential wizards. Lester had also been a member of the Brotherhood's inner circle, with his sons destined to succeed him. But when the dust had settled, Kendra alone remained.

It was a feat that had shocked onlookers to the core, and the Brotherhood, committed chauvinists that they were, had parted ways with the Harrington dynasty.

In the process they had lost access to a considerable store of wealth. It was that unfortunate event that had started to apply pressure for me to sign on with the Brotherhood and take my oath. They needed to ensure the Caldwell succession went more smoothly.

In some ways, her survival had brought us here. In spite of that macabre fact, I was quite glad she came. She was a capable witch, and a shrewd tactician. She might well make the difference.

The fourth chopper opened and a well-tanned Greek man stepped out. His complexion was a rich olive tone, his dark hair swept back. He wore an all black suit with a gold belt and suspenders. The bulges at his sides indicated that he was indeed armed.

I suspected he seldom went anywhere otherwise. Behind him, four men in black body armor, tactical harnesses, and black and red masks carried assault rifles.

I'd seen the Helldrakes at Madison Square Garden. Hades hand-picked his elite from ex-servicemen and women. I'd have wanted a few more of them, but I imagined Kendra wouldn't let them on her plane leaving New York.

Hades was my ace in the hole, my plan for ridding myself of Aleida.

I strode across the south lawn as staff moved to greet our guests.

"Kendra, thank you for coming." I rushed to help her across the lawn.

She kissed me once on either cheek.

"My pleasure, Seth. I wouldn't have missed this for the world."

"I trust Dizzy has kept you in the loop,"

Kendra leaned close. "I'm well aware of the danger, Seth."

I looked down at her heels. "Would you like me to fetch you something a little easier to walk in?"

Kendra raised an eyebrow. "We're heading to the dinner now, aren't we?"

"We certainly are. It's in the marquee." I eyed the lawn between here and there.

"And Dizzy is there?" Kendra asked, her voice low.

"Of course. She's been helping Lara."

"The heels stay," Kendra replied.

"If you insist." I chuckled, waving to her escort. "Assist Ms. Harrington to the marquee. Ensure she doesn't break her ankle on the way."

Kendra fixed me with a stare. "Are you going to explain why you burdened me with the company of that scoundrel?"

"He was in your company when I met him." I winked. "I've brought him here to see to a personal matter. Don't worry, he's out of your hair now."

Kendra lingered, waiting for an explanation, but I gave her none. Hades was here at my invitation, and I intended to keep that business between us.

"Head on over to the marquee. The staff will see to your luggage and get everything settled into the manor. In the meantime, let us relax. Tomorrow we'll have the most spectacular wedding you've ever seen."

Kendra took in the improvised wedding venue.

"Good thing you Caldwells have deep pockets. I have to imagine all this set you back a pretty penny."

"Pocket change for either of our families," I answered. "And I'd have spent it a hundred times if it made Lara smile."

Kendra smiled and headed for the marquee. "I'm glad you finally found someone who makes your heart sing."

With Kendra taken care of, I ambled toward to the fourth helicopter.

Hades greeted me, a note of mirth in his voice. "Master Caldwell, you were most cryptic on the phone. Care to tell me why I'm here? Why I'm really here?"

"You don't think I'd invite you to my wedding for the pleasure of your company, Hades? That's a little cynical. I quite enjoyed the time we spent together in New York City."

He put his hands on his belt, the motion exposing the pistols holstered beneath his arms. "Level with me now, or I get back on the chopper. I don't gamble my life on a whim."

I swallowed. There was clearly no stalling him. "When I was at the Grand Trial, I fought in an arena in the Underworld. It was an unsettling battleground with a well of swirling souls at its heart. There were hosts of them, the restless spirits of the dead."

"I know the place," Hades replied. "What of it?"

"Last time I was there, I was sent by Ares. If I had a desire to return, could you make it happen?"

"What makes you think I could?" Hades' voice turned cold.

"Call it a hunch," I replied. "Can you do it or not?"

"You want to return to the halls of the dead, having been lucky enough to survive them once. Did you learn nothing while you were there?"

"I learned a great deal. Like the fact that spirits cannot hide there. They are drawn inextricably to that well and into the great beyond."

"Yes," Hades replied with the tired tone of a teacher wrangling a daft student. "It's also the playground of Eurynomos, a flesh-eating demon, and a dozen other horrors that would make your blood run cold. Even with my master's blessing, I wouldn't deem it wise to travel there. Without it, it's certain death."

"Then it's a good thing you won't be going. I plan to go alone."

"Have you completely lost your mind?" His jaw sagged. "You'll be killed."

"Quite possibly. But if you do this for me, I'll give you anything you want, Hades. Think of that."

"Only a fool would take a marker from a dead man."

I laughed. It seemed he knew only too well the score, but I tried to appeal to his greed, nonetheless.

"Oh Hades, come now, you haven't got where you are today by taking the safe road. If I survive, I'll be one of the most influential men in the world. I can open opportunities to you the likes of which you never dreamed."

He stared at the marquee. "Is Kasey in there?"

"She is," I replied. "I fished her out of some trouble in Wales yesterday. She's now our honored guest."

Hades poked his finger into my chest. "This I will require of you. Should you somehow survive this insanity you have planned, I would have you put in a good word for me."

"What?" I replied. "You want me to vouch for you?"

That I'd not expected. I didn't know what to say.

Hades tucked in the back of his shirt. "Clearly, she values your opinion. She is willing to die for your cause. Should we all survive this madness, she will no doubt ask you why you brought me here. You will tell her you begged this favor of me and I asked nothing in return. You'll tell her you don't know why."

I stared down at the ground. If those words ever came out of my mouth, it was going to be a lie. I was pretty sure I knew exactly why Hades was here. The poor fool was in love.

I couldn't fault him for trying.

"I can do that, Hades."

"Good. I'll arrange your ticket to hell. The consequences of that journey, my friend, are on you, though."

My heart beat a little faster and I stretched out my hand. "You have a deal."

Hades gripped it. Power resonated through my arm and into my chest.

The bargain had been struck.

Hades chuckled. "Come, let us enjoy our Last Supper then."

"You think Lynch will come?" I asked.

Hades glanced around, checking for eavesdroppers. "Oh, almost certainly."

"How can you tell? Have your sources picked up something we haven't?"

"I feel my master's eyes on this place, which means he knows something that we do not."

I swallowed. That wasn't comforting at all.

"Come, Seth. Let us eat and drink, for who knows what tomorrow may bring."

I led Hades and his helldrakes to the marquee. "I took the liberty of seating you with our friend. I hope you don't mind."

There was a single banquet table in the middle of the marquee. Stationed along the edges of the room were a series of smaller round tables. Kendra's strike team sat at one. Manor security sat at another.

There was still plenty of room for the helldrakes among them.

I pointed down the table, where there was a vacant seat across from Kasey. "Thank me later."

My father sat at the head of the table. Beside him sat Lara. Opposite her was my seat.

Lara was dressed in a white evening gown and looked positively radiant. Dizzy and Kendra sat at our sides. Then there was Kasey, her face still not having recovered from Hades' entrance.

Whatever relationship existed between them, it was clear Hades wanted more. And he was willing to pay almost any price to get it. He might just be another Greek tragedy in the making, but I'd sworn an oath.

I hoped to live long enough to deliver on it.

At the far end of the table sat Levi. I met his eye, but he gave no indication that anything was amiss.

I took my place at the head of the table and raised a glass. "Friends, family, and honored guests. It's good to have you here to celebrate with us. Lara and I are mindful of the sacrifice and risk that this is for each of you."

I paused.

"Some have wondered why we would press on with this wedding in light of all the opposition we have faced. Considering what may yet lie ahead, I thought it only right you should have an answer."

My eyes met Lara's. "The day I met you, I walked into that museum thinking it was a grand joke. Normals hoping to catch a glimpse of the arcane. I was a wizard in their midst, and they didn't have the faintest clue. It was all a laugh until you walked down those stairs."

A lump formed in my throat. "I spoke to you, and it was immediately apparent that your passion for your craft burned with an intensity that I'd never before seen. And by its light, I realized a stark truth. I was the joke."

Picking up my glass, I continued. "I was a liar and thief who had never wanted anything half as much as you wanted to learn. But that night, everything changed for me. The truth is, Lara, you make me want to be so much more. I've spent every day since trying to become the man you deserve, and while I may not be there yet, I don't want to live one more moment without you. So if I only have one day left to live, I want to spend it with you, fighting for another. I would gladly walk through hell for the chance to spend the rest of my life with you."

A tear ran down her cheek as I struggled to control my own.

"So I raise a toast to you, my dear. You bring out the very best in me."

"To Lara!" the table chorused as we raised our glasses.

My wife rose from her seat. "My dear, you have always been so much more than you believe. I saw it in you the night we met, and I'm an excellent judge of character."

Laughter rose from the table.

"You will have the chance to hear my vows tomorrow," she said. "In the meantime, I wish to raise a toast of my own. A toast to all of you. Thank you for being here."

She hefted her glass aloft and our guests followed suit. Everyone that was, but Kasey.

In the distance, a whirring sound signaled the departure of the helicopters that had brought our guests to the manor.

The whirring grew louder, as if the choppers were buzzing right over the top of the marquee on their way off the grounds.

The guests drank to my wife's toast. Everyone except Kasey. Her glass was still clutched in her hand as she stared vacantly past Hades.

Her lack of participation did not go unnoticed. Lara stared at her as the rumble grew louder and louder.

Suddenly, Kasey's head snapped to the left as she looked straight at me.

"Seth!" she called. "He's coming."

CHAPTER 17

The dull roar of engines grew louder as they approached.

I was expecting Lynch to attack the wedding. If Kasey was right, he was early, but how could she possibly know that?

My heart sunk. Had Lynch got to her first? Surely not.

"How do you know it's him?" I shouted over the noise.

"The same way I knew you were coming to rob me," she replied as she rose from the table. "They have a cargo plane and a convoy of trucks inbound. They are aiming for the eastern wall."

My father pulled out his phone, presumably to call in the attack, but after pressing it to his ear, he cast it aside. "They're jamming our signal. She's right."

I set down my glass. "Alright, everyone, on your feet. Let's move."

If Lynch was attacking the east wall, our forces there should buy us some time to regroup. I just needed to get word out and get our own personnel moving to intercept.

Racing to the back of the marquee, I stepped out into the cool evening air in time to see a massive green cargo plane descending from the sky. It had no lights on, no landing gear lowered, but from the whine of the engines it was decelerating.

From the look of it, the carrier was a C-5 Galaxy. There was no airstrip near here, and not nearly enough room to land for a vehicle that size.

But on he came, dropping lower and lower. I watched, transfixed, as the massive cargo plane set itself down, bouncing once as its underbelly kissed the grass before landing heavily in the eastern lawn. Grass and sod were torn up as the plane plowed a huge furrow. As its momentum slowed, the plane started to turn a little, but not nearly enough. The vehicle's momentum carried it right into the eastern wall.

The entire wall exploded outward, bricks and steel flying everywhere as the Galaxy tore right through it. The plane came to a halt only when its wings caught on what was left of the wall's pillars.

Scattered gunfire bracketed the plane as the security forces engaged the downed aircraft.

Anyone inside the plane was likely reeling from the impact but wouldn't be for long. If they had a convoy on route, they'd intentionally taken out a section of the wall.

This was Lynch's play.

As if in answer, the rear cargo ramp dropped and three army jeeps rolled out of it, circling around the plane as they turned their heavy machine guns on the walls. Our fortifications had been intended to keep others out, not repel an assault from inside. Security forces fell back to the armored towers as the heavy weapons fire cut down a number of them.

A clanking rattle signaled the arrival of an M1 Abrams battle tank as it rolled out of the Galaxy super carrier.

"Sweet Lord, they have a tank," Hades muttered from my side.

Three more jeeps rolled out. Behind them, several lorries, presumably full of assault troops, brought up the rear.

Ignoring the wall, they started across the lawn toward us.

In the distance, more trucks pulled up outside the wall. They disgorged more troops. Heavy machine-gun fire from our security towers greeted them. The towers were defensible emplacements of bullet proof glass and steel, designed to allow our forces to provide devastating cover fire.

The tower exploded, raining bricks and steel everywhere as the fortified emplacement turned into a cloud of debris. Three Apache attack helicopters raced in low over the wall.

"He bought a whole army," I said in disbelief as the attack choppers buzzed past us, strafing up the lawn and the manor.

My heart raced. The majority of our security was stationed around the outer perimeter of the estate. But Lynch was already inside the walls, secured in an armored convoy heading right for us. If I had to guess, he would be in that tank.

The jeeps provided covering fire, as the tank's turret swiveled toward us.

"Run! Take cover by the lake," I shouted. The embankment ought to provide us with at least some cover from incoming fire.

With a roar like thunder, the tank fired, sending a shell right through the marquee. It punched clear through the wall about thirty feet away, obliterating the chairs stacked behind it.

"Jonas, get Lara to choppers and get out of here," I said. "We'll deal with those Apaches. Once you're airborne, you should be able to outrun them."

"If you think I am leaving you, you're as mad as he is." Lara pointed at Lynch's tank.

"Lara," I said, raising my voice, "we have too much to lose now. Get out of here. I'll find you when it's safe."

"I'm not going anywhere."

We were out of time to argue. I couldn't bear the thought of our unborn child getting caught up in this war. I could only hope her father would prevail.

"Kendra, Hades, have your forces fan out," I said. "Loose formation. Any form of battle line is going to be obliterated by that Abrams."

"You can't expect to hold that off," my father replied. "We need to retreat."

"If we run now, we'll be cut down in the open ground. Clearly, Lynch knows we were in the marquee. If we draw them here, they will be in a crossfire between us, the snipers on the roof, and the converging security forces. We'll turn the eastern lawn into a killing field."

"We have no comms. How do you plan to coordinate the defence?" my father countered.

"And what about those gunships?" Kasey asked. "When they turn around, we're going to have no cover from the rear."

"One at a time." I tried to focus, but the constant crises were wearing me down. "Dizzy, get word to the wall. Have the teams converge on this position. We break them before the manor. If they can hold the wall against the outer forces, all the better."

Kendra kicked off her heels, the barefoot billionaire ready for war. Knowing Harrington industries, that dress would be bullet-proof, but there was still an awful lot of exposed flesh.

"I'll be right back," Dizzy reassured Kendra, then she shifted into an eagle and took to the skies. With the radio out, she was my only choice for spreading the word. Not that we could afford to spare Dizzy, but if we didn't start gathering and coordinating our forces, Lynch would roll right over us.

The three helicopters strafed the back lawn before banking over the manor and heading back for us.

"Levi, I'm going to need you to take out those choppers." I pointed at the Apaches.

"Are you quite sure?" Levi asked. "Your guests cannot un-see this."

"This is your home now, Levi, as long as you wish it to be. Everyone was going to find out eventually. I'll have your back. Have you got mine?"

"I swore it." Levi pushed off the embankment and headed straight for the choppers. Peeling off his jacket, he cast it aside.

"A bartender against three attack craft. Are you quite certain you haven't lost your mind?" my father asked.

"Watch and learn," I replied. "The rest of us need to get to those trees, to make us harder to spot from the lawn."

The helicopter gunships ignored Levi and loosed a series of hellfire missiles into the marquee. Tables, chairs, and white linen went everywhere as the entire marquee infrastructure was blown to hell.

Kendra shouted orders to her team as the helldrakes spread out on our right flank. High-powered rifle rounds punctured the evening air as the snipers on the manor roof opened up on the charging convoy.

A gunner in the lead jeep slumped forward, leaking blood and brain matter out of what was left of his head.

The marquee destroyed, the helicopters roved, searching for us. As we raced into the tree line, they repositioned for another strafing run, all the while ignoring Levi as he crossed the field.

I wondered what manner of magic he'd worked on their minds to accomplish that.

A brilliant flare of golden light swept the field, and Levi disappeared into the glare. As the light expanded, I was forced to cover my eyes lest it blind me. When I could open them again, Levi was gone and in his place was the most majestic creature I had ever seen: an adult dragon, gold and glimmering like the sun at noon day. His wings were more than thirty feet across, and his considerable bulk was larger than the three helicopters combined.

The ground trembled as he loped forward and sprung into the sky.

The Apaches broke formation, splitting as they tried to peel away from him, their chainguns scoring across his scales.

Levi spun, passing upside down underneath them. He grabbed the undercarriage of the first Apache with one claw and rolling in the air, hurled it at another chopper.

The two Apaches collided, their rotor blades obliterating one another before the fuel tanks exploded.

Fire washed over the golden dragon, but Levi seemed utterly unaffected by it. Snapping his wings, he changed course and went after the third. Levi was in its blind spot and closing fast.

The chopper tilted forward, trying to gain speed, but Levi was faster. As the Apache sailed over the eastern lawn, running for the hills, Levi's jaws opened and a massive gout of flame spewed out of his mouth. The superheated fire melted right through the Apache's tail, sending the helicopter careening out of control.

As it wobbled, Levi went right for it. Its rotor blades smashed into his armored hide, sending sparks flying before the dragon dropped his shoulder, slamming into the rotor fixture.

The rotors shattered and the Apache became a flaming meteorite that Levi sent sailing into the jeeps racing across the lawn.

The Apache struck the lawn and cartwheeled right through a jeep, demolishing them both and sending twisted steel in every direction.

The ground convoy opened fire, 50. cal heavy machine-guns hunting Levi as he climbed higher. Orange muzzle flare leaped from the barrels of the weapons, but Levi gained altitude, putting himself well and truly outside of their line of fire.

With the helicopters dealt with, the ground force was the next threat.

In my gut, I knew Lynch would be in that tank. He would never trust someone else with this task.

Drawing on my power, I summoned and shaped a sphere of ruby red arcana. Drawing back, I hurled it at the closest Jeep.

The red orb blazed through the sky and struck the front of the nearest Jeep. It melted straight through its engine block and found the fuel line. The detonation caused the vehicle to land on its roof, before the Abrams tank rolled straight over its broken frame.

"Lynch is going to be in that tank," I called. "We need to stop it dead, then go in and fetch him out. Any volunteers?"

No one said a word.

"I didn't think so. Lay down some cover fire. When they get closer, we'll make our move."

The security teams, including Kendra's forces, opened fire. But even the high-powered rifles they brought failed to scratch the hull of the tank. We were going to need something more potent.

We fanned out along the tree line, studying their advance.

The jeeps opened fire, the heavy weapons cutting down two of the helldrakes as they sought more cover.

"There's too many of them," I shouted. "Don't leave cover, and whatever you do, don't run. We stop them here. If we break, we'll die on that lawn."

"I'm open to any suggestions," Kendra called. "Surely you have some heavier munitions here, or have the Caldwells fallen on hard times?"

"The security teams have armor piercing weapons, but most of them were deployed on the wall. That's where we figured they'd be needed. They'll be repositioning, but it will take time, and Lynch is moving too quickly. We need to bring that convoy to a halt."

"On it," Kasey called back. "Give me all the cover you can."

"Kasey, no," Hades shouted as she broke cover.

She didn't look back.

"Dammit," Hades said, racing after her.

Kendra's team provided covering fire, but the tank sent an explosive shell into their midst. Screams, dust, and sod rose at the blast. At least three of them fell.

"Get Lara to the chopper," I shouted to Jonas. "The Apaches are down. Now's your chance."

"They're already a smoking ruin, son," Jonas called back. "None of us are leaving now."

I stole a look over my shoulder and realized he was right. The four choppers Kendra and her team had arrived on were a smoldering heap of twisted metal. They must have been the first thing the gunships went after.

Lynch didn't want anyone leaving here alive.

I hurled spells at the armored vehicles, trying to draw them off Kasey. I burst one tire and sent a blast through the windshield of another, but it wasn't nearly enough.

As Kasey and Hades advanced, the convoy focused its efforts on them. Hades gestured frantically and it took me a moment to realize what he was up to.

Fifteen feet in front of Kasey a shifting black shadow, twenty feet wide, swirled like a vortex.

The ethereal fog spread before her. Bullets rained down on her, but as they struck the snaking shadow, they simply whiffed out of existence. Hades fought to keep the shield intact, but sweat rolled down his brow.

Kasey chanted in Welsh, her voice laced with power as she bellowed loud enough the dead could have heard her. She was the calm at the eye of the storm, and power streamed toward her.

She dropped to one knee and slammed her palm into the ground. "*Tamaid!*"

The earth before her split asunder. The jagged chasm grew deeper as it raced away from her. The spell split into three forked crevasses that tore through the ground ahead of the convoy, growing deeper by the meter.

The first two jeeps went over the edge, disappearing into them, grinding crashes marking the bottom of the pits.

One of the chasms arced toward the tank.

The tank fired another shell, right at us. I summoned a shield and willed it forward. I couldn't take a tank, not on my best day. Shaping the shield on an angle, I tried to deflect the shell away from us. The shell struck my spell and shattered it. The munition slammed into the ground twenty feet to my left. Two of Kendra's team died instantly. The billionaire heiress was thrown to the ground. As the smoke cleared, I could see the blood running down her dress from the wound in her shoulder.

"Seth," my father groaned.

I turned to him. A six-inch shard of steel shrapnel was buried in his chest. blood seeped down into his cummerbund. If we didn't stop that tank, it was going to be the death of us. It teetered on the edge of the chasm, one track over the side, its tread spinning uselessly.

It was so close. Breaking cover, I raced at the tank.

"*Fuerza,*" I bellowed.

The blast of magic struck the teetering tank. It slid an inch. Then the earth beneath it gave way, and the Abrams slid into the chasm.

Levi descended, bathing the entire convoy in superheated fire.

"Get Kendra to the manor," I shouted back at her team. "Lara, Jonas, you take my father. Get him to the east wing, now."

"You can't go alone," Lara called after me.

"I'm going to deal with Lynch," I replied, racing across the lawn.

Kasey and Hades rained destruction on the flustering convoy. The gaping chasms stalled their progress, as Levi poured fire from above. Hades struck without mercy, shadowy blades of magic striking down anyone who strayed into his line of sight.

The fighting at the wall was turning. I only had small window of opportunity to cut Lynch out before his reinforcements arrived.

I made straight for the tank. One of Lynch's soldiers raised his assault rifle, but his head exploded, the report of a rifle shot echoing over the field.

The snipers lit up the halted convoy with unrelenting fire.

I reached the first Humvee as one of the soldiers kicked open the back door to dismount.

Pointing at the door, I bellowed, "*Fuerza!*"

The wave of force struck the door, slamming it into him so hard it knocked him unconscious. His body went limp as he collapsed. I bent down and picked up his assault rifle. I wasn't much of a shot, but it was an automatic weapon and at this range, even I couldn't miss with a full magazine.

Lynch's soldiers scattered, fleeing from the shadow cast by the golden dragon. I could almost feel the terror, and I wondered what manner of psychic assault Levi was subjecting them to. Grown men cried before being immolated.

Reaching the crevasse, I found the tank. It was trapped between the two soft sodden walls of the trench, fifteen feet down. The tank was sliding slowly into the earth. Two soldiers stood beside its open hatch. Neither of them seemed to see me through the smoke.

"The coast is clear, sir," they called. "We need to get you out of here."

"We're not leaving till those Caldwells are dead," Andrew Lynch barked back.

I would have recognized that arrogant tone anywhere.

Dropping onto my arse, I slid down the bank of the chasm toward the tank. The descent tore up my suit as I went over sod and stone. The two soldiers turned towards me. I squeezed the trigger of the assault rifle. The weapon bucked, but the sustained burst tore through both of them. As my feet struck the tank, the rifle clicked dry. I cast it aside and kicked the hatch shut, buying myself a moment to think.

"What the devil is going on up there?" Lynch shouted.

"You're going to die in this hole, Andrew!" I bellowed. "You should have let me walk away. You could have kept your little band of murderous puppeteers. Now what have you got to show for it? Nothing. The Brotherhood are done."

"Is that you, Seth?" Lynch chortled. "You should have sent me an invitation. I wouldn't have had to crash the party."

I panted and gasped as I jammed my foot down on the hatch, I couldn't go through it to get to him. It would be like shooting fish in a barrel.

"I gave you a chance, Lynch. You should have taken it. No one's coming to save you."

"I don't need saving, Seth. Your father's little betrayal will be in vain. Tell me, did I hit him with that last round? I could have sworn I saw him go down before we fell in this damned hole."

"Just a flesh wound," I called back, hoping it was true.

The top of the tank glowed angry red, and I staggered back, tripping over the body of the solder I'd just killed. A lance of red energy punched through the top of the tank, passing through where I'd been standing only a moment earlier. Lynch channeled the spell, carving a gaping hole in the top of the tank. The steel roof collapsed inward leaving the Abrams open to the air.

Lynch pointed his palm at me. A fist of air struck me in the chest, throwing me back against the dirt side of the crevasse.

I hit the door and collapsed on the prone corpse. Lynch started climbing out of the tank, gloating.

"Foolish boy, when I'm done with you, I'll kill your wife for good measure. Ensure there is nothing left of this forsaken family."

"You'll leave her out of this," I grunted.

"Or what?" Lynch replied. "You'll turn me to gold?"

"I think shit is a little more your color," I said. "Come a little closer and I'll see to it."

"I don't think I will," he replied as he stood up on the top of the tank. He was less than three feet from me and holding a Glock. "Any last words, Seth?"

My hand rested against the sod wall of the crevasse. I nodded slowly so as to not cause him alarm.

Looking him dead in the eye I chanted, *"Terremoto!"*

The earth trembled, lynch fired, but in the chaos of the tank sliding another six feet, the bullet struck nothing but dirt.

Lynch was knocked sideways, falling back into the tank. I grabbed the steel superstructure of the tank, holding tight until it came to a stop. The body of the dead soldier was pinned in place by the turret.

I plucked the grenade off his belt and pulled the pin. As Lynch cursed inside the tank, I tore out the pin and slid the grenade along the chassis of the tank. It skittered twice before dropping into the tank.

I smiled.

"What the...?" Lynch gasped.

The grenade couldn't have been more than a foot from him when it detonated and left him no time to react. The explosion rocked the tank, causing it to drop another foot as its heavy frame ground through the soft earth.

I clung to the tank for dear life, panting as I tried to catch my breath.

I couldn't leave until I knew the grenade had done its job.

Staring down into the Abrams, I noted the shredded remains of Andrew Lynch. There was no coming back from that.

Brushing myself off, I started the slow climb out of the crevasse. By the time I reached the surface, what was left of Lynch's forces were in a full-blown rout.

Kasey, Hades, and Levi harried them toward the wall.

"Lynch is dead," I shouted after them. "Spread the word."

With Lynch gone, I headed back for Lara and my father.

I wanted to ensure they were safe.

The mixed security detail made slow progress as they carried the wounded between them.

Two of Kendra's security were carrying my father. Dizzy in her gorilla form had scooped up Kendra and was bounding across the lawn, heading straight for the healers and the east wing.

Jonas and Lara were right behind them, providing covering fire with the Section 9 commandos.

I caught them before they reached the manor.

"Seth," Lara called, "are you alright?"

"I am, which is more than I can say for Lynch."

"You got him?" Jonas perked up.

I nodded. "I made sure of it. The rest of them are on the run. Without Lynch, they are falling back in disarray. There are still enemy on the grounds though, so look alive. If anyone tried to storm the manor, gun them down. Levi, Kasey, and Hades are driving them out."

"No, I'm not," Hades said. "I came to help you see to your father."

"My father? What do you mean?"

Hades looked past me to my father. "That battle is already won. This one remains to be fought."

There was something in the way Hades looked at my father that was disconcerting.

"You're not going to make it, Frank," Hades said.

My father stared up at him, his eyes glassy but resolute. "I know."

My heartbeat sped up. "Don't talk like that. We need to get you to the healers."

Even as I said the words, I knew the chances of my father pulling through weren't great.

"Take me to my study," my father said.

Did he want to die at his desk? I expected him to have a little more fight in him. My father had never given up on anything in his life. It hurt to see him so content to slip out of this world.

"We can still get you to the east wing. There's time," I whispered.

"The study," my father grunted. "Now!"

I couldn't take them all inside, and I didn't want an audience for what I feared was to come.

"Jonas, have your team hold the balcony," I said. "Make sure no stragglers make their way to the manor."

"On it," Jonas replied. "We'll keep those bastards out."

Lara and I propped up my father and carried him into the house. We were almost at the study when Lucky appeared in the hall before us.

"Lucky, what the hell are you doing up here?" I shouted. "There's a war on out there."

"I know," he called back, sweating profusely. "The comms are down. I wanted to help."

"Then open the study. We need to get him inside. We've got our hands full as it is."

"Frank's been hit?" Lucky's voice broke.

He pushed open the doors, and we started down the hall.

As we approached, Lucky reached behind his back and pulled out a small pistol. It was a Walther PPK.

He pointed it at me and stuttered. "S-Sorry, Seth. Lynch's orders."

My heart seized.

Lucky was the traitor. No wonder Lynch had known our every move.

Burdened by the weight of my father, I was helpless to stop him.

As his finger tightened around the trigger, Hades materialized behind him. Lucky yelped as his right arm fell to the floor, severed just above the elbow, taking his pistol with it.

Hades' lips moved and another shadowy blade burst through Lucky's throat.

"Bloody backstabbing traitors," Hades muttered.

Was there no one Lynch couldn't get to?

We left what was left of Lucky in the hall and carried my father into his study.

"Set me down on the rug," he wheezed.

We lowered him gently onto the rug. Blood soaked his white shirt. He looked up at me.

"Hold on," he whispered.

Reaching for his watch, he pressed a button on the band.

There was whir as somewhere beneath us a mechanism tripped and the entire rug, along with the floor beneath it, dropped like a rock.

And so did we.

CHAPTER 18

My stomach flipped weightlessly as we plunged downward, descending into a basement I didn't even know existed.

We had to have gone the best part of fifty feet when the platform slowed to a halt.

"What the hell, Dad?" I groaned as I found my footing.

Lights flickered to life around a room that was little bigger than the platform we'd arrived on, fifteen feet across and perfectly square. On one side was a pair of sliding steel doors and a keypad with a biometric lock.

"Get me to the lock," my father said.

Lara and I staggered forward, carrying him between us. He was growing weaker by the moment and was bearing less and less of his own weight.

We reached the door, with Hades watching our backs.

My father pressed his hand to the lock and the steel doors slid apart, revealing a pentagonal chamber inside of which a brass pentacle had been inlaid in the stone floor.

Set between the pentagram and the circle were a series of arcane components and the sacrificial knife I'd recovered from Aleida's corpse.

Set in the wall at each of the five points were columns of a strange sapphire stone. They glowed with arcane energy.

"Dad, what is this place?" I could sense the magic here enveloping me. There was a familiar feel to it that I couldn't quite put my finger on.

"Somewhere I've been researching our curse problem," he replied.

It was more than that. I could feel it, and I knew from experience when my father was giving me half the truth. The entire space had been rigorously constructed to exact specifications. There was a precision to it that was unmistakable.

It was meant for ritual work.

"What are those pillars?" I pointed at the walls. "And why do they feel so familiar when I've never seen them before?"

"They are formed from berydiam calcite, a rare mineral that is remarkably good at storing power. Each of them has been charged at our ancestral temple. That's our power you're feeling. It's been a painstaking effort for the last three months. But I thought the day might come when we would need it."

"Need it? For what?"

"Seth, I'm dying," my father said. "I can feel it. She taunts me even now."

"Then cast her out," I pleaded. "We should be seeking a healer, not suffering that wretch."

"It's okay, Seth. This is what I want. Set me down inside the circle."

Lara and I lay him inside the center of the pentagram. He reached out and grabbed the sacrificial knife.

"Dad, you don't have to do this."

"I'm going out on my terms, son." He gripped the blade tight. "You're going to want to step outside the circle now."

"Not until you tell me what you're doing."

Lara grabbed me by the arm, dragging me out of the pentagram. "This isn't the time to argue."

"I'm doing things over," my father called.

His eyes held my gaze as he raised the blade high above his chest.

He reached out with his free hand and touched the circle. "*Comenzar!*"

His voice was little more than a whisper, but power filled the room. The five columns hummed with arcane might.

My dad chanted weakly, his voice fading until it was no longer audible. Then he plunged the knife into his chest.

"No!" I shouted.

I'd told him about that knife. It could drag a person's soul from their body. I'd seen it in action myself. Was that what he intended? Who knew what other consequences it might cause.

His body went limp, blood running from the new wound.

Then as suddenly as it had begun, the ritual was over. My father's lifeless body lay in the centre of the pentagram, the knife quivering in his chest as power dissipated.

I rushed to his side. Placing my hand on his neck, I checked for a pulse, but there was nothing. Tears ran down my cheek. I wasn't ready for this. We were so close. We'd even beaten Lynch. Somewhere in my heart, I'd been hoping we would spare my father from the curse, but that was a pipe dream now.

My emotions welled up, choking my throat.

"Seth, what's that?" Lara pointed at my father.

A faint wisp of ethereal mist started rising from the wound. It grew and expanded until it formed a shape before us. I recognized it immediately. It was the perfect likeness of my father, only devoid of the substance of his physical form.

And for the first time in years, he was smiling. Not the cocksure grin of a man who had outmaneuvered an enemy, but my father's broad smile of genuine joy.

"It worked," my father shouted, punching the air. "It actually worked. I can't believe it."

"Worked?" I shook my head. "What do you mean worked? This is what you wanted?"

"I felt the pull trying to drag me beyond, but I bound myself to this place, just like she did. Only I wasn't fool enough to bind myself to a living being."

I stared at my father in disbelief. "Why would you do this to yourself?"

"To get the life that was taken from me," he replied. "For the first time since I was a boy, I can't even hear her. It wasn't until I spoke to Kasey that I realized. Aleida can't haunt another spirit. If only I could work out how she hides from view. That seems like a useful trick."

"Well, she's had a four-hundred-year head start," I replied. "This is necromancy. It perverts the natural order of life. I can't believe you'd do this, and without even speaking to me."

"I did this for you, Seth. And for your mother. She woke last night and when I told her all that was happening, she only asked me for one thing. And that was to not leave her alone in this world."

I shook my head. If the Congress were upset before, this would send them over the edge. Necromancy and anything like it was utterly Forbidden.

"Don't worry for me, Seth. Now I can help you. I can be the father I wasn't the first time around. Who knows, with a clear mind, I might even be able to kick her to the curb."

Aleida. My heart pounded. She had to be here. The only living Caldwell was right here, in this room, watching my father's plan unfold.

"What exactly did you bind yourself too?" I asked.

"The manor," my father replied with a grin. "I will endure as long as it stands. Now with a dragon watching over it, that should be just about forever. Nice work with that, by the way. I assume you promised him the vault?"

I couldn't believe how calm he was being right now. He'd just died. I didn't want to delve into the semantics of my deal with the dragon.

"Yes. Why does it matter?" I set my hands on my hips.

Dad smiled. "Just glad to see you fighting for what you want again. If Lynch is dead, and his forces are on the run, the manor should stand. Now we just have to find and fix that witch, Aleida, once and for all."

He strode over to one of the sapphire pillars and examined, before nodding. "Yes, this will do nicely."

A soft cackle emanated inside my mind.

"You amateurs think you can hurt me? Please." Aleida dissolved into a fit of laughter. "I have lived a dozen lifetimes and know things you can scarcely dream of."

I stood alone in the ritual circle, Aleida's voice haunting my mind. Which meant I wasn't alone. She was here with me.

"Aleida, I'm coming for you," I whispered, my voice wavering as I gave one final thought to the plan I'd been considering for the last few days. It was insane, but with Lynch gone, she was the biggest threat to my unborn child.

"Your time is numbered. How long do you think it will take us to break the curse now that we've been able to reproduce what you did? Days, weeks, a month perhaps? You're as good as gone."

"Foolish child," she hissed. "You think you can defeat me. The moment your child is born, I will drive your mind from your body. You will beg for mercy, and it will not come."

The voice echoed in my mind, just like it had in Panama, and I knew that she was here. Occupying the same space as me. Just like Kasey had warned.

I bent down, palmed the brass circle, and willed my power into it, forming a barrier no matter could cross.

"What exactly do you think you're doing?" Aleida taunted. "You can't even see me. How do you intend to fight me, child?"

"I don't," I replied, "but right now, anywhere I go, you go. We're bound together, right?"

There was silence, as she considered the implications.

"You will never have my child." I turned to Hades. "Send me now."

His face twisted up with concern. "Are you sure?"

"This was the deal," I replied. "The rest is on me. Get it done."

Aleida slammed against the barrier, pitting her will against mine, but I focused all my effort into maintaining that barrier. If I was stuck with her, she was going to be stuck with me.

"Seth, what are you doing?" Lara called.

My lip trembled. I hadn't confided in her my intentions. She would never have agreed. Her brow was furrowed, her face long with concern.

"Whatever it takes, dear. This is how it has to be."

"Don't you dare, Seth." She raised a pistol, pointing it at Hades. "If you say one word, I will blow out what's left of your brain. So help me, God."

Hades looked up at her. "Then you would be undoing his final gift to you. Don't make this all for nothing."

"Seth, no," Lara said, tears streaming down her face.

"I told you, my dear. I would go through hell for you. And that is exactly what I'll do. She'll never hurt our child.

Lara's pistol hand trembled, and Hades closed his eyes.

"*Metaforá*."

The stony room vanished, and I was falling. My stomach writhed and flipped as weightlessness engulfed me. I plunged through inky darkness. The journey bothered me less, this time around. I knew what to expect.

In the distance, a sickly sea green light emerged. It was a tiny speck at first but grew swiftly as I hurtled toward it.

The light took form as I descended, growing into a sprawling labyrinth beneath me: Hades' Arena.

The ground rushed up to meet me. Just moments before I hit it, I felt something pull hard on my back, yanking me skyward. I felt like I had driven into a wall with a seatbelt on. I jerked violently, before falling the last five feet to the ground.

I looked around to get my bearings. Faint green light lit the place with its unearthly hue. It was cold and dank in a way that seemed to permeate even the air I breathed.

The arena was eerily quiet.

"Fool," Aleida hissed. "What have you done?"

I turned. Replete in the blood red and turquoise robes of the high priestess, was my forebear. She wore a headdress of feather and bone designed to strike terror into the hearts of men.

Her brown eyes seethed with malice.

"Welcome to the underworld," I replied with a broad grin. "All your effort to thwart death and now you're here anyway."

"You doomed us both," she shouted, power crackling madly along her fingertips.

"Go on, do it," I replied, taking great pleasure in her discomfort. "You kill me and your soul will have no binding. It'll be drawn inexorably into the well of souls, and that will be the end of you. The curse stops with me. My child will be free of you."

"But you will be dead." Aleida raised her hands, power gathering rapidly.

I might have underestimated both her spiteful nature and her sense of self preservation.

I took off, racing around the nearest corner. I knew the maze better than she did. I'd been here before, where she'd spent four hundred years avoiding it. Lightning scored along the wall behind me as I darted around the corner. The entire arena was a grand circle. The twelve outer gates would be inactive, but I didn't care.

I just wanted to get closer to the Well of Souls, and I wasn't taking any chances with Eurynomos, Hades' pet demon.

"There is no point running, Seth," Aleida called. "I do not tire or grow weary. Sooner or later, you will fatigue and I will claim one more Caldwell before I die."

I rounded another corner as a scratchy crackle filled the air. It was manic, and hauntingly high pitched.

I knew it all too well: Eurynomos the flesh eater. Aleida was drawing it to us with her incessant talking.

I couldn't worry about him, now. I had places to be. I turned left, and then right, and then left again, moving steadily toward the center of the maze. I hadn't been here in months, except for in my nightmares, but I could never forget my time here. The maze's construction worked in my favor. It was already designed to funnel champions toward the centre, away from the outer gates. Only by skipping the pattern could one break free, and I had no intention of doing that.

My leather soled wingtips scuffed at the floor as I ran. My heart pounded in my chest, sweat running down my brow. My breath seemed heavy as Eurynomos' howl carried through the arena.

When it went still, I could make out Aleida's cursing as she trailed along behind me.

"You can't run forever, Seth," she said. "You're only mortal."

"Exactly," I called back. "And hoping to stay that way."

I rounded another corner and entered the central chamber of the arena. The Well of Souls yawned open before me in a massive cavern of unfathomable depth. The sound of thousands of souls meandering in it filled the air with a faint whooshing noise.

On the other side of the massive abyss, blotting out the faint glowing green of the wall, was the eerie black silhouette of Eurynomos. He was twice as large as I remembered, his beady red eyes staring at me as his jaws opened wide.

"I'm starving," he rasped, "so the master sent me a snack. It's been too long."

I ignored him. Not a sound long-term strategy but I couldn't afford to be distracted now.

I raced around the outer perimeter of the Well of Souls, heading for the demon. Madness, perhaps, but I needed Aleida in this room.

Glancing over my shoulder, I caught her incorporeal form round the corner.

The second she did, the pull from the well started to suck her in. The edges of her intangible being seemed drawn toward it like a vacuum.

It was far stronger than it had been when the priestess of Hera had confronted me here. I could only suppose that had been the work of Hades interfering in the natural order of things to make our challenge harder.

Aleida hissed as the pull carried her closer to the well. Rather than attack me, she was straining to withstand the well's pull.

Which is exactly what I'd been hoping for.

I dropped to my knees, placed my hand on the ground, and chanted, "*Latón.*"

I couldn't transmute the entire floor, but I didn't have to. I just needed a circle. Where my finger traced, the stone floor shimmered and shifted, before setting into a bronze circle. It was a crude approximation of a circle, but it would have to do. Drawing a perfect summoning circle while a demon bore down on you was not an easy feat.

Aleida's eyes grew bloodshot at the strain. Her hands rose as she shouted, "Iluminación!"Lightning arced toward me, but I completed the circle and willed power into it, sealing myself inside.

The arcane assault played off the surface of the shield. The entire circle was only three feet wide and barely fit me, but it would have to do. Eurynomos charged, throwing himself at the barrier. The impact rattled through my mind, but I shut it out.

"Eat her," I shouted, pointing to Aleida who was trying to flee, but seemed trapped in the well's vortex.

"Spirits don't sustain," he said. "All taste, no substance."

"That's a shame," I replied, closing my eyes.

"You teased me once before, mortal. Today, I will consume you, body and soul."

The demon struck the barrier again, but it held fast. I wouldn't be able to maintain it forever. Reaching beneath my shirt, I pulled out the leather thong with the obol hanging from it.

Gripping it tightly in one hand, I called, "Charon, I summon thee."

I willed power into my words, hoping the ferryman of the river Styx would hear them. It was a difficult effort to maintain the shield whilst summoning but I had no choice. To fail was to be consumed by the demon.

"Charon," I bellowed louder. "The ferryman. He who bears souls to their eternal rest. I summon thee."

Eurynomos cackled and pounded against the barrier. I could feel the exertion of the past few days building by the moment. My barrier was starting to wane.

I glanced down. The bronze of the circle was diminishing, shifting back into the strange green stone.

Even the arena was fighting me.

If Charon didn't show, this whole plan was going to end poorly. I might have saved my baby, but I'd left Lara to raise our child alone.

"Charon, I have brought payment for my journey across the river Styx. Answer me!"

The veil rent as the skeletal prow of a canoe burst through the air inside my circle. The vessel was fashioned from the bones of an unrecognizable creature and glided through the air as if it were bobbing on water. Charon stood at the prow, his hands, covered in steel gauntlets, gripping a wooden paddle. The rest of his being was clothed in a ragged cloak that seemed to be made of thousands of strips of billowing grey and black fabric. The cloak's cowl hid his face, but a pervasive sense of dread attended him.

He raised his paddle as my circle's barrier exploded.

Eurynomos squealed with glee as he descended on me. Charon swung his paddle with the confidence of a major league baseball star.

"Depart, you accursed creature," he shouted as he belted the demon straight over the edge and into the Well of Souls.

No doubt Hades would reincarnate him again, but I breathed a sigh of relief as he vanished from sight.

Aleida lashed out with her power, the lightning playing across Charon's cloak cackling as it ground itself into the boat.

The ferryman swept his gauntlet through the air. Aleida screamed as she was sucked over the edge and into the Well of Souls.

The angry witch howled all the way down.

When the arena was silent once more, Charon turned to face me where I still knelt on the ground.

"What madness is this? A mortal in the underworld demanding passage of me. You are misguided, child. I bear passengers here. I don't take them back."

My heart sank. "But I have payment."

I held the obol up for him to see. "Ares gave me this, I know it is good for one trip. Take me home."

Charon regarded the obol but said nothing.

"Please, Charon. There is nothing to say you can only ferry your souls one way. Make this trip for me. Your masters on Olympus are not finished with me yet. They gave me the coin and expect me back in my own realm."

I was way out on a limb, but this had to be what Hera and Ares had meant. Both of them, in their own way, had tried to ensure I would have a life left to give in their service.

I shook the obol. "It's good for one trip."

"I do this," Charon said, "and this place will become grand central station for mortals who think they can come and go from the underworld for a coin."

"I won't tell a soul," I replied. "I swear it."

"It is most unusual." Charon stared down at me. "Most mortals never see me and now you have looked on me twice and lived. Hear this, Seth Caldwell. The next time we meet, I shall be ferrying your soul to its eternal rest."

"Is that a yes?" I asked, rising to my feet.

Charon pointed a gauntlet at the vessel. "Get in."

I grabbed the bleached bone lip of the boat and leaped over the side.

The canoe launched forward, and I fell into the seat behind me as the veil before the boat rent in twain.

My heart hammered in my chest as I silently prayed he was taking me home.

CHAPTER 19

It wasn't the wedding day I had pictured. The manor grounds were trashed. Shrapnel and empty casings lined the lawn, which might never recover from the gaping cleft Kasey had put in it.

I stood in a tiny gazebo beside the lake, Lara's hands in mine as we stared into each other's eyes.

No, this was so much better than I ever believed was possible for me.

There was nowhere near the number of guests that had been invited. I didn't blame them. I wouldn't have wanted to walk into this battleground either.

Even the celebrant had chickened out. Fortunately, Levi was an ordained minister and willing to fill the void. He stood with his back to the lake, a gold gleam in his eyes.

Inside the gazebo rested a small number of chairs. Dizzy and Kendra sat together, their hands entwined. Beside them sat Kasey and Hades, who was clearly enjoying himself while Kasey did her best to not encourage him. Jonas sat beside Hades, his eyes not leaving us for a moment. Beside him sat my mother in a wheelchair, still recovering her strength, and behind her stood my father. There was a huge grin on his incorporeal face.

I'd never seen him so happy. Perhaps because I'd never seen him before the curse started weighing on him.

Aleida was gone. The Brotherhood was in ruin, and for once I had no idea what the future held for me. All I knew was that I wanted it to be so many more days like this.

I spoke my vows, straight from the heart and full of the hope I now felt.

"Lara," Levi said, "I think I speak for everyone when I say I'm eager to hear the thoughts you promised us when we were so rudely interrupted last night. If you would give us your vows, please."

Lara nodded.

"Seth," she began. "When you walked into my museum, I never took you as the sort to rob the place."

Dizzy's laugh filled the little gazebo.

"To be honest, I had no idea what to make of you. You came into my life at a time when everyone was calling me crazy for wanting to believe in and study the supernatural world. I was alone with my work, and thought I was alright with that. Until I met you."

She took a hurried breath, her eyes welling up.

"You brought magic into my life where there was none, and every day since has been utter madness, but I wouldn't have it any other way. I love you, my wizard, and will till the day we die."

She swallowed to hold back the tears.

Levi continued. "Then, by the power vested in me, by the church of Our Lady of Perpetual Exemption, I now pronounce you man and wife. You may kiss the bride."

I pulled Lara into me and kissed her deeply. Somewhere behind us, Kendra wolf-whistled and Kasey cheered.

When we finally came up for breath, Lara was blushing furiously but was no longer on the edge of tears. I took her hand in mine and led her past our friends and out onto the lawn.

All around us, the signs of the Brotherhood's wrath scarred Weybridge manor, but still it stood proudly. We had endured the worst the world had thrown at us, and it had only made us closer.

I squeezed my wife's hand and for the first time since I turned eighteen, I was looking forward to the future.

Eight months from now we would be welcoming a child into a world where their future was bright and not predetermined by the obligations we'd borne for four hundred years.

The government and the Congress still had their questions, but with Lynch dead and his deeds becoming public knowledge, that too looked likely to dissipate.

I'd spent my life trying to cure my curse, and with Aleida gone, I wasn't sure what I was going to do.

I did have an open job offer from the mother of Mount Olympus, but Hera was going to have to wait. Lara and I had a baby to prepare for and I didn't know the first thing about being a good parent.

Perhaps if I was lucky, someone might have a book laying around that I could borrow.

If not, I was sure I could steal one. What could possibly go wrong?

The End

Seth is taking some well-earned time off. If you enjoyed *Urban Arcanology*, I'm sure you'd enjoy *Conjuring a Coroner*. You've met Kasey here, why not check out her adventures? She regularly encounters mythical beings, murderous creatures, and shadowy organizations trying to destroy New York City.

You can start the series with the prequel here.

Visit – https://readerlinks.com/l/2615538
Or if you'd prefer to explore the mythological beings that live beyond the veil, why not dive into Magical Midlife Crisis? Nora is a lovable forty-two-year-old single mom who turns to bounty hunting to make ends meet. Unfortunately, that leaves her as the last line of defense when the Fae come for her small Australian town.
Visit – https://www.samuelcstokes.com/boun-ty-hunter-down-under

THANKS FOR JOINING ME ON THIS JOURNEY

When I set out to write this series, I couldn't wait to share Seth's adventure with you. Born with unusual talents and a curse that would kill him, Seth has battled men, demons, arcane practitioners and cabals, in order to get his life back.

But along the way, he's found so much more. I hope you enjoyed seeing him grow as I did. It's a difficult thing to end a series, but I hope you found it as satisfying as I did. I took care to try and tie up all the loose ends and leave few questions unanswered.

There is, of course, that job offer from Hera. Who knows, we may have to revisit that down the track. Trouble is brewing among the Olympians, but Seth has a family to focus on. So, for the time being we leave our hero at Weybridge manor, building a life with Lara and his soon-to-be born son. I'm sure some of you will have questions; be sure to ask them in our Facebook group, or shoot me an email.

If you enjoyed this series, I'd encourage you to pick up the others in the Arcanoverse. There is definitely an overlap between them and the Brotherhood's fall which will certainly send ripples through the Arcanoverse.

You can start Kasey's adventure here: A Date with Death is the action-packed prequel. You can dive in for free when you join my newsletter.

Or join Nora in a magical midlife crisis that will leave you laughing and reading long into the night.

Thanks again for joining me on this wild ride. If you loved Seth, please share him with a friend who loves a great adventure or leave a review for the series (particularly book 1, Half-Blood's Hex). It helps more than you will ever know!

See you in the next adventure,

S.C. Stokes

P.S. I've included a preview of my other series below. So, scroll on and check them out. You can also contact me using any of the links below.

You can find me on:

Facebook

Bookbub

Email: samuel@samuelcstokes.com

Want to see my other titles? Head to my website

https://www.samuelcstokes.com/

Or sign up to my newsletter where you'll receive exclusive short stories, giveaways, behind the scenes look into my series, and so much more. My newsletter is the place to go to never miss sales, new releases and special merch. Click the link below or type it into your browser.

https://www.books.samuelcstokes.com/jointhevips

If you enjoy social media, I have a growing group of readers who love to hang out, share their favorite reads, funny animal pictures, and torment me about when my next book is coming out.

www.facebook.com/groups/scstokesarcanoverse/

A Date With Death Preview

Murder in New York City had been on the rise lately, and while Kasey felt for the poor souls and their families, she couldn't help but feel a little relief. For a graduate struggling with her student loans, the job security couldn't have been better.

Life wasn't all sunshine and fresh corpses though. The steady supply of new 'clients' had created some competition in the workplace. Not that Kasey minded a challenge, but her success had brought notoriety, and the unwelcome attention of John Ainsley.

After four years of school, a cross country move, and a name change, she wasn't going to let a spoiled brat ruin her career. Not when it was just starting to take off.

"Who else would want to do this?" Kasey muttered to herself as she caught her reflection in the polished aluminum examination table. Normal people feared death but for Kasey, death was a part of life. The part that she chose every day, due largely to her unnatural connection with it.

Unlike the poor man lying on the table before her, she could see it coming.

That edge had given her an unfair advantage over her fellow examiners. Her findings were second to none, often uncovering insights into cases that other seasoned examiners had overlooked. It wasn't their fault, really.

Kasey simply wasn't normal. She was not a 'normal.'

Kasey sat the scalpel aside and tucked her fingers into the large Y-shaped incision. With practiced hands, she lifted and rolled back the flesh, revealing the cadaver's rib cage and vital organs. As she did, a green mist descended, completely obscuring her sight.

When the mist cleared, she was no longer in the morgue. She found herself in a loft apartment somewhere in Manhattan. From the view, she guessed she was in SoHo, or at least her consciousness was.

Born a witch, Kasey had inherited the gift of magic from her parents. Old wizarding stock, their blood carried with it the arcane gifts of the Welsh Druids. While the ancient sects had all but faded from the public eye, they were well remembered in the World of Magic—a formidable bloodline once feared for their blood magic and ritualistic sacrifice.

No, Kasey was no normal, but even among the magical community she was an oddity. She had been born prescient. The ability to see the future was rare, even in the magical community. Her true sight manifested as it willed, sharing invasive and often unpleasant views into the lives of those she came in contact with, and that included cadavers like the one whose chest cavity she had just opened.

Now she found herself floating in a New York City loft, as a wine glass hurtled past her face into the exposed brick wall beside her. The glass shattered, its contents running down the brickwork.

In her incorporeal form, Kasey was invisible, so she knew she wasn't the intended target. She turned, searching for the source of the flying wine. A brunette in a tauntingly high split obsidian cocktail dress stomped through the loft. Mascara ran down the woman's red face as she cried.

"There's nothing to worry about, Tina," the woman sputtered, "Tayla's just a friend from work."

The woman stomped over to the couch where a man lay comatose, his mouth hung open as his head dropped over the back of the couch.

"Well, Jim, just how many of your work friends sext you?" the woman, presumably Tina, held the phone over him, as she scrolled through a sea of images. "There are hundreds of pictures of her on here, Jim, and most of them are nudes!"

Jim didn't stir.

"She's very cute, Jim," Tina said scrolling through the messages, "and impossibly flexible. But we're meant to be getting married next month, you unfaithful ass."

Tina hurled the phone at Jim and stormed into the kitchen.

"What am I meant to tell my family? They're flying in for this sham!" she shouted as she opened a drawer and began rummaging through it.

Kasey's heart ached for the woman. She hadn't had a great deal of luck with men herself but finding out your fiancé was cheating on you weeks before your wedding had to be soul crushing.

When Tina re-emerged from the kitchen, she held a set of silver scissors. She sniffed as she strode across the loft, her eyes red and puffy as she stood over her wayward fiancé.

"I know what I'll tell them, Jim. You had a terrible accident and we've had to postpone the wedding. I just hope Tayla will understand."

Sticking the scissors between her teeth, she crouched down and began fiddling with Jim's belt. Still, he didn't move. Kasey was beginning to suspect he'd had a little more than just the wine.

Tina unzipped his pants and yanked them off, leaving Jim in his boxers.

As Tina reached for the boxers, Kasey whispered, "Oh Tina, don't do it."

There were some things Kasey never wanted to see, and a castration was one of them. Unfortunately, her second sight seldom gave her much of a say in the matter.

This time, however, it seemed her gift was listening, as the familiar green mist descended just as Tina raised the scissors.

When the mist cleared, Kasey was back in her morgue, standing over Jim's body, her sympathy for him dissipating by the moment. Unfortunately, Tina had gone too far. There would be a price to be paid for her drunken revenge. As much as she sympathized with the bride-to be, justice had to be served. Otherwise what was the point of the wretched visions if not to balance the scales?

Justice was a dish that seldom served itself. Often, it needed a little help.

That's where Kasey found herself: a foot in either world, just trying to make the best of it. She had not always been at peace with her gift. As a child, seeing a continual stream of agony and death had been torture, but in time, that panic turned to purpose. In a world of suffering, her macabre visions and medical expertise could grant a measure of peace and justice to the families of her clients.

The World of Magic seethed and bubbled below the surface of the natural world. Witches and wizards living in secret, their presence concealed by the hustle and bustle of a busy world. In a world that worshiped technology, the arcane had faded into myth. The world was divided between witches and wizards; those who understood magic, and everybody else. The normals. They lived in blissful ignorance of the supernatural world that surrounded them on a daily basis.

Her gift could be fickle though. Feast or famine. There was little middle ground and even less explanation as to why. There was no Doctor On Demand for psychics, not real ones anyway, so she did what she could with the cards life dealt her.

She suspected Jim had been slipped some kind of sedative. Toxicology tests would show which had been administered. The results would take hours yet, but that would leave plenty of time for the autopsy she had been procrastinating.

It felt a little redundant, but not performing the autopsy would raise more questions, so Kasey set about the task. She bent down, leaning in to examine Jim. Two of his ribs showed signs of having been broken in the past. No recent bruising around the site indicated an old injury. Irrelevant, perhaps, but she made a mental note of the wound for later, just in case.

As she worked her way over the body, the pronounced click of the door being opened echoed through the silent morgue. She spun to confront her unexpected guest, and the scalpel swung from her hand. It hurtled toward the door. She stared as the world slowed. Each revolution of the blade took an eternity. With an eerie *shick*, the blade buried itself in the drywall inches to the right of the open door.

Her hands balled into fists as she noted John's arrogant smile and his all too perfect teeth. His eyes traveled from Kasey to the quivering blade and back to Kasey.

Her jaw sank open, her feelings torn between regret for damaging the wall versus a small part of her that fervently wished she'd hit the unwelcome interloper. Karma could use all the help it could get when it came to John Ainsley

"Your surgical skills could use a little work, Kasey," he said with a grin. "One of these days, you're going to injure someone."

"One can only hope," Kasey muttered as she leaned back against the countertop.

John sauntered into the room. His unbridled sense of self-importance was as unappealing as the Ivy League side part he sported proudly.

At first glance, one could be mistaken by thinking him handsome, but such a notion would soon be shattered by the disappointment that would follow meeting him. John Ainsley oozed entitlement, and his behavior around the office reeked of someone used to getting their way. His Rolex served as a constant reminder of both his affluence and poor decision-making ability.

After all, who wears a sixteen-thousand-dollar watch while performing autopsies? Even more curiously, who performs autopsies for a living when they have the cash to drop on a Rolex? Surely there were more promising career paths for Ivy League graduates drowning in enough familial wealth to build a modern dynasty.

"What are you doing here, John? Can't you see I'm busy?" She gestured over her shoulder at the open body behind her.

"I can see that," John said, glancing down at the cadaver. His eyes widened and he took a step backward, shaking his head. "Kasey, what—"

"It wasn't me," she interrupted.

"Why did you cut his balls off?" John asked, ignoring her denial as he leaned forward to examine the body closer. "Where did you get your degree? Prison?"

"NYU," she said, pushing John away from the table. "Where I earned my place. Daddy didn't have to buy them a new laboratory to secure my spot."

John batted away the insult as if it were a bothersome fly. "Well, if this is how they taught you to perform an autopsy, I'm glad I went elsewhere."

Kasey rolled her eyes. "He came in like that, John, but if you don't get out of here, I'll see that you leave sporting a matching tribute. I'm sure I'd be doing the ladies of New York a favor."

John grinned as he cocked his head. "Come now, Kasey. How would you know? You still haven't taken me up on my offer." The corners of his mouth peaked up into a grin. "Afraid you might like it?"

"Afraid I might catch something," she said. "I'd sooner trade places with our friend on the table. Now, get out."

"But," John protested, trailing his hand along the autopsy table, "this looks far more interesting than the massive coronary sitting on my table."

"Out!" Kasey bellowed, pointing at the door.

"No fun at all," John muttered as he slipped out of the lab.

As the door clicked shut behind him, Kasey sucked in a deep breath to calm her frustration.

She looked at the scalpel still buried in the drywall by the door. Glancing around to ensure she was alone, she lifted her hand and whispered, "*Gwys.*"

Power pulsed through the examination room, and the scalpel twitched as strands of magic wrapped themselves around the silver haft of the scalpel. Then with a pop it sprung free, hurtling through the air back into Kasey's open palm.

Raising her other hand, Kasey chanted, "*Atgyweirio.*"

The drywall bubbled, liquefying before her eyes as it simmered and knit itself together as if nothing had ever happened.

After placing the scalpel down on the table, she retrieved a fresh blade from her surgical tray.

"Yes, the last thing I need is John to have any evidence of that little outburst," she said aloud to herself.

Her arcane gifts had certainly complicated her life, the visions in particular, but it was times like this she was glad she'd been born a witch. Not having to deal with some of the more tedious mundane tasks in life definitely had its perks.

She lifted the new blade and was about to resume her work when the lab's phone rang.

"This is going to take all day at this rate," she muttered as she dropped the blade back on the tray.

The clatter of the scalpel echoed through the lab.

"If this is John again, I swear..." She let the threat go unfinished as she trudged across the room, and then sighed as she lifted the phone of the receiver. "Kasey speaking."

"Kasey, this is Dr. Sampson. Is everything alright?" There was a note of concern in the otherwise friendly tone.

Aw, crap. Dr. Julie Sampson was New York's Chief Medical Examiner, the head of her field and one of the country's foremost experts in forensic medicine. She was one of the only women to hold that particular office in three decades.

She also happened to be Kasey's boss.

"Yep. Everything fine. Just a little bit of a slow start down here today, that's all," Kasey said, regretting her tone immediately.

"Hoping to chew through some of the backlog before lunch?" Julie asked.

"I had planned to, but things just aren't going my way."

Click-click. The sound of Sampson's pen carried down the line. Sampson was cool as ice; if she was fidgeting with the pen, it didn't bode well.

Sampson broke the silence. "I thought I might catch you in the lab. What are you working on?"

"The one with the mutilated manhood," Kasey said, figuring the odds would be with her that it was the only case of its kind in the office.

"Oh," Sampson said. "How's it looking?"

"This one's cut and dried," Kasey said, and then grimaced.

Sampson burst out laughing. "Oh, Kasey, that was terrible."

"I didn't mean it like that," Kasey said, pacing circles with the phone against her ear. "Now that I've put my foot in my mouth, what can I do for you?"

Sampson cleared her throat. "Well, I know you were hoping to clear a few files, but I'm wondering just how far you are into your current procedure?"

"I've just begun the autopsy," Kasey replied. "Not a lot of mysteries here, though. Clearly someone with an axe to grind. I suspect he was sedated and then mutilated while he was out cold. All that remains is to determine what sedative was used. Hopefully it will give the police something they can use to work out who did it."

"Good," Sampson said. "Sounds like an easy one. No match for your talents then."

Kasey felt the color rise in her cheeks. Praise from Dr. Sampson was hard earned. She didn't know what to say. Her pause grew awkward as the void lengthened.

"Or at least I hope it's an open and shut case," Sampson continued, "because I have something else for you. Something I want you on, and no one else. I'm going to need you to give Mr. Mutilation to someone else."

"Um, sure, I guess," Kasey mumbled.

"Excellent, because I have someone else that needs your attention."

Kasey felt uneasy. Something wasn't quite right. She ran her fingers through her dark brown hair as she considered Dr. Sampson's words.

Shifting her weight from one foot to the other, she asked, "So, when are they coming in?"

There was another pause. Not a good sign. "That's the thing, Kasey. They aren't. You'll need to go to them. Grab a field kit and be waiting downstairs. They've sent a town car for you. It will be here shortly. Don't worry, they will return you at the completion of your examination."

Kasey scratched her head. "The field. Where am I headed?"

"I can't say, I haven't been given the details, but the request came direct from the mayor's office. So, grab your kit and head down to the street. They will be there any minute."

Kasey nodded although no one could see her, and then felt a little sheepish.

"Kasey, are you still there?"

"Yes," she stammered. "I understand. I'll go grab a pack now."

"Excellent. And Kasey?"

She paused. "Yes, Dr. Sampson?"

"Tread carefully. These aren't the kind of people you want to antagonize."

Kasey bit her lip. What did that even mean? "Yes, Dr. Sampson. I won't let you down."

She hung up the receiver and pondered the bizarre phone call. Field trips were a little unusual, particularly with the city's resources spread so thin. Medical examiner offices in two boroughs had been closed. The staffing shortages had left the three remaining offices overworked and understaffed.

She wandered back to the examination table, popped the wheel locks off, and wheeled John Doe over to the freezer. Later, the police would learn his name was Jim.

Gingerly, she shifted him onto the cool steel tray and locked him away. After peeling off her gloves, she threw them in the trash, grabbed a field kit from the supply closet, and headed downstairs.

As she stepped outside, she slowed her pace to weave her way through a crowd of pedestrians thronging the street.

A horn blared as a black town car pulled to a halt in front of the building. An angry taxi peeled around the Lincoln and tore off down the street.

The Lincoln came to a halt, and a driver stepped out. He was wearing what looked like a pressed uniform from a hotel, complete with a chauffeur's hat.

"Are you Miss Chase?" the man called.

"That's me," Kasey replied, starting toward the town car.

"Marvelous. Come with me, please." The driver opened the rear door. As Kasey approached the vehicle he reached for the kit. "Let me pop that in the trunk for you."

Kasey surrendered the kit and slid into the back seat of the Lincoln, fastening her seatbelt.

The trunk slammed behind her and a moment later, the driver was back in his seat. Popping his turn signal, he slid back into the traffic.

Leaning forward, Kasey asked, "So, where are we going?"

The driver tilted his head, finding Kasey's eyes in the rear-view mirror. "I'm not at liberty to say, Miss Chase. We'll be on the road for a little while though, so you just relax back there."

Kasey nodded as if she understood, but everything about her current situation made her uncomfortable. The unusual request from Dr. Sampson, who was clearly nervous. This entire unexpected field trip, not to mention the chauffeured town car whisking her off to an unknown destination.

She settled down into the rich Corinthian leather. As nice as it was to be out of the lab, she couldn't ignore the uncomfortable pit that was forming in her stomach.

What could the mayor possibly want from me?

Find out in A Date With Death.

Visit – https://readerlinks.com/l/2615538

BOUNTY HUNTER DOWN UNDER PREVIEW

Alasdair laughed, the rich throaty rumble filling the room. In the library, I had found his laugh endearing. Now that I was the object of his mirth, the sound was quickly wearing on my nerves. Particularly after I had passed their silly little test and found the Camp.

"You can't just walk in off the street and take a bounty, lass," Alasdair said. "Even the least of those creatures will maul you if you get in their way. This is a trade to be learned, not a charity. You must apprentice to someone who knows what they're doing, or you won't last a day."

"Unfortunately, we only have one Master Hunter who would be available for such tutelage," the Old One added. "And he's a grumpy old Scottish bastard. I doubt you'd find him pleasant company."

"Don't even think about it." Alasdair set down his cup.

I wasn't sure whether he was talking to me, or the Old One, but I needed this job and I was just about to protest when the Old One intervened.

"Think about what?" the Old One asked, cocking his head to the side. "I'm in the habit of giving the orders around here, not taking them. Remember your place."

Alasdair stiffened, pointing his finger at me.

"You want to saddle me with Sally Homemaker here? She won't last a day."

"I lasted yesterday, didn't I?" I snapped.

"You survived," Alasdair replied, looking down his nose at me. "Don't mistake luck for skill, or competence. It's that sort of thinking that will get you killed."

He turned to the Old One, addressing him like I wasn't even there. His tone was more deferential this time. "Look at her, Master. She's been favoring her hip since she walked through the door. She's likely to blow her hip out at the first sign of combat."

"Hey," I interjected. "I'm forty-two, not sixty-five."

Alasdair ignored me. "Hunting is painful, gruelling work. If someone is going to watch my back, I need to be able to rely on them. Otherwise, I'm better off alone."

"I can do pain," I replied. "I have given birth, twice."

The Old One chortled. "Certainly a glutton for punishment, aren't you?"

Turning to Alasdair, he rested a gloved hand on his shoulder. "I am inclined to give her a shot. I have a good feeling about this one."

"That's what you said about the last one," Alasdair growled. "He lasted all of three months, before the arrogant little sod went after the Red Cap. Now he's dead, and his wife is in a psychiatric institution. Heaven forbid you have a bad feeling about someone."

Three months. That was how long my predecessor had lasted.

I shuddered. My eyes rested on the photo of the hook-nosed creature occupying the top of the bounty board. A hundred thousand dollars was a lot of money, but you couldn't spend it if you were dead.

"I didn't have a good feeling about him," the Old One replied. "I said he had talent, and beneath that facade he was a psychopath. Using a monster to kill monsters was a healthier outcome than what might have occurred, had nature been left to run its course."

The Old One looked at me. "She is different."

Alasdair turned to me. "You said it yourself. You've got two children. That's two very good reasons to turn around and walk right out that door. If you insist on following through with this, I can't make you any promises. No one can. Who will care for your children if you're dead?"

"If I can't put food on the table and keep a roof over their heads, I'm not caring for them now."

Alasdair leaned on the table. "She can't be reasoned with. I'm sure she'll be a right pain in the arse to teach."

"No more than you were, I'm sure," The Old One said, his voice rising in its inflection.

Well, that explained their unusual dynamic. The Old One wasn't just the boss; he was Alasdair's mentor.

"How long are you going to hold that over my head?" Alasdair asked.

"Until the day you die," the Old One replied, letting out a wheeze. "May it be in your sleep, many years from now."

"Not bloody likely," Alasdair said, "and you know it."

"So it's settled then," the Old One replied. "Nora, you will accompany Alasdair and learn to be a hunter. Learn well, child, because he is right—there is no room for error here. Your next mistake could cost you your life, and I don't need any more coins on my wall."

As morbid a warning as it was, I couldn't help but smile. He was actually giving me a chance. What that entailed, I wasn't yet sure, but I had my foot in the door.

A klaxon-like siren reverberated through the confines of the building. I ducked, grabbing at my ears to prevent the din from deafening me. It sounded like an old air raid siren and was emanating from a rusty apparatus hanging on the back wall of the office.

"What on earth is that?" I shouted over the racket.

"It's the *aláram tairseach*," the Old One said, his voice weary and dry. "It warns us when the Veil has been parted within the city limits."

The Veil was the divider between our world and the supernatural realm. My mother had been lecturing me about it since I was a child.

The Old One trudged toward the office at the back of the Camp. He pushed open the door and the klaxon rattled in its mount.

Alasdair followed, and so did I.

The door led into a small boardroom. As the Old One passed through the door, he waved a gloved hand through the air and whispered something I didn't quite catch. The alarm abruptly stopped, and I was able to uncover my ears.

The boardroom was dominated by a large table covered by a miniature model of a city. It was not unlike those models architects used for their 3D representations of projects to be constructed. I took a step closer and found I was looking at a top-down view of Beenleigh.

I picked out the courthouse and the library. The model had all the streets marked out carefully and to scale. Worked into the streets and the buildings were carved runes which set it apart from the map I'd been using all day. The runes appeared to be some sort of Gaelic but for the life of me,

I couldn't make sense of them. My eyes were drawn to a flashing red light at one end of the board.

The Old One moved toward it, leaning closer to the board as he studied the runes etched into that section.

I recognized the location: the Logan River Parklands, a sprawling park built along the twisting bends of the Logan River. It had plenty of exercise equipment and playgrounds for the kids. It was a common stop for parents and their children. Conor and Shay had loved it as youngsters.

It was also home to the local park run, not that I'd been in a year. Or three. I was going to have to remedy that if I took this bounty hunter gig seriously. I couldn't afford to be huffing and puffing from a stroll about the town. Maybe I'd head down there this weekend.

If you last that long.

"It's in the Parklands," Alasdair said. "On a weekday, plenty of people about. Another creature of Winter causing chaos?"

The Old One studied the glowing runes. "Crisp working, modest opening, short duration. Certainly Sidhe, but the location does make me wonder. Tread carefully, Alasdair, and take the rookie with you."

Rookie? It had never felt so good to be considered an amateur.

Alasdair grumbled, "Fine. Come on, comet," as he left the boardroom. "Let's see if we can't get you killed your first day on the job."

He left the boardroom and strode over to a bank of lockers, fiddled with a well-oiled padlock on one, and pulled it open. He took out a helmet and handed it to me.

"What's this for?" I asked, hoping my eagerness could dispel his gruff demeanor.

"Protection," Alasdair replied, shutting the locker.

I looked at the helmet and considered my encounter with the troll yesterday.

"This will really help protect me from the Sidhe?"

Alasdair gave me a look like he had sucked a lemon.

"No, from the road. Do try to hang on."

I felt like an idiot as he pushed open the back door and led the way to a large black and silver Harley-Davidson sitting behind the building. A second helmet waited for him on the seat.

He threw his leg over the bike, as I pulled the helmet down over my hair.

"What are you waiting for? An engraved invitation?" he asked.

I'd been trying to win him over with optimism and cheeriness, but if he was going to be an ass, in the hope he could drive me off, he would be bitterly disappointed.

I stepped into his space, right up against the bike.

"Alasdair, I get it. You don't want me here. You don't like having to drag a newbie around. Fair enough. Whether that's because I'm a woman or threw up the first time we met, I don't know. But what I do know is this—I need this job. Which means I need you. And as far as I can see from that empty room and wall full of coins, you're just about the last man standing. How long can that last?"

"What do you mean?" he asked, not moving an inch.

"Well, the other hunters are gone, aren't they?"

Sure, there was a chance there could be other hunters out roaming the town as we spoke, but that wasn't the vibe I got talking to Alasdair and the Old One. They were tired and worn out. The air in the Camp was thick with resignation. It felt like defeat that just hadn't happened yet.

I poked my finger into his chest. "Only a man could think that being the only bounty hunter in town is a good thing. You might as well paint a target on your back."

"What do you know about it?" he replied, his voice rising an octave.

"Only what you've told me. Which isn't a helluva lot," I said. "But if the Sidhe are half as wily as you seem to think, you've got to realize that if you're the only game in town, sooner or later they're going to start hunting you. The sooner they punch your ticket, the sooner they have free run of the place. I get the feeling the Old One doesn't hit the streets too often. Am I right?"

"He's retired from the field. Someone needs to run the Camp."

"Precisely. So unless you want every otherworldly creature in town coming for you, you need to recruit. Create a target-rich environment, so to speak. So stop moaning about my presence and get invested in my training. Because one of these days, they're going to come for you, and you're going to want someone watching your back."

Alasdair sat, silently considering my point, before nodding at the seat behind him. "Get on the bike."

I'll take that as a yes.

Men weren't particularly inclined to acknowledge when they were wrong, and I figured my gruff Scottish mentor was no exception. I swung my leg over the Harley and clambered on behind him. I looked around for somewhere to hold onto and realized there was nowhere else to put my arms but around him.

So, I wrapped them around his broad chest and found only muscle. Part of me was acutely aware of just how much of me was pressed up against his back, and just how good that felt.

Dammit, Nora, focus. This isn't the time to let your libido do the thinking for you.

Alasdair peeled out of the car park, sending a spray of gravel out behind the bike.

I hung on tight as we wound through town, rolling through the set of traffic lights at the top of City Road and down toward the Parklands at the edge of town. The road led to a round-about with an on-ramp to the freeway and another exit that I knew would take us to the park.

The question was, what was waiting for us there? What had caused that warning siren in the Camp?

Alasdair leaned to the left and my body followed his lead. We rounded a rocky plateau and the murky brown waters of the Logan River came into view. Alasdair slowed as we approached, scanning the vast green expanse before us.

The road through the Parklands itself ran in a large loop. It had been laid between the Logan River on the left and a small marsh surrounding an island on the right. The outer rim was where the play areas had been built, along with the walking trails and a few pontoon jetties leading down to the river.

Several narrow land bridges led through the reeds and marshes to a grassy mound that formed an island in the midst of the marsh. Sometimes local reenactment groups frequented the area, building forts and battling each other for control of the island. Today the area was vacant. The small gate leading to the causeway was locked.

Alasdair taxied into the car park. There were a dozen other vehicles, as well as a handful of families scattered about the play equipment.

A mother was walking a stroller along the outer circuit while another was doing her best to push two kids on the swings. A small fitness boot camp occupied a large grassy field.

There was no sign of an otherworldly presence anywhere.

Alasdair cut the engine and we climbed off the bike. He set his helmet down, raised his hand over the bike, and whispered something.

I felt a faint whiff of power that sent a tingle down my spine.

"What was that?" I asked.

"Just a little something to make sure the bike is still here when we get back. It wouldn't be the first time someone has tried to steal it."

Fair enough. This was Beenleigh, after all. It had something of a reputation for things disappearing when they were not bolted down. I imagined that the pristine Harley might be a tempting target for a thief or a teenager wanting a joyride.

"What will happen if they try?" I asked, my curiosity piqued.

Alasdair glanced at the seat of the bike. "The next person to sit on that seat without uttering the right counter-spell will feel like their ass is on fire for a week."

"Isn't that dangerous?" I asked.

"Only to them," Alasdair replied with a shrug. "In my experience, they don't make it more than about twenty feet before they decide to leg it. It's a teachable moment."

"You don't have any children, do you?"

"No," Alasdair replied. "Why?"

"Oh, it just shows in your teaching manner," I replied before realizing I probably shouldn't criticize my mentor to kick off our relationship.

Alasdair appeared unfazed. "Any complaints, take it up with the Old One. Rest assured that, next to the Old One, I'm a saint."

I thought back to meeting the Old One at his caravan. I could still recall the feel of the knife in my back.

I didn't doubt Alasdair for a minute.

"What do we do now?" I asked, hoping to change the subject.

"We keep our eyes open," he replied. He hadn't stopped scanning the park around us for any sign of trouble. "Just because we can't see it, doesn't mean it isn't here. The Sidhe are masters of deception, glamours, and veils. You can't trust your eyes when it comes to them."

"Then how will we know when we've found them?"

"Oh, you'll know," he replied cryptically. "Let's go. We won't find them here in the car park."

We started out of the car park, strolling along the footpath like a couple out for a late afternoon walk. Not that we held hands or anything. Something told me Alasdair wasn't interested enough in maintaining a cover to weather a public display of affection.

"The first thing you need to know about what we do, is the rules," Alasdair began.

I couldn't help but grin.

He took one sideways glance at my face and asked, "What are you smiling about?"

"You said *we*. I'm on the team," I replied with giddy excitement. It was far more than I'd expected when I set out this morning.

He shook his head. "You won't be for long unless you pay attention. Listen up."

"I'm listening. Hit me," I replied as my gaze followed the mother walking her pram. There wasn't anything unusual about her, but knowing the Sidhe were about gave me anxiety for her, and her baby.

"The first is that we are a part of society, not apart from society. Consider the consequences of your actions and those your actions expose to the supernatural world. Not everyone is cut out for handling it. You have some talent. I saw it in the library. Learn when to use it and when to hold it in reserve. The town trusts us because of the good work we've done. You take out a family as collateral damage, or vandalize town property, and that can turn everyone, including the authorities, against us. Got it?"

I nodded. "The good we do can't be outweighed by the damage we cause. Understood."

"That's one way to look at it," he replied. "The second is sacrifice. Hunters do what we do, so that others can have a better life, safe from the perils of the Otherworld, safe from the danger, stress, and trauma that we face every day. Embrace that sacrifice; use it to drive you. The path of the hunter is a lonely road. I know you are in it for the cash, but you have to understand it isn't all bounties and celebrations. The longer you do what we do, the more likely you are to mess up and when you do, you will get hurt. That is the price we pay, so others don't have to."

"Have you ever messed up?" I asked as we made our way around the circuit.

He pulled up the sleeve of his jacket. The flesh of his left arm above the wrist was dark and discolored. I'd never seen anything like it.

"Everyone makes mistakes. Rule three. Learn from them. You will live longer."

I reflected on the rules. "So, when it comes down to it—don't get caught, take a flogging for those who should never know about it, and don't get beaten the same way twice?"

"More or less," Alasdair replied.

We reached the end of the circuit and stood beneath the painted red bridge that spanned the Logan River.

We'd walked the length of the outer path and found nothing out of the ordinary.

"There's nothing here," I said. "Could the Camp's alarm system have malfunctioned?"

"If it can, I've never seen it," he said, turning away from the river to survey the marshes and the island on the other side of the ring road. "Which leaves us with that mess over there."

We set out toward the island, crossing the ring road and strolling down the grassy embankment toward the causeway. The island looked deserted, but as he walked, Alasdair's posture changed from casual stroll, to coiled and ready to strike, his hand never far from the machete in its sheath at the small of his back.

"Whatever you do, stay beside me or behind me where I can look out for you, and do exactly what I say. Now is not the time to be a smart ass, got it?"

I considered a quip, but I could read the room and thought better of it.

"Perfectly," I replied, wanting my reluctant mentor to know he could count on me.

A tingle started like a pinprick in my fingers, but after a few more steps, the hairs on the back of my neck stood on end. As we walked, the sensation grew stronger.

"Alasdair, can you feel that?" I whispered.

"Yes," he replied, pushing me behind him.

"What is it?" I asked.

"Sidhe magic," he said. "A lot of it."

We reached the island, but there was nothing except grass and trees as far as the eye could see.

Alasdair cleared his throat, loudly addressing the empty island.

"What's it going to be?" he called. "Are you going to skulk behind your glamours? Or are we going to talk?"

Only silence greeted him, and I wondered if I'd imagined the whole thing.

He raised a hand and whispered, *"Teine!"*

Flames rose from the palm of his hand until a broiling inferno roughly a foot high billowed from it.

"It looks like there isn't anyone here, Nora," he announced theatrically. "Guess we're okay to do a little back burning. These trees are looking out of control."

He strode toward the nearest tree, the white-hot flames above his hand wisping toward the bark.

"Stop!" A shrill voice cut through the warming air.

Alasdair closed his hand and the fires flickered out of existence. He had a smug look of satisfaction on his face.

Before us a shimmer rippled through the air, like an invisible curtain parting, and five beings appeared before us on the island.

Join Nora, her found family, and her lovable hound, Bran, on this action-packed adventure.

Visit – https://www.samuelcstokes.com/bounty-hunter-down-under

ABOUT THE AUTHOR

Sam is a writer of magically-charged fantasy adventures. His passion for action, magic and intrigue spawned his Arcanoverse—a delightfully deluded universe that blends magic, myth, and the modern world in a melting pot that frequently explodes.

When he isn't hiding away in his writing cave, his favorite hobbies include cooking, indulging sugary cravings, gaming, and trying to make his children laugh. You can find more of his work at www.samuelcstokes.com or connect with him at the links below.

f facebook.com/SCStokesOfficial

g goodreads.com/author/show/3043773.S_C_Stokes

BB bookbub.com/authors/s-c-stokes

The S.C. Stokes Library

Conjuring A Coroner Series

If you love witch and wizard thrillers where the mythology and monsters are very real, enter the world of Kasey Chase—a medical examiner taking on shadowy organizations, vampires, and the Fairy Courts, one spell at a time.

A Date With Death(Prequel) – When a wealthy, reclusive wizard is found dead in his mega-mansion, Kasey Chasey is sent to determine the cause of death. Unfortunately, it's almost certainly one of the five entitled wizarding heirs she's now locked in a mansion with

Dying To Meet You- Born a witch, Kasey Chase went into forensics so she could use her talents to close cases. This worked great in the morgue, but she's just been transferred to active duty at the 9th Precinct, and performing magic in front of normals is strictly forbidden.

Plus 11+ other action-packed urban fantasy adventures are waiting for you in the Conjuring a Coroner series.

Magical Midlife Crisis Series

Do you enjoy your heroes with a little more age and wisdom under their belt? Nora's a librarian suffering from a magical midlife crisis who turns to bounty hunting to make ends meet. If you love adventures featuring the fae, found family, and urban fantasy adventures set in unusual locations (Australia), then you'll likely get a real kick out of Nora's Magical Midlife Crisis.

Bounty Hunter Down Under- My mother always warned me about the creatures of the Otherworld, but I never expected an ice troll to show up at my work.

A Bay Of Angry Fae- When I imagined my forties, I didn't anticipate quite so many severed heads.

Ghosts At The Coast- It never snows on the Gold Coast. They call it the Sunshine State for a reason.

Urban Arcanology Series

When you're looking for a world where magic and mythology are very real, my Urban Arcanology series will hit the spot. Seth comes face-to-face with Greek Gods, angels, demons, and ancient relics in his quest to cure the curse he was born with.

Half-Blood's Hex- I should have been an archaeologist. They have the good sense to only steal from the dead. I can't afford to wait that long.

Half-Blood's Bargain- There was a time when a deadly curse was the worst of my problems.

Half-Blood's Debt- When I woke up face to face with the God of War, I knew there had been a terrible mistake.

Half-Blood's Birthright- The Libro Sanguis contains the secrets I need to survive. Unfortunately, it's located back in New York City in the possession of one Kasey Chase.

Half-Blood's Quest- The Holy Grail is meant to grant eternal life, but it seems more likely to be the death of me.

Half-Blood's Betrayal- Lynch and his army are coming to ensure my extinction. It's shaping up to be one hell of a wedding.

Milton Keynes UK
Ingram Content Group UK Ltd.
UKHW040648191223
434651UK00001B/116